"I'VE NEVER BEEN ABLE TO FORGET YOU."

Sloane heard her gasp at his words, and he searched her face. "Don't get the wrong idea," he said, smiling cynically, "I haven't been carrying a torch. Except . . ."

"Except what?" she demanded angrily.

"Except that I want to be completely free. And I couldn't be until I knew you were happy. Tell me you are."

"No, Sloane, I can't." Elise felt like an open wound, but she willed herself to sound calm.

"I'm exactly what you see. An old maid living in an old house. But I've taken more risks than you'll ever take, even though I stayed while you went off to see the world. I've given love, with absolutely no guarantee of having it returned. I may be weak, afraid of change, as you say. But I'm not afraid to give myself. Will you ever say the same?"

ABOUT THE AUTHOR

Named this year's Outstanding New Author for a
series by the *Romantic Times*, Emilie Richards
has gained a large following of loyal readers in her
new career as a romance novelist. Presently on
sabbatical in Australia with her minister husband
and their four children, Emilie makes her home in
New Orleans. This is her third Superromance.

Books by Emilie Richards

HARLEQUIN SUPERROMANCE

172–THE UNMASKING
204–SOMETHING SO RIGHT

These books may be available at your local bookseller.

Don't miss any of our special offers. Write to us at the
following address for information on our newest releases.

Harlequin Reader Service
901 Fuhrmann Blvd., P.O. Box 1397, Buffalo, NY 14240
Canadian address: P.O. Box 603,
Fort Erie, Ont. L2A 5X3

Emilie Richards

SEASON OF MIRACLES

Harlequin Books

TORONTO • NEW YORK • LONDON
AMSTERDAM • PARIS • SYDNEY • HAMBURG
STOCKHOLM • ATHENS • TOKYO • MILAN

Published December 1986

First printing October 1986

ISBN 0-373-70240-X

For my children:
Shane, Jessie, Galen, Brendan,
who sometimes have to point the way.

CHAPTER ONE

THE FIRST THING she noticed was the silence. It hovered in the August morning air like a patient vulture waiting for his prey to cease its struggles. Elise had never realized that silence, something she had experienced little of in her thirty-five years, could be so foreboding.

Forcing herself awake she sat up in bed, pushing long strands of black hair away from her face with the palms of her hands. She listened carefully, but the silence remained unbroken. Through sleep-swollen eyes she gauged the time. There was no clock in her bedroom. Sleeping late had been one of the problems Elise had never had to worry about.

The heavy sunlight beating relentlessly through her window told her that the morning was at least half gone. *Why? Is Mama sleeping late too?*

The question triggered its own answer as she became more fully awake. *Mama.* No, Mama would sleep forever. Elise waited for the familiar sadness but this morning she could detect no signs of it. Her mother was gone; Jeanette Ramsey's death was unalterable. Elise Ramsey was alive, possibly for the first time in seventeen years.

And the house was silent.

Swinging her legs over the side of the bed Elise stood, her long cotton gown falling in snowy swirls around her bare feet. She drew aside the curtains at her window and peered out at the sun-dappled avenue. The town of Miracle Springs was awake, going about its business with slow-moving enthusiasm. Elise stood at the window for long minutes counting cars. One...two... Satisfied that by sleeping late she had missed absolutely nothing, she turned and began to search her closet for the coolest dress she owned. The day was going to be a scorcher.

The dress she chose was one her mother had never liked—not that it had been easy to please Jeanette Ramsey, anyway. But this particular dress had elicited comments about gypsies and dressing to suit one's age and position in the community. It was white with a full embroidered skirt in a style that was never quite in or out of fashion, and Elise felt young again when she wore it. She realized that in her mother's eyes, that had been the whole problem.

Elise fastened the dress and pulled a brush through her long hair, twisting it into a cool knot on top of her head, and wondered fleetingly how much longer she'd be able to get away with the severe hairstyle that did nothing to soften the inevitable signs of approaching middle age. She wasn't much of a judge, never having wasted time examining her appearance for innovative ways of dealing with its flaws. Elise had worn her hair long since she was a child. She loved it. Glossy, still black and utterly unstylish, it was an important part of her image of herself. If it emphasized features that were less than perfect, it also emphasized the high cheekbones and smooth olive skin that she liked to think were her best assets.

As she wandered around the room her movements made little noises, disturbing the intimidating silence and shaping it to suit her. Now that she was wide-awake Elise wondered why something she had longed for all her life—freedom, a chance to think her own thoughts—had seemed so threatening this morning. Undoubtedly, living alone was going to take some getting used to.

"But you will get used to it," she said out loud, "because you're probably going to spend the rest of your life alone." It wasn't a new thought or a particularly sad one. It was something she was just beginning to come to terms with, and like a child reciting a Bible verse, she spoke the thought as often as possible to commit it to memory and internalize it.

Downstairs, Elise stopped to throw open the heavy draperies in the living room before moving on to the kitchen to fix her breakfast. The old frame house was already beginning to soak up the day's sunshine. August in central Florida was as predictable as anything in life could be. It was hot and humid, guaranteed to slow the average person's pace by fifty percent. Most of the inhabitants of Miracle Springs cut their losses by air-conditioning their houses and places of employment.

Elise's house had one small air conditioner in the room that had belonged to her mother. The rest of the house had been left to the ravages of the Florida summer. Now Elise turned on a circular fan that was sitting on top of the kitchen counter and began to slice a grapefruit. She hummed as she worked, keeping the silence at arm's length with her own music.

This day would pass, and with it, the other sultry days of August. September would come, and with its arrival her life would once again be filled with the noise and confusion of teaching tenth grade English at

Miracle Springs High. Elise, who had spent most of her life wishing for silence, put down her grapefruit knife and picked up a pen. As she slashed an X through the date on the calendar above the counter, she wondered why that simple act gave her so much satisfaction.

"SO AFTER ALL THOSE YEARS of faking illness, Mrs. Ramsey just up and died last month. Just like that. Nobody even knew she was sick. She complained so much all the time Dr. Mooney didn't do more than give her a quick checkup. Next thing anybody knew, she keeled over in his parking lot. Gone in a minute."

Sloane Tyson sat in his aunt's living room and twisted the brim of his panama hat. The malleable straw crackled and popped as he ruined the shape of it forever. "So what happened to Elise after her mother died?" he asked, his voice a shade more enthusiastic than mere politeness dictated.

"Oh, she's still here. She'll be teaching again this year, I suspect. Best teacher at Miracle Springs High. Prettiest, too." Lillian Tyson looked at her nephew with interest. "Weren't you sweet on her years ago?"

Sloane had forgotten how every detail of life in a small town was collected and stored in the minds of its inhabitants. The system was more efficient than a computer bank and only slightly more personal. Today he had sat quietly and listened to his aunt's recital of the intimate details of the lives of Miracle Springs citizens, not expecting himself to be drawn into the conversation. He should have known better. He should have realized that Elise Ramsey would be on Lillian Tyson's list.

"You remember farther back than I do," he said nonchalantly. But of course, what he said wasn't true.

He'd forgotten a lot about Miracle Springs, put it out of his mind as if he'd never lived there, but he'd never forgotten Elise. No, he'd never forgotten Elise.

Lillian would not be daunted. "Well, it seems to me that you went steady with her your senior year."

"That was seventeen years ago."

"Around here, nothing much happens in seventeen years."

Sloane smiled wryly. His aunt was right, and it was precisely the reason he had left the small town of three thousand where he'd been born. He'd left at the first opportunity and never come back—except once, for his mother's funeral.

Lillian Tyson seemed to read his mind. "Are you going to make it, Sloane? Can you stand living here for a year?"

"My choices are limited." Sloane stood and began to pace the small living room that was crowded with old furniture and assorted knickknacks. He was a large man, and he dwarfed his surroundings as well as the old woman who fondly watched his pacing.

"You're like a tiger in a cage," she pronounced, proud of her analogy. "Always have been. Miracle Springs hems you in."

And it was precisely that "hemming in" that had brought him back, Sloane admitted to himself. For the first time he was in need of the sheltering influences of the little town, its slow, easy pace, its acceptance of its own. The last thought made him pause. "Do you think they're going to accept Clay?" he asked.

Lillian watched her nephew and her unfailingly cheerful face remained open and smiling. She didn't have to ask who "they" were. She knew Sloane referred to the citizens of Miracle Springs. "He's your son, isn't he? He's a Tyson. He may have some trouble, but he'll make it here.''

"He wouldn't have made it in Cambridge," Sloane said to himself as much as to his aunt. "The kids there would have eaten him alive.''

"They may try that here, but he'll be protected.''

"I guess that's a start.''

The living-room door swung open and a slender young man entered the room, his hands jammed in the pockets of stiff new blue jeans. "I fed your cats, Lillian,'' he said.

"Aunt Lillian,'' his father corrected him sharply.

"It's all right,'' Lillian said, waving aside Sloane's protest. "Clay doesn't know me from Adam. I don't seem like an aunt to him yet.''

"He's still got to learn the proper forms of address,'' Sloane said, his hat brim crackling anew in his hands.

"Aunt Lillian,'' Clay said pleasantly, stressing the first word. "All this relative stuff seems strange.''

"I suspect everything seems strange,'' Lillian said, a smile directed at her great-nephew. "But you don't seem strange to us. You're the spitting image of your daddy there. Right down to the way your hair swirls off your forehead.''

Clay nodded, glancing at his father to see what impact his aunt's comment had made on Sloane. With an insight far beyond his years, Clay suspected that their resemblance was not a source of pleasure to his father.

"Resembles you right down to the ponytail,'' Lillian said, this time to Sloane.

"Sloane had a ponytail?'' Clay asked.

"Nothing like yours,'' Lillian said, reaching out to tug the brown hair that fell in restrained waves to the middle of Clay's back. "When your dad was growing up around here, nobody'd even seen long hair on a man. Your dad's was short, barely long enough to put in a rubber band, but I'll tell you, it caused a stir in this town you wouldn't believe."

"What happened, Sloane?" Clay turned to his father and monitored his expression again.

"My uncle hauled me off to the barber shop. He was bigger than I was." The ghost of a grin lit Sloane's face.

Clay was encouraged. "Are you planning to repeat history?"

Sloane's expression became serious. "I'm not going to force you to do anything, Clay. It's your hair. I have no opinions about it one way or the other."

"Well I do," Lillian said firmly. "You want to fit in at Miracle Springs High, you get that hair cut before you go the first day. Kids'll like you better if you look like them."

Clay considered her words. "Why would they want me to look like them?" he asked finally. "That doesn't make any sense."

Lillian's jaw dropped a little, and Sloane shook his head. "You've got a lot to learn about teenagers, Clay," he said.

Clay shrugged. "I haven't even seen any teenagers here."

"Hasn't he been to the springs?" Lillian asked Sloane.

"I've been too busy settling in to take him."

"He can go by himself," Lillian admonished. "He's fifteen. This isn't Boston. Fifteen's old enough to go anywhere around here. Do you have a swimsuit?" she asked Clay. At his nod she added, "Do you want to go?"

Clay nodded again.

"Then go home and put it on. You can swim while your dad takes care of business this afternoon. I'll walk you down to show you the way."

Sloane waited until Clay was gone. "Are you sure that's a good idea?"

"He's got to start somewhere." Lillian observed the tiny frown lines on Sloane's forehead. "It's not like Clay's got something seriously wrong with him. He's going to be fine."

"He's got such a long way to go before he understands what this crazy world is all about. I feel like I'm throwing him to the lions."

"All parents feel that way," Lillian said, trying to soothe him.

"But not all parents are suddenly raising a son they didn't even know existed," Sloane said bitterly. "Not all parents have a son who didn't even know he had a last name until a month ago."

"And not all parents in that situation would care," Lillian reminded him gently.

"I never wanted to be a father."

"Give yourself time. Give Clay time. Give Miracle Springs time."

"Miracle Springs will have to bring me a miracle. I'm afraid that's what it's going to take."

"It's happened before." Lillian stood too and set her frail hand on her nephew's shoulder. "The first miracle was finding Clay; the second one will be really finding him."

Sloane's taut body relaxed under her touch. "I appreciate your optimism."

"I appreciate your coming back here. I may be a selfish old lady, but I'm glad you're home. Even if it's just for a year. You were always more like a son than a nephew."

Sloane's expression softened. "By the time we leave, you may be glad to see us go."

"Not likely."

Sloane put his arms around his aunt and hugged her much as he had as a young boy. There were some things that time and distance and endless mistakes never changed. Sloane knew that his aunt's love was one of them.

Lillian's eyes were teary when the embrace ended. "Don't go getting all soft on me, boy." She stepped back to search Sloane's face. "You know, as much as you dislike this town, you might find some things here for yourself this year."

"Such as?"

"Such as a mother for Clay."

Elise's name lay unspoken between them.

Sloane shook his head, his features fixed in decisive lines. "Clay will have to do with one parent. But then, that's more than he's ever had before."

"Just give this year a chance," Lillian said softly. "Let time take care of the rest."

But Sloane, who had never believed that time took care of anything, was lost in his own thoughts.

As Elise strolled under the succession of canvas and fiberglass awnings that were strung over Hope Avenue's sidewalks she wondered if she'd live long enough to see any changes in Miracle Springs. She had often thought that the only miracle the town had to offer was the way it had avoided entry into the twentieth century. Even if changes occurred, they were so subtle as to be invisible to the human eye.

The sameness of everything was like an opiate to creativity and to growth. It was a potent drug that lulled Miracle Springs residents into accepting the inevitability of their lives.

"This town'll kill you, Elise. It'll sneak up on you and bury you in its sameness until you don't know you're different from everybody else. And you'll die not remembering."

Elise stopped in the middle of the sidewalk and wondered at the voice she had just heard. She wasn't going crazy. There was no doubt where the voice had come from. It was in her memory, locked tightly there for safekeeping. It was Sloane's voice, and the words were some of the last he had ever spoken to her. She hadn't let herself think about that conversation for years.

She shook her head, not to banish the voice, but in distress at her own vulnerability. Seventeen years had passed and Sloane was still with her.

"Morning, Elise."

Elise looked up to see Olin Biggs, Miracle Springs mayor, bearing down on her. "Good morning, Olin."

"Hotter than Hades today. Same as yesterday. Probably the same tomorrow."

Funny. Those had been her thoughts exactly, only she hadn't been thinking about the weather. "It is hot," she agreed politely. "How's Sally?"

"She's doing fine. I think she's actually looking forward to school starting. You wouldn't consider moving up to eleventh grade English, would you? I know she'd like to have you as her teacher again."

Elise shook her head regretfully. "I can't do it. But tell her to come by and see me. She was a wonderful student." Elise fielded Olin's condolences about her mother's death and walked on. By the time she reached the post office, she had encountered two former students and one more parent. The students were now gainfully employed residents of Miracle Springs with families of their own. Elise felt the distinct sensation of middle-age settling over her. All she needed was a cat or two and a few gray hairs, and she'd be the sterotypical old maid schoolteacher. If she wasn't already.

She was sorting through her small collection of bills and advertisements when she heard a familiar voice behind her. "Elise. What a nice surprise."

Her smile as she turned was hopeful. "Hello, Bob. Is Amy with you?"

Bob Cargil shook his head, displacing the hair that was carefully combed to cover the widening bald spot at the center of his scalp. "No, she's at the springs. You look lovely this morning."

"Thank you." Elise smiled again. It was nice to have someone notice what she looked like. "You look like you're feeling fit this morning."

"I can't really complain."

A rebellious voice inside her proclaimed that if Bob couldn't really complain, it was the first time such a thing had happened. She squelched the voice with stern self-control. "How's the book coming?"

Bob shrugged. He was a history teacher at Miracle Springs High School and for the past five years had been working on a textbook for high school classes in Florida history. He had been stuck for the past four. "It's hard to work in this heat." he said.

"I'm sure," Elise commiserated. The rebellious voice reminded her that Bob's entire house was air-conditioned. Once again, she squelched it.

"Is our date still on for tonight?"

"I'm counting on it," she said with as much enthusiasm as she could muster. Then her voice brightened a little. "Is Amy coming?" Amy was Bob's fifteen-year-old daughter and Elise's biggest reason for tolerating Bob's presence in her life.

"No. This one's just us."

"Tell her I said to come by and visit."

"You know she will. She's always pestering me to let her come see you. But I know..." Bob's voice trailed off.

"Bob, I've told you, I'm not in mourning. Having Amy visit is something I look forward to."

"I'll tell her."

"Good." Elise reached out and squeezed his hand. "I'll see you tonight." She watched his retreat. Bob had recently developed a peculiar shuffling gait as if he were practicing for the old age that was still a safe distance away. Although he was ten years Elise's senior, there was nothing wrong with his health that exercise and diet couldn't cure. But Bob enjoyed the aging process and everything that went with it. Not for the first time Elise thought of the similarities between Bob and her mother, and shuddered delicately.

The chimes in the town hall tower announced that it was eleven o'clock. Elise knew that meant it was actually 11:06. The tower chimes had been six minutes off as long as anyone could remember. No one had ever bothered to fix them, and now if anyone suggested it, the town fathers pointed out that fixing the chimes

would only confuse people. It was better they reasoned, to leave them alone.

The prospect of a long hot afternoon stretched in
front of her, and on the spur of the moment, Elise decided not to spend it at home. There nothing awaited
her except silence, unrelenting heat and a few unnec-
essary household chores. For the first time in her life
she was really free to explore other options, and although there weren't many options to explore in Miracle Springs, there were a few. She stopped at the
drugstore, bought a turkey sandwich to go and took a
shortcut down Faith Street toward the source of the
town's name.

There was no silence at the springs. Crowds of teenagers with blaring radios littered the sandy brown
beach. The dock stretching from the beach out over the
water was covered with glistening, oiled bodies, and
underneath it small children darted in and out between the piers that had been sunk deeply into the
sand. Benches enameled a forest green sat in the shade
of palm trees and moss-draped live oaks at the beach's
edge, and Elise settled herself on one to enjoy the
clamor.

She wasn't alone for long. Former and soon-to-be
students dropped by to say hello. She had known most
of them since they were small children. Some were the
sons and daughters of her own high school friends;
others she had met at church or in her volunteer work
teaching reading at the tiny Miracle Springs library.
Elise was as certain of her popularity with the town's
young people as she was about anything in her predictable life.

A petite teenage girl with a cap of curly blond hair waved and then came to stand in front of her. "Hi, Elise. I've never seen you here before."

Elise patted the bench, and the girl sprawled beside her, spreading wet sand in her wake. Elise didn't even notice. "Hi, Amy. Where've you been all summer?"

"Here mostly." Amy's face grew suddenly serious. "Dad said you wouldn't feel like visitors because of your mom. But I've been wanting to come and see you. He was wrong, wasn't he?"

"Yes, he was." Elise put her arm around Amy's shoulders and gave her a quick hug. "But he was thinking of me so we won't be mad at him."

"Like I said at the funeral, I'm sorry about Mrs. Ramsey."

"Thank you." Elise smiled to let Amy know that she didn't have to remain so serious. "Now tell me what you've been doing."

They gossiped for a while and then Elise watched as Amy was pulled away by boisterous friends. It was only as she finished her sandwich and settled back to watch the teenagers' antics that Elise noticed the boy standing underneath a nearby tree.

She had heard Sloane's voice in the middle of a nearly deserted sidewalk. Now she was seeing his image and it was just as clear. She resisted the desire to squeeze her eyes shut. The voice had been a product of her memory. The image was real. And it obviously couldn't be Sloane himself.

Elise watched with fascination as the boy turned slightly, giving her a better view of his profile. She drew in her breath sharply as she cataloged his features. He had Sloane's wide forehead and his golden-brown hair waved back with the same determination Sloane's had always shown. Of course, this boy's hair was much longer, but cut short, Elise knew it still wouldn't settle down neatly. It would always be unruly and the girls would always ache to smooth it for him.

The straight nose was Sloane's; the deep-set eyes were too. Even though Elise couldn't see their color, she'd bet her life they'd be that peculiar shade of pecan-shell brown that almost bordered on gray. But it was his mouth that gave away his relationship to Sloane. It was a perfectly formed mouth, chiseled by a master hand, a mouth that could draw back in a sardonic grin or remain locked shut in an effort to avoid trouble.

Was the boy Sloane's nephew? A cousin? A son? The last seemed the most and the least likely. Elise hadn't seen Sloane in seventeen years, but she'd heard all about him. There were enough Tysons living in Miracle Springs to keep her informed, although Sloane's mother had died years before. She knew that he'd made a name for himself as an author. In fact, she'd read all his books. She knew that his personal life had been less successful. There'd been one marriage and one divorce a year later. To Elise's knowledge there'd been no child, but even if she was wrong and Sloane had had a son by that union, the boy would only be five or six. This boy was a teenager.

And yet, how could a cousin or a nephew emerge with Sloane's body and face? For that matter, as far as Elise knew, she had met all the Tysons. This boy was new in town.

As if he could feel her stare, the boy turned to face Elise. Even though politeness dictated that she look away, Elise could not. Instead she smiled tentatively. "Hi."

Elise accepted the fact that the boy would probably nod and move away. Talking to strange older women was no teenager's idea of a good time. Instead, he moved closer. "Hello," he responded.

"You're new here, aren't you?" she asked, encouraged by his proximity.

"Yeah. We just got to town last week."

And I've been out of touch, Elise thought to herself. *Or I'd know who you are.* "I'm Elise Ramsey. I teach English at Miracle Springs High. Will you be a student there this year?"

"I guess. If they let me in," the boy said candidly. "My name's Clay."

"I'm glad to meet you, Clay."

He nodded as if it only made sense she'd be glad to meet him. "What grade do you teach?"

"Tenth. What grade will you be in?"

"I don't know yet. They're having trouble deciding what to do with me."

Elise frowned. "How old are you?"

"Fifteen."

"Well, most fifteen-year-olds are in tenth grade. Did your other school hold you back or push you forward?"

Clay smiled. "I've never been to school."

It was an answer Elise hadn't expected. "That's surprising," she said as nonchalantly as possible.

"Yeah, I guess it is." Clay came to stand beside her. "If they put me in tenth grade English, what will I be studying?"

"I put a lot of emphasis on writing," she told him, studying him with undisguised interest now that he was closer. His eyes *were* the color of Sloane's. The confirmation gave her a slight jolt. After all these years she could still remember exactly what Sloane Tyson's eyes looked like.

"What kind of writing?" Clay asked.

"Creative writing. Poetry, short stories, plays. We read a lot, too."

Clay nodded. "I'll like that. I've done lots of writing. I started a novel when I was thirteen but I needed help getting over a hump and nobody at the ranch that year was a writer."

"The ranch?"

"Destiny Ranch, in New Mexico. I grew up there."

The name struck a familiar chord in Elise's memory, but she couldn't decide why. "I think I've heard that name before," she ventured.

"You probably have. They were always writing us up in the newspaper." Clay pointed at a group of kids standing by the water. "Do most of these kids go to the high school where you teach?"

"All of them and more besides. It's the only high school in the county, so kids are bused in from the surrounding area, too. You'll make lots of friends." But even as she said the words, Elise wondered how true they were. With his extravagant ponytail and his curious combination of adult intelligence and child-like candor, Elise wondered if Clay would stand out in a school where standing out was thought to be the worst possible crime.

But Clay had already shrugged off her optimistic prophecy. "I'm more interested in just finding someone I can talk to."

"Clay!" a voice on the other side of the dock shouted. "Clay!"

Without turning, Elise knew whom she would see. Somehow the day had been leading up to this. The foreboding silence that had punished her with images of her lonely future, Sloane's voice on the sidewalk, Sloane's image stamped on the boy sitting next to her. They had all been warnings of a confrontation that was yet to come.

"Sloane's calling me." Clay stood. "I'd better go. He hates to be kept waiting."

Not "Uncle Sloane," or "Dad." Not even the more formal, "my father." "Clay," she said, her courage failing rapidly, "are you talking about Sloane Tyson?"

The boy nodded. The too familiar lines of his jaw were set now, and his body was suddenly tense. "Yeah. See you later."

Elise raised her hand in salute as Clay walked away. She knew that all she had to do was turn her head. A slight rotation of her chin and she would see, once again, the only man who had ever meant anything to her. But it was no surprise to Elise that instead she continued to stare at the sparkling turquoise spring and the raucous children on the beach. No, it was no surprise that she lacked courage where Sloane Tyson was concerned.

Seventeen years had passed, but she, like the town Sloane had hated, was still essentially the same. She could take no risks; she could not reach out for what she wanted. She was no different than she had been the day she told Sloane she would not marry him and leave Miracle Springs forever.

Long minutes passed and finally Elise stood, turning to begin the walk back home. The laughter and shouts from the beach were no longer comforting. They only reminded her of what was missing in her life

CHAPTER TWO

"I MET A NICE WOMAN at the springs," Clay told Sloane, although Sloane hadn't asked about his day. As a small child, Clay had learned that if he wanted to talk about himself, he had to initiate the conversation and pick an adult who would be receptive. Since Sloane was the only adult available, he would have to do, even if his eyes were shuttered and his arms crossed firmly in front of his ribs as they walked down Faith Street. Clay, a master at reading body language, gave the conversation no more than a fifty percent chance of success. But it was worth a try.

"Good," Sloane replied.

Clay tried again. "She teaches English at the high school."

Sloane nodded but the length of his step increased. Clay, who was tall for his age, had to hurry to keep up.

"Her name's Elise Randall or something like that."

"Ramsey. Elise Ramsey. And yes, I know her."

"I hope I'll be in her class."

This time Sloane didn't even nod. He hadn't been close enough to get a good look at the woman sitting beside Clay on the bench, but his gut level reaction had assured him that it was indeed Elise Ramsey talking to his son. He had had a perfect opportunity to approach her, say a casual hello and permanently loosen the knot in his stomach that formed every time her name was mentioned. Elise Ramsey, for God's sake. Seventeen years had passed, and he had lived the equivalent of several lifetimes since then. So why was he behaving like an anxious adolescent, letting his reactions build up and submerge his common sense?

All it was going to take was one simple conversation, one short series of pleasantries to put Elise in the proper place in his psyche. The longer he waited the harder it was going to be. She was nothing to him but a woman from a small Florida town, a schoolteacher whose idea of fun was probably dinner at one of the two local restaurants and a drive to Ocala to take in a first run movie. She had undoubtedly absorbed Miracle Springs's value system, and now that she was finally free of her mother, she was probably hunting a husband with the frenzied tenacity of a spinster who sees her biological time clock winding down.

Sloane shook his head at his own conclusions. Why was he trying so hard to convince himself that Elise was anything other than the warm, intelligent, sensitive woman he had known? Of course, she hadn't quite been a woman seventeen years ago. She'd been poised on the razor's edge between adolescence and maturity. He had gone that far with her himself, and by now the years would have completed the transition. There was no reason to believe that all that had been wonderful about Elise had changed.

Nor was there any reason to believe that all that was not wonderful about Elise had changed, either. Underneath the warmth, the intelligence, the sensitivity had been a woman too weak to stand up for herself. In the end she had taken the easiest road. And with a flash of insight, Sloane realized that he had never forgiven her for doing so.

"Sloane?"

Sloane grunted, too lost in his own thoughts to pull himself out of them easily.

"I asked you if you used to go to the springs when you were a boy." Clay's tone was patient. Adults didn't like petulance. In that way he was sure Sloane was no different from any of the dozens of adults who had taken care of him throughout his fifteen years.

Sloane realized he was leaving Clay behind, and he slowed his pace a fraction. "I practically lived there when I was your age. Did you enjoy the water?"

"I didn't go in."

"Why not?"

"I never learned to swim."

Sloane flinched. There was so much he didn't know about this boy, this son who was a stranger. "I guess you didn't have much of a chance to learn in the desert," he conceded. "I'm sorry I didn't realize it before, Clay."

Clay heard the genuine regret in Sloane's voice and it surprised him. "What could you have done about it?" he asked curiously. "Besides, I always figured I'd learn how to swim once I got the chance."

"I'll see about getting somebody to teach you."

"Thanks, but I'll teach myself."

Sloane was intrigued, in spite of himself. "How do you propose to do that?"

"I've taught myself to do lots of things. I have a system." Clay paused. "Do you want me to tell you about it?"

"Go ahead."

Encouraged, Clay began. "First you have to divide everything into parts. Take swimming, for instance. You have to decide exactly what part of swimming you want to learn. If you want to learn more than one part, then you have to decide what order you want to learn the parts in.''

"Go on." Sloane realized that Clay was communicating more than a personal theory of learning. He was telling his father about his upbringing, and Sloane wasn't sure he could handle the revelations to come. But how could he explain that to Clay?

"Well, then you have to observe someone swimming. You have to concentrate only on the part you want to learn and tune everything else out. Then, when you can verbalize exactly what that person is doing and memorize it, you try it. But not before, otherwise you can get yourself in trouble.''

"What have you learned to do that way?"

Clay hesitated. The conversation had gone so well that he hated to spoil it by talking much longer. "Lots of things. Baking bread, riding a horse . . .''

"No one taught you those things?"

"Not those things. Mostly no one wanted to bother. They said if the environment was right, we'd learn without being taught." Clay recited the last words as if he were mouthing sacred doctrine.

"Page twenty-two of the counterculture bible," Sloane said, trying to keep the anger he felt out of his voice.

"It wasn't a bad life." Clay defended his past. "I was happy.''

Sloane clenched and unclenched his fists as they walked in silence the rest of the way home. Discussion of Destiny Ranch and what the community of people who lived there had and hadn't done for his son shortened his fuse to the point where it was almost nonexistent.

How had it happened that a son of his—a son he hadn't even known about—had been sentenced to fifteen years of exile in the New Mexican desert with a continually revolving community of dropouts from American society? Of course Sloane had to take some of the blame himself. He had fathered Clay, never considering the fact that Willow, Clay's mother, wasn't using birth control. He had been nineteen at the time, blissfully unaware of the most important fact of life: one always reaps what one sows. He had been drunk on freedom, drunk on the number of women who were his for the taking, drunk on the thought of a life without the fetters of Miracle Springs.

And now he was paying the price. No, that wasn't quite true. Clay had already paid the price. Sloane himself would be witness to that for the rest of his life. Somehow, he'd have to find a way to ease the growing burden of guilt and fury that threatened to overwhelm him every time he thought about his son.

Now he turned down Charity Street, oblivious to the curious looks of his neighbors as he and Clay passed.

"I'll take you swimming myself," Sloane said gruffly as they reached the steps of the house he had rented for the next year. "Tomorrow morning, first thing."

Clay watched his father enter the house and disappear. "That'll be fine," he said, although there was no one to hear his answer. Then he followed Sloane inside.

ELISE WASHED HER HAIR and parted it neatly in the middle. The late-afternoon sun was her hair dryer as she lay outside on a blanket, thumbing listlessly through an old magazine. The backyard was beginning to show signs of the drought that had lasted for more than three weeks. Elise considered turning on the sprinkler, then thought better of it. It would mean moving her blanket, and that seemed like too much trouble.

"Go ahead and burn up," she muttered to the surrounding foliage. "I'll just plant cactus."

The elephant ear plant nearest her nodded in the light breeze, and Elise shut her eyes in exasperation. Talking to plants was bad enough; having them answer meant she had hit bottom.

She hadn't felt this low, this abandoned, since the hours immediately following her mother's death. Then she had cried and the release had been welcome. There were no tears today.

How could she cry for something that had ended almost two decades before? Sloane had been out of her life for years and with him had gone possibility. Now possibility had returned, and so had Sloane. There was a message here somewhere, but it was in a language she obviously didn't understand.

Rationally she knew that Sloane's return to Miracle Springs at this crucial time in her own life was a coincidence. What else could it be? She had lived her thirty-five years in this little town that had been founded around a miracle—or so the story went—but Elise had never believed in miracles. At least not for herself.

Somehow, whether she believed in miracles or not, it was still as if the hands of fate had reached down to pat her on the head. She couldn't believe that she and Sloane were being brought together. That was too sentimental to be palatable. But it did seem that she was being given a chance to put her past in order, to de-mythologize it so that she could begin to imagine a new future for herself.

A future far away from Miracle Springs. A future with only the silences I want.

Even the thought of that much freedom shot ripples of fear through her body. The thought of facing Sloane again had the same effect.

Elise rolled over and then stood, lifting the blanket to shake and fold it. Inside, the house seemed cooler as she busied herself getting ready for her dinner with Bob. But nothing could keep her from remembering that she had purposely avoided Sloane at the springs today. And that memory triggered another memory of an evening at the springs when she hadn't avoided Sloane at all.

Sloane Tyson had been a remarkable young man. At least that was the way he was described by the few people in town who saw beyond the cynical smile and the saber-sharp tongue that ruthlessly flayed anyone who crossed his path going in the wrong direction. And Sloane had always been absolutely certain about the right direction. For everyone.

Still, Elise had known, even at sweet sixteen, that there was more to Sloane than intelligence and cynicism and arrogance. He was the only son of a widowed mother who had no talent for or interest in controlling him, and Sloane had always run wild with only the occasional firm hand of an uncle or two to keep him in line. But underneath his wayward exterior Elise had sensed a gentleness that only needed a chance to grow, a sensitivity that had to be hidden behind the facade of a rebel without a cause. She had also known that in order to recognize these parts of Sloane and treat him like the young man she instinctively knew him to be, she would have to face the wrath of her mother who was sure "that Tyson kid was going to ruin his family's good name.'' She would also have to face the scorn of her goody-goody friends and most of the population of Miracle Springs.

Even then Elise had known herself to be weak. While other teenagers were cheerfully using emotional blackmail to get what they wanted, whether it was a new curfew or the keys to the family car, Elise always swallowed her resentment and did as she was told. She was a dutiful daughter, a fact that brought her little recognition, and she succumbed time and again to pressure from her mother on almost every issue.

The exception had been Sloane Tyson. Years later she could recognize her fainthearted rebellion for what it was: a last-ditch attempt to stand up for herself, even if she had to do it in Sloane's sheltering shadow. But at the time it had been the most significant act of her adolescence. At the beginning of her junior year she had simply decided that the entire population of Miracle Springs could be damned. There was something about Sloane Tyson that she liked, and she had set out to discover exactly what it was.

It hadn't been easy. Sloane himself had shown no interest in her attempts to draw him out. He'd sneered at her friends, made fun of her interests, asked her if he was the September selection for her charity-of-the-month club. But once committed, Elise had refused to accept his hostility at face value. More and more she wondered if his reaction to her was fear that she might not turn out to be genuinely interested in him.

Not that Sloane didn't have girls interested in him. Half the female student body at Miracle Springs High—the wrong half—was rumored to have fallen prey to his restless vitality. In a school where getting close enough to unhook a girl's bra was an occasion for locker room rejoicing, Sloane was known to have moved to a new level of expertise without having to lift a finger. No, some of the girls had loved Sloane, had loved his sardonic good looks and his ability to make hash out of every teacher to cross swords with him. It was the others, Elise's friends, that amorphous group known as the "good girls," who wouldn't give him the time of day. And Sloane would no more have asked them for anything than he would have joined the Marines.

By late fall of her junior year, Elise realized her plan—Be Nice to Sloane and He Will Respond—was not going to work. His only response had been ridicule, and she was wearing down under his barrage of insults. She had decided to switch tactics in one final attempt to make him realize she really wanted to be his friend. With her heart in her mouth, and her reputation on the line, Elise had asked Sloane to be her date at the Miracle Springs homecoming dance. The invitation had been especially meaningful because Elise was one of two junior girls elected to the homecoming queen's court, and they would be spotlighted at the dance.

Sloane's reaction had been devastating to a girl whose riskiest act up to that time had been to pet a stray dog during rabies season. He had laughed at her. He had laughed so hard that he couldn't even answer, and Elise, to her chagrin, had burst into tears and run all the way home.

Her romance with Sloane had begun that night. The sensitivity she had felt in him had actually existed. He had called to ask if she would see him, and Elise had agreed because he couldn't hurt her any more than he already had. They had met at the springs so that Elise wouldn't have to argue with her mother about the company she was keeping.

Sloane was late, a habit that never changed in all the months they spent together, and Elise had become increasingly nervous as she waited. Had he set her up, hoping she'd come while he was off somewhere laughing about her interest in him? More and more certain she was being played for a fool, she had decided to leave when she heard his voice behind her.

"I'm glad you came."

Afraid to turn around, she had sat motionless on the green bench at the edge of the beach and waited for him to join her.

"I really didn't expect you to be here," he said, sliding into place beside her.

"I told you I'd come."

"And I'll bet your word is sacred." There was only a faint hint of cynicism in his voice.

"It is," she agreed. "I like people to feel they can trust me. Is trust one of those things you think is silly, Sloane?"

He hadn't risen to the bait. "No."

Mollified, she tried to smile. "I'm glad."

They sat in silence as the night breeze warmed them. Finally Sloane shifted his weight to face her, and Elise could feel his eyes on her. "What kind of Girl Scout game are you playing with me, Elise? I'm not your type, and I sure don't need to be rescued."

He might not need rescuing, but she did, and on some level, she had realized it, even then. "I know we're different," she said cautiously, too nervous to meet his eyes, "but there's something about you I like, Sloane, although today I've been having trouble remembering what it could possibly be."

"My good manners?" he asked helpfully.

Elise sighed. "I thought I saw something buried deep inside you that obviously isn't there."

"And like the good girl you are, you felt compelled to go for a treasure hunt."

"I'm going home." Elise stood and shook out the full red skirt of her dress. "We're wasting time."

In a moment she was back beside him and his fingers were locked around her wrist. "You're not going anywhere. You've been hounding me for weeks. I want to know what's going on."

"I have not been hounding you!"

"What do you call it?"

"I wanted to be your friend. I was being nice to you, just like I would be to anyone I wanted to be friends with. Now let go of me."

"Just friendship, Elise?" He had moved closer, pulling her arm around his neck as he inched forward. "Or were you hoping the rumors you'd heard about me were true? Were you hoping you'd get a chance to live dangerously?"

She had opened her mouth to protest and in a split second, he had covered it with his own, kissing her with a thoroughness that left her gasping for breath when he withdrew.

"Is that what you wanted?" he asked.

It had been, although she had not known it before. But she hadn't wanted to be kissed with Sloane's taunts still between them.

"Maybe it was," she said, stumbling over the words. "Maybe I have wanted you to kiss me, but I've wanted more than that, too."

"We can arrange that," he said pulling her closer to kiss her again, his hands beginning to wander over her slender curves.

Elise had begun to cry.

"Scared, Elise?"

She had shaken her head, sobs racking her body. She wasn't afraid of Sloane. It had never entered her mind that he might try and force her to do anything.

Surprisingly, he had loosened his hold on her and of her own volition, she had rested her head on his shoulder until she could calm herself. "I'm not scared of you," she said finally. "I'm just tired of your insults. I want to get to know you, and all you do is push me away."

"I was doing exactly the opposite."

"No you weren't." She straightened and slid a safe distance to the other side of the bench before standing. Sloane didn't try to stop her. "I'm going home." She had almost reached the street when Sloane called after her.

"Do you still want me to take you to the dance?"

She could have exacted retribution with a haughty no. Instead she shrugged helplessly. "Only if you'll call a truce for the evening."

"I'll pick you up at seven."

She had turned to give him a watery smile, tossing her long black hair over her shoulder as she did. "I'll be waiting."

And after that she was always waiting for Sloane, sometimes on her front porch, more often on the same green bench at the springs. She had waited for more than his presence. She had waited for him to kiss her again; she had waited for him to touch her, and finally to make love to her. She had waited for him to tell her he wanted her to come away with him, and at the end, when she couldn't go, she had waited for his understanding.

Only the last wait had been without end.

Now, as she dressed for her date with Bob, Elise realized that she was waiting for Sloane again. And what did she hope would happen when they were forced to confront each other with the barriers of seventeen years firmly in place between them? Forgiveness? A chance to ventilate self-righteous anger? The realization that the chapter of her life entitled Sloane and Elise had truly come to a close?

She didn't know. The only thing she knew for sure was that she was scared. And the thing that scared her the most was that Sloane might not even remember her name.

"YOU LOOK LOVELY as usual, Elise." Bob bent to kiss her cheek and then straightened slowly as if his back might be thrown out of shape by the subtle movement.

"Thank you." Elise took the bouquet of exotically hued zinnias that Bob handed her and automatically began to strip off the lower leaves to place them in water. "These are beautiful. I'm surprised they've made it through the drought."

"Amy waters them every day. She sent them for you."

"That's my girl."

"She might as well be. You're the only mother she's ever known." Bob followed Elise into the kitchen as she got a vase out of the cupboard.

"Amy's very special to me," Elise said matter-of-factly.

"Sometimes I think you wouldn't even bother with me if I didn't have a daughter."

Bob's comment was uncharacteristically revealing. Elise felt a flutter of surprise. After thirteen years of a relationship that could only be described as placid, were she and Bob finally going to talk about their feelings?

"Well," she said tentatively, "sometimes I think you wouldn't bother with me if you didn't have her. I've been a handy mother-substitute for Amy, haven't I?"

"You could have been more. I've offered you marriage more than once."

"Yes, you have." Elise ran water in the vase and waited while it filled.

"And you've always said no."

"And you've always been glad I did." Elise turned off the faucet and began to arrange the zinnias.

"That's not true."

"You don't love me. And I don't love you." Elise's tone was still matter-of-fact. "We both tried to make love happen. As lovers, we were complete failures." Without wanting to she thought of the nights in Bob's arms when she had found herself thinking of Sloane Tyson. Those nights had ended years before. A mutually agreeable but unspoken pact had put a stop to them trying to force feelings that weren't there. Elise wondered why Bob was discussing matrimony now. She wondered why she was, too.

"Maybe we don't love each other the way you mean, but I care about you. I respect you," Bob insisted. "Good marriages can be built on less."

Elise was surprised that the word "marriage" had crept into the conversation again. "What are you trying to say?" she asked, her curiosity aroused.

"What I'm trying to say is that now that your mother's gone, Elise, I want you to marry me." Elise turned to face him and watched Bob anxiously smooth back his hair. "I can't stand the thought of you alone here in this big old house. When Jeanette was alive, I didn't worry about you. You had her, and I knew she'd watch out for you."

Elise crinkled her brow, amazed that Bob had ever believed that Jeanette Ramsey had watched out for her daughter. In reality, Elise had spent the last seventeen years of her life watching out for her mother. Everyone in Miracle Springs understood that. Everyone except Bob. "What do you think is going to happen to me?" she asked him.

Bob avoided her gaze. "I just think you'd be better off married to me. We're both getting older. We can take care of each other in the years to come."

"I'm not exactly decrepit."

"Of course you're not," Bob tried to soothe her. "You're still a lovely young woman. But..."

"But I won't be for long?" Elise tried to decipher Bob's blank expression. Was there a flicker of fear behind the horn-rimmed glasses? Was Bob afraid for her? Elise abandoned the thought immediately. Bob was not the type to worry unduly about others. He was a good man, but he was tied up in his own little world. And she had always refused to share that world with him.

"If we marry, neither of us will have to be lonely," he said flatly.

"Do you really think marriage can prevent loneliness?"

Bob seemed startled by her words. He recovered quickly. "Obviously this isn't the right time for this conversation. I know you're still getting over your mother's death.''

''I'm fine, Bob.'' She tested his understanding. ''In some ways Mama's death is a relief. I'm free for the first time in my life.''

His look was disapproving. ''You never seemed to mind taking care of her.''

''I minded a lot.'' The strength of her words even surprised Elise. Not because they weren't true, but because she had finally spoken them out loud. Since her tongue seemed to be properly loosened for the first time, she continued. ''My mother was never sick a day in her life until the day she died. But I spent seventeen years waiting on her hand and foot, catering to every little whim. Now that she's gone, I feel like a tremendous burden has been lifted off my shoulders.''

''She was your mother, Elise.''

Elise nodded. ''She was. And I gave her a big chunk of my life. But I'm not going to waste any more of it wallowing in sorrow I don't really feel.''

''You surprise me.''

Since she had surprised herself, too, Elise could only nod.

Bob looked at his watch. ''We can continue this later. I made reservations at the Inn for seven.''

''I'm ready.'' Elise set the zinnias on the kitchen table and led the way to the front door.

As they drove along in silence, Elise wondered about the spurt of courage that had allowed her to say things to Bob she rarely had even allowed herself to think. At least part of her reason for being so honest had been to keep him at bay. She didn't want to marry Bob Cargil, but neither did she want to lose his friendship and, more importantly, the friendship of his daughter. Perhaps if he realized she was someone other than the selfless martyr he believed her to be, Bob would think twice before trying to push her into marriage.

They parked in front of the Miracle Springs Inn. The inn bordered the Wehachee River, whose source was the crystal-clear springs further down the road. The inn itself was a century-old ramshackle hotel with Victorian gingerbread outside and a mural in the lobby depicting the legend that had given Miracle Springs its name. It was a story of Indian lovers and untimely death, and the local Chamber of Commerce exploited it without a shred of guilt, as did the inn. It was terrific for business.

Bob and Elise ignored the fading painting as they walked directly to the dining room to claim their reservation. The room was crowded as always, and they were seated before Elise could scan it for friends. It would be an unusual night if she didn't know at least two-thirds of the people around her. She nodded to acquaintances and waited patiently while Bob went to greet one of the town's matriarchs at her table. It was only as she turned idly to examine the rest of the room that Elise realized that Clay and a man in a brown suit were sitting two tables away. The man was staring at her.

He had to be Sloane. So much was the same, and yet so much was different, too. Elise could almost feel her mind whirling as it adjusted to this new image of the boy who had never matured in her mind. Seventeen years. He was thirty-five, not eighteen anymore. His hair was still the same abundant golden brown, his body—at least what she could see of it—still hard and fit. Perhaps when he stood she'd see a protruding belly, a slackness of muscles, but she didn't think so. He had kept himself in shape.

The face was very different. The cynicism had hardened into harsh lines. He had a mustache now, a luxuriant one that drooped over the brooding lines of his mouth, giving him the appearance of a hard-boiled private eye. His nose seemed slightly off center as if he'd had it broken once. Elise didn't find that surprising. Sloane had always been the kind of man who could push others to the boiling point without even trying.

His eyes were unfathomable. Elise could feel their probing even though a table separated her from him. He was examining her intently but his expression was so distant that she couldn't tell if he recognized her. Her eyes flickered to Clay. His expression was unguarded and surprisingly warm. He, at least, knew who she was.

Her reaction took only seconds, yet it seemed to her as if she had sat there for years allowing Sloane his examination before she forced herself to stand and walk to his table. She could feel her hands perspiring, and she wiped them on the full skirt of her dress as she moved toward them.

She spoke to Clay first. "It's good to see you again, Clay," she said with a smile that took a surprising amount of energy.

"Hello, Elise."

She smiled again and then turned slightly to face the man she had not been able to face at the springs. "Hello, Sloane. It's been a long time." Silently she thanked Clay for having said her name. At least she didn't have to introduce herself to Sloane. That would have been more than she could bear.

Sloane stood, dwarfing her as he had always done. "Hello, Elise."

Elise inclined her head. They stood quietly examining each other. Elise wondered what he saw. Did he see the same woman he had known, older but not so old as to be unattractive? Did he remember the things about her that only he knew? Could he read the turbulence of her feelings in the black eyes that he'd written poetry about?

"You've hardly changed at all," he added finally. The words were said with no warmth. Elise suspected that no compliment had been intended.

She shrugged. "We all change. Even in Miracle Springs."

His mouth twisted into a humorless smile. "Funny. I've never been sure that's true."

"I know." She stepped back a little. If she'd had any doubts that Sloane didn't remember her, they'd been put safely to rest. Their simple conversation was charged with unspoken energy. Yes, Sloane remembered, and he'd never forgiven her. "You've changed," she said quietly.

"How?"

She examined his stylish haircut and expensive clothing. "You're more civilized somehow."

"It would be a mistake to think I'm much different," he said, a warning clear in the deceptively soft-spoken words.

Elise nodded. If she'd hoped for a simple conversation to destroy her memories, she had been mistaken. "I'd better get back to my table," she murmured politely. "It's nice to see you again." She turned to Clay. "Have a good dinner." After a nod to them both she made her way to the table where Bob was seated once again.

"I see you've rediscovered Sloane Tyson," Bob said dryly as Elise stared with unseeing eyes at the menu.

Elise heard the disdain in his voice, and it shocked her out of the near trance she had fallen into. "What does that mean?"

"You two were a couple in high school, weren't you?"

Elise nodded. Denial was useless in a town that remembered everything. "But I haven't seen him since the day we graduated."

"I knew he was back."

And Elise understood that those five words explained Bob's latest marriage proposal. At least they explained some part of it. She probed for further understanding. "Does it bother you that seventeen years ago I went steady with Sloane Tyson?"

"You did more than go steady." Bob's words were an accusation.

Elise carefully closed her menu and laid it next to her plate. "Why that should bother you now is beyond my understanding."

"It's always bothered me."

"Go on."

"I don't think so." Bob snapped his menu shut and without it to shield him, Elise saw that he was pouting.

"Seventeen years ago you were a twenty-eight-year-old married man with a wife who adored you. What does any of that have to do with today?"

"My wife isn't sitting in this room."

"Your wife is dead."

"I don't want Sloane Tyson making a fool out of you, Elise."

Elise counted the heartbeats throbbing in her neck. Twelve passed before she took a deep breath to answer him. "I don't think Sloane Tyson is the man in this room who's trying to make a fool out of me, Bob."

"I don't want you to get hurt." Bob picked up his menu and buried his face in it again.

Elise folded her hands in her lap, swallowing angry words. Unwillingly her eyes were drawn to the man two tables away. Sloane was staring into space, his eyes carefully veiled. Elise studied him for a moment before she forced herself to look away.

She wanted to believe that Sloane was not unaffected by their meeting. She wanted to believe that he, too, had felt the hidden energy coursing between them. They would never have a relationship again; the days of their love and their lovemaking were over. But suddenly, irrationally, it was important to know that Sloane was not oblivious to her.

She risked another glance, and this time she found his eyes on her. There was self-mockery in his stare as if he could not believe that he was being drawn into this intimacy. But he did not look away.

Defiantly, Elise stared back. She was not afraid of being hurt or of being made to appear foolish. She was not afraid of Sloane Tyson or even of herself. If she had a fear now it was that the years had wiped away all traces of the girl Sloane had once loved and with them, the one love affair of her life.

As if to reassure her, Sloane slowly lifted the glass of wine in front of him and held it out to her in a sardonic toast. Without thinking, Elise responded with her water tumbler. And for a moment, they were the only two people in the crowded little room.

CHAPTER THREE

SLOANE BARELY TASTED the fried catfish he had ordered and partially demolished. It was overcooked and bony, two trademarks of the inn's seafood menu, and not tasting it was a blessing. Out of the corner of one eye he could see Elise finishing a salad and talking to the man she was sitting with.

Lord, she was still beautiful. He had meant what he'd said to her. She had barely changed at all. It was as if she had been caught in a time warp, suspended like Sleeping Beauty, waiting for someone or something to come along and awaken her to the real world once again.

He gave a cynical snort at the last thought. How could she reawaken to the real world if she'd never been in the real world? Miracle Springs *was* a time warp. There was nothing here to make a person grow older. Nothing but heat and humidity and a mercilessly plodding progression of days that stretched into infinity until...

"Sloane?"

Sloane lifted his head to gaze at his son, and for a moment he felt caught in the time warp, too. There he was at age fifteen. The same face, the same color hair, the same lithe body. He blinked and cleared his mind of wandering thoughts.

"How do you like the seafood platter?" he asked, finally.

Clay nodded, surprised his father would want to know. "Well, I like it, but I don't know what I'm eating."

Sloane sighed. Everything was new to Clay, even the very food he ate. His son had survived fifteen years on vegetables and whole grains like a damn milk cow. Before anger could overwhelm him, Sloane allowed the calm voice of reason to intervene. There was nothing wrong with vegetables and whole grains. Most of the country would be better off with just such a diet. He took a deep breath, lifting his fork to point at the different things on Clay's plate. "Shrimp, oysters, some kind of fish—probably catfish—hush puppies."

"Hush puppies?"

"Hush puppies. I'll take you fishing for hush puppies someday, Clay."

Clay, who had already eaten one of the fried cornmeal nuggets and recognized the taste, smiled at his father. He wasn't used to Sloane's warmer side, and he found that he liked it. "You mean I can go fishing in the middle of a cornfield?"

"You're a Tyson. Around here that means you can do just about anything and get away with it."

"That should be interesting."

They lapsed into silence once more, and it continued until the end of the meal.

Several tables away Elise tried to concentrate on Bob's monologue. It was a useless exercise. She was as acutely aware of Sloane's presence as she would have been had he been sitting across the table from her. She could see him out of the corner of her eye, silently eating his dinner. She had noticed one brief exchange with

Clay, and then nothing more. Curiosity was the least of the emotions she was feeling, but she did wonder what relationship Clay had to Sloane. Whatever it was, it wasn't a comfortable one.

She had carefully avoided Sloane's eyes again after their impromptu toast. She was sure that he had been able to read the turmoil of her emotions in that one gesture. It would be just like Sloane to assume he had scored a point. She could almost hear his thoughts. *Well, little Elise never married. There she sits, growing older by the moment, just waiting for the right man to come along and claim her. There she is, just ripe for a brief love affair.*

Her own thoughts startled her. Was she imagining Sloane's words or were they her own? Was she indeed waiting for the right man? Was she indeed ripe for a brief love affair?

She continued to nod at Bob at the appropriate moments and smile when necessary, but her mind probed her emotions. It only made sense that seeing Sloan would resurrect the feelings she'd carefully put in storage all those years ago. That did not mean that she was still in love with him; that did not mean that she was even attracted to Sloane himself anymore. What it meant was that she was a woman who had denied herself one of the basic pleasures of life for too long. Feelings long repressed tended to make themselves known eventually. Sex was just one more factor to sort out in the jumble that was her life right now.

Having talked herself into accepting her feelings for what they were, Elise hazarded a glance at Sloane. He and Clay were standing to leave, and Sloane was watching her. There was nothing covert about his gaze. He was daring her to notice him, to respond to him in some way. Without thinking of the consequences, Elise lifted her hand and motioned for Sloane and Clay to come to her table.

When they were standing beside her, she gave them both her warmest smile. Already Bob had stood for the introductions. "Bob Cargil," she said, her voice steady, "I'd like you to meet Sloane Tyson and Clay..."

"Tyson," Sloane supplied. "My son."

Elise nodded as if that only made sense. She would puzzle out Sloane's and Clay's relationship later.

Bob and Sloane shook hands, but Elise noticed that Bob did not extend his hand to Clay. "Sloane's back in town for a visit," Elise continued, her intonation making the statement a question.

"Actually I'm back for the next year," Sloane explained to Bob. Elise knew that the explanation had been for her, however.

"It's nice to meet you," Bob said, his voice coldly polite. "I know most of the Tysons. I went to school with your Uncle Jack."

Sloane nodded. "It's almost impossible not to have gone to school with somebody from my family."

"Jack was a real hell-raiser, as I remember," Bob said.

"One of the three black sheep in the family. My father started the tradition, so I hear." Sloane's voice left no doubt as to who the third black sheep had been.

Elise interrupted before they could go on. "Well, it's good to have you here, Sloane, Clay," she said. "I'll look forward to seeing you both around." She wondered at her own words. They had sounded like an invitation.

Obviously Bob thought so, too. "Miracle Springs is so small, we're bound to run into you, aren't we, Elise?"

She nodded, but she couldn't keep a small smile from framing her even white teeth. Bob as protector. It was a role she was having trouble imagining. She raised her eyes to Sloane's, and for a moment their gazes locked. Then he inclined his head and turned to make his way out of the dining room with Clay following him.

"Black sheep," Bob scoffed as he took his seat. "From what I've heard, Sloane Tyson was the blackest sheep to attend Miracle Springs High. And I wouldn't be surprised if that son of his plans to set a new record."

"Clay seems like a very sweet boy," Elise protested. "Not rebellious at all."

"What do you call that ponytail? And did you see what he was wearing? A Save the Whales T-shirt in the Miracle Springs Inn dining room!"

"Do you really think it was any less appropriate than the way those kids over there are dressed?" Elise pointed to a table where two teenagers sat with their parents. The girl was wearing a flowered Hawaiian shirt and enough brightly colored plastic necklaces and bracelets to add five pounds to her weight. The boy was wearing a conservative blue polo shirt but his hair stood up in neatly arranged spikes all over his head.

"Tourists," Bob said.

Although Miracle Springs depended on tourism for some of its income, the local people looked down on the sightseers who thronged to the area in the summertime. Elise knew that Bob's use of the word "tourist" was one step away from profanity.

"Keep an open mind about Clay," Elise warned, knowing all the while that she was asking the impossible. "He may be in one of your classes this fall. If you let yourself, you might enjoy getting to know him."

The look on Bob's face rivaled Sloane's for cynicism.

CLAY WAS ENDLESSLY FASCINATED with television. Sloane was not. Tonight as Sloane sat in the tiny living room of the house he was renting and listened to the television blare, he thought he would go crazy with unreleased energy.

He had got exactly what he'd bargained for. He'd wanted a safe, small-town environment for his son. Clay needed a secure stopping place between the unreal world of the commune where he'd been raised and the dog-eat-dog world of urban America. Sloane had known that life in Miracle Springs wouldn't be exciting or challenging for himself. But he'd forgotten what it felt like to have the pressure build up inside him until he knew he was a walking time bomb.

What had he done as a teenager when he'd felt this explosive tension? He remembered he'd done crazy things. He'd gone skinny-dipping in the ice-cold water of the springs; driven his uncle's pickup at eighty miles an hour over sandy paths in the turkey oak and pine wilderness of the Ocala National Forest; taken a pup tent and a case of beer to some sweetly scented orange grove south of town and spent the night seeing how much of the illegally purchased beverage he and his buddies could consume. Just because it was something different to do.

Then there had been the other way he'd eased his restlessness. Elise.

"Clay, turn that thing down!" Sloane stood and lowered the volume himself before Clay could even move a muscle. Sloane hit his fist lightly on the top of the television. "I'm sorry," he said contritely. "I think I just need some fresh air."

"Did you want to go for a walk?"

Sloane nodded his head, and Clay stood, his eyes flickering back to the screen.

"You're in the middle of your show. I'll go by myself," Sloane told him. Clay, without a change of expression, sat down again.

Outside, the night air still held the day's heat. Despite the recent drought, the humidity was high and Sloane could feel it shimmer around him. He had grown used to the crisp, bracing air of New England and this steam bath felt strange and unpleasant. As he walked, Sloane paid little attention to where his footsteps were taking him. He crisscrossed Faith, Hope and Charity, grimacing at the ridiculous street names.

Years before, Miracle Springs, to get its share of Florida's billion dollar tourism business, had decided to go all out on a publicity campaign. Sloane remembered that he had been about eight years old when the city fathers had decided to change the street names to attract more attention. In addition to the three main streets downtown there was a Love Lane, and two others roads were called Grace and Mercy. Luckily, the town council had run out of inspiration at that point— or else they had run into opposition from citizens who wanted no part of the sham. The rest of the county had been spared from suffering the embarrassment of the people who lived in the center of town.

Back on Hope Avenue, Sloane began to head away from the springs. His steps slowed and he paid careful attention to his surroundings. There was a house missing here, a new house there, but essentially Hope Avenue hadn't changed much. Mayor Biggs's house had just been painted, a real estate office had been opened in the home of a childhood friend. And then there was Elise's place.

Sloane stopped pretending that he had been going anywhere else. He was standing exactly where he had meant to stand, standing where he had stood countless times before. For a minute he could almost pretend he was seventeen or eighteen, waiting on the sidewalk for Elise to come down the steps and join him. Now there were no parents to disapprove of his visit. Only Elise, who would probably disapprove just as much as her parents had ever done. Sloane looked up at the two-story frame house and considered his next move. He could go home again, or he could walk up to the front door and hope she was home alone.

And then what would he say? *Hello, I just dropped by for a chat? Hello, I thought we could catch up on seventeen years?* Sloane felt a surge of disgust at his own ambivalence. He couldn't remember a moment since leaving Miracle Springs when he'd been so confused. He felt like a teenager; he was acting like a teenager. Sloane Tyson, a man who had no tolerance for weakness in himself or others, stood on the sidewalk and wondered exactly what had brought him to such a state.

THERE HAD BEEN NO PARTING KISS when Bob dropped her at her front door. He seemed to have taken Sloane's presence at the inn as a personal insult, an insult for which he blamed Elise. Considering Bob's mood for most of the evening, Elise hadn't been surprised when he'd taken her key, unlocked her door and said a chilly good-night. Then he had got in his car and driven away.

Now, Elise undressed leisurely in her bedroom with the lights off and the windows and shades wide open to capture whatever breeze was stirring. It was too late to catch the beginning of anything on television, too early to go to bed. She knew if she tried to read, the words would blur in front of her.

She pulled on a long summer nightgown of cool white cotton and sat on the bed, taking the pins out of her hair. It fell almost to her waist, and she brushed it absentmindedly as she thought about the evening.

She had finally faced Sloane. It hadn't been as hard as she had imagined; she had handled herself with aplomb. She was not a confused adolescent. She was Elise Ramsey, popular teacher.... She could think of no other description that was flattering. Spinster. Old maid. Unclaimed treasure.

What was wrong with her? From what corner of her mind had the self-doubt emerged? She had nothing to be ashamed of. Whatever her life lacked in excitement, she could at least be proud of the respect with which she was held in Miracle Springs.

But somehow, tonight, respect seemed a poor substitute for something else.

Her thoughts were interrupted by a series of knocks on her front door. Elise stood, dropping her brush on the bed, and then reached for the robe that matched her gown. The cotton was sheer, but not sheer enough to be revealing, and she gathered it around her as she hurried down the steps.

Sloane was just turning to leave as she opened the door. For a moment they stared at each other, both surprised. Elise, who'd felt perfectly modest in the gown and robe, now felt unclothed. Sloane, who'd convinced himself he knew what he was doing, felt tongue-tied.

"Well, I didn't expect to see you here," Elise said finally, pulling the robe a little tighter.

"I didn't expect to be here," he murmured, taking in the picture she made with her black hair falling over the gossamer white fabric. His body's reaction was unmistakable and he felt a surge of anger at its betrayal. He forced himself to speak calmly. "Would you believe I was in the neighborhood?"

"That's one excuse that always holds water around here. Everything's in the neighborhood." She frantically searched her memory for the appropriate etiquette. There was none. Sloane seemed to be waiting for something, and finally, she shrugged. "Would you like to come in?"

"Yes."

Elise stepped back and opened the door wider. Sloane brushed past her, and Elise felt crowded by his presence in the hallway. Sloane had always been big, and although her height was almost average, he'd always made her feel tiny and fragile. She wondered if he enjoyed having that effect on women.

"Are you here to pass the time, Sloane? Or did you have a reason for coming?"

"I had a reason." Sloane turned and without asking for an invitation, made his way into the living room. Elise had no choice except to follow. "Are you alone?"

"I always dress this way for company," she chided him gently.

"Bob what's-his-name left early," he said with satisfaction.

Elise felt small flickers of anger beginning to kindle. "That's no concern of yours, is it?"

"Only that I don't want to make small talk with him."

"You never were much good at small talk."

"I never wanted to be."

Elise realized that Sloane was still standing. "Sit down," she said as graciously as she could manage. "Would you like iced tea? I'd offer you coffee, but it's too hot even to think about it."

"Nothing, thank you." Sloane sat on the sofa, and Elise chose an overstuffed chair across the room, arranging her gown and robe around her as she sat. She was suddenly conscious that her feet were bare. That small intimacy left her mouth feeling dry.

"Did you have a nice dinner?" she asked, simply because it was the only thing she could think of to say.

"Does the Miracle Springs Inn serve nice dinners?"

"You have to know what to order."

"Obviously I didn't."

Elise fidgeted in her seat. "How does Clay like living here so far?" she asked after a few moments of silence.

"We haven't been here long enough for him to form an opinion."

This time the silence stretched for a full minute; Elise realized she found it unbearable. Sloane was staring at her and even in her agitation, she couldn't miss the cool, male appraisal. Finally she stood. "This is awful," she said with heartfelt honesty. "Even if you don't want tea, it'll give me something to do while we talk or don't talk." Without another word she marched into the kitchen, and Sloane, with a slight smile, followed her.

"I didn't come to make you uncomfortable," he said, standing in the doorway as she moved gracefully around the old-fashioned kitchen.

"Didn't you?"

"Actually, I lied a little while ago. I don't know why I came."

"Sloane Tyson? Unsure of himself?" Elise heard the challenge in her voice, and it surprised her. All day she'd dwelt on the fact that Sloane had not forgiven her for her actions of seventeen years before. Now she realized that she had never forgiven him either.

He went on as if she hadn't spoken. "I guess I'd like to put the past to rest. We'll be seeing each other; this town is too small to hide in."

Elise nodded. "All right. How do you propose that we put the past to rest?"

"We could catch up on each other's lives."

What a deadly game that would be. Sloane would tell her of his fame, his success, his loves. And she would tell him of endless years of caring for a petulant mother and teaching English. Then Sloane would be vindicated, knowing that he'd been right when he'd told her that Miracle Springs would strangle her, cut off her life's blood and her spirit's sustenance.

And yet she wanted to know about him. She wanted to know what he'd done and who he'd become. She wanted to know exactly whom she would be dealing with for the next year.

"All right," she conceded. "You go first." She held out the glass of tea and Sloane took it politely. Elise leaned against the sink and Sloane leaned against the stove. They measured each other across the narrow space.

Sloane began. "Seventeen years is a long time to cover."

"I know some of it. I heard you got married and divorced. I know about your success as an author." She weighed her next words and decided to go ahead. "I've read all your books. You're very good."

"I'm surprised you've read them."

"Why? Didn't you think people in Miracle Springs might be interested in philosophy or sociology? I particularly liked the one you did comparing the problems of Vietnam veterans and those who resisted the draft. I find your viewpoints stimulating. But then, I always did."

Sloane held out his glass in a mock salute. "Touché."

"No one likes to be patronized, Sloane."

"Was that what I was doing?"

"I think so, yes."

Sloane sipped his tea. "What else do you know?"

Elise shrugged. "That's about it."

"When I left here I traveled out west."

"I know that's what you'd intended." She knew because she'd intended to go with him. Even now she felt a pang at the lost opportunity. Especially with the real Sloane Tyson standing mere inches away, overwhelming her tiny kitchen.

"I hitchhiked for a while and then I ended up with a group of people in the Destiny Community. Have you ever heard about them?"

Elise drew designs on her foggy glass as she tried to remember. "Clay said something about a Destiny

Ranch today when I was talking to him at the springs. It rang a bell but I can't remember why.''

"Same group. But seventeen years ago they were a traveling commune. They sold food and provided medical care at rock festivals.''

"Sort of a hippie Red Cross. Now I remember. And you got involved with them?''

"It was a way to see the country. When we weren't traveling we stayed at one of their five farms. I met lots of different kinds of people. For a kid hungry for new experiences, it was wonderful.''

"And then?'' Elise looked up.

"I got tired of the whole scene.'' Sloane smiled at his own lapse into sixties vernacular. "Drugs were plentiful and I got tired of seeing people freaking out. There were always good, stable people with real ideals trying to keep Destiny on an even keel, but there were the crazies, too. One day I realized I was having trouble telling the difference.''

Elise tried to imagine a life like the one he was describing. "It sounds . . . colorful.''

"It was that.''

"Your books are so knowledgeable about the counterculture. Now I understand where you got a lot of your ideas. It wasn't all impersonal research.''

"No.'' Sloane finished his tea and set it on the stove. "I decided to go back to school when I turned twenty. Goddard College in Vermont had a program that was liberal enough to interest me. I was liberal enough to interest them, and they gave me a good-size scholarship. Then I went on to Boston University and finally Harvard where I was given a job as assistant professor of sociology.''

"You're still there, aren't you?''

"I'm on sabbatical for a year. Actually I don't teach many classes. They give me lots of time to write and do the lecture circuits."

"And you like Boston?" Elise wondered just how long she could make her final swallow of tea last. The glass was a useful device for keeping her hands busy.

"I live in Cambridge near the campus. Yes, I like it."

"Where does Clay fit into all this?" Elise realized her glass was finally empty and set it down, folding her arms.

"Now that the conversation is rolling, do you think we could go back to the living room?"

Elise nodded and followed Sloane back through the house. They resumed their original seats, and suddenly they were both wary again.

"Clay," Sloane began, "is my son by a woman in the Destiny community. We had a short . . . relationship, and when I moved on she didn't see any point in letting me know she was pregnant with my child." His voice had turned bitter.

"How could she do that to you?" Elise imagined that the anger she felt was nothing compared to what Sloane must have experienced when he discovered he had a son.

"She didn't do it to me. You'd have to understand Destiny to understand how it happened. Pregnancy and childbearing were thought of as natural functions—impersonal natural functions. Everyone liked the idea of children, although how many people actually liked kids, I can't say. Most of the women there got pregnant at one time or another. The children were raised by the community. Family ties weren't forbidden, but they weren't encouraged. As it happened, Willow, Clay's mother, was a die-hard supporter of the Destiny concept. Since everyone was supposed to help raise the kids, no one thought to make a point of whose child Clay was. He never knew; I never knew. Only Willow knew.''

Elise sensed the emotion behind the clipped words. ''And how did you find him?''

''Destiny's time came and went. Their numbers dwindled. They sold one farm, then another. Eventually what was left of the community settled on their New Mexico ranch where, as near as I can tell, Clay has been since he was a toddler. Finally, even that property had to be sold several months ago. There was only a handful of people left at the end. Seven of them were kids under the age of sixteen.''

''And Willow contacted you?''

''Willow had been gone for years.'' Sloane put his hands behind his neck as if to ease the tension there. ''The authorities were called in, and the kids whose parents weren't on the ranch were put in foster homes. Eventually they traced Willow to California. She's married with a new baby. Her husband's an accountant. He didn't want Clay; Willow didn't want Clay. She told the authorities to find me.''

Elise couldn't think of one thing to say. Obviously, however, her eyes betrayed her feelings.

''Yes,'' Sloane said softly, ''it was the surprise of a lifetime.''

''I'm sorry. You've been cheated so badly.'' Elise cast about for words to better console him, but found none.

''Clay's the one who's been cheated. A mother he never really knew, a father who doesn't have the faintest idea how to be a parent.''

''Then you're finding it difficult?''

"We're getting by."

"Clay seems like a nice boy. I think he'll be a son to be proud of."

"Your turn, Elise."

Elise was jolted by the back-to-business sound of Sloane's voice. She realized that her sympathy had made him cautious. Evidently the atmosphere had warmed up too much. She tried to sound matter-of-fact. Actually there was so little to say about her life that there was no other way to sound.

"After you left I commuted to the University of Florida and got a degree in English education. I've taught at the high school ever since." She searched for details to make her existence sound less dull. "I like teaching, and that part of my life has been more than satisfying." Damn, why had she said that? She might as well have announced that the rest of her life had been anything but.

"You never married." Sloane's face was carefully blank, but Elise could read his thoughts anyway. There was no point in trying to pretend.

"No. I lived here with my mother until she died last month."

"This house hasn't changed a bit. It's exactly as I remember it."

"Mother got more and more rigid as she grew older. Change frightened her." Elise tucked her feet under the folds of her gown and crossed her arms in an instinctive gesture of self-protection.

The gesture wasn't lost to Sloane. He was torn between wanting to comfort her and wanting to rage at her for sacrificing her life for the whining, peevish woman who had given birth to her. "Did she ever love you for it, Elise?'' he asked finally. ''Did your sacrifice ever make her love you?''

Elise could feel the blood drain from her face. How could he? How could he take her life and reduce it to a pathetic quest for maternal love? Seconds passed as she tried to force words past the lump in her throat. ''I think you'd better go,'' she said finally. Her voice was as cold as his words had been.

''Not until you answer me. I want to know if staying here was worth it for you. I'd like to think it was. I'd like to think your life hasn't been a waste, that you got something important from remaining in Miracle Springs.''

''None of this is your business!''

''I wish to God that were true.'' Sloane stood and for a moment Elise thought he would leave. Instead, he began to pace the length of the room. ''I made it my business seventeen years ago. I haven't forgotten what we meant to each other; I haven't forgotten you.''

He heard her gasp and he stopped to search her face. ''Don't get the wrong idea,'' he said with his familiar cynical smile, ''I haven't been carrying a torch. When you refused to go with me, it destroyed whatever we'd had. Except...'' His voice trailed off.

''Except what?''

''Except that I wanted to be completely free of this place. I wanted to leave without another thought. Instead, you kept a part of me behind with you. I've felt the pull all these years. I've never been able to forget Miracle Springs the way I've wanted to forget it.''

''And you blame that on me. Convenient.'' She was surprised that she was capable of such cold sarcasm. Inside she felt wounded, bleeding.

"You were the only person in this town besides a few relatives who ever meant anything to me."

"You have a funny way of showing me I was once important to you." Elise stood, too. She felt much too vulnerable sitting while he towered above her. "You come into my house and demand to know if I've wasted the last seventeen years of my life. You haven't written or called or visited me in all those years, and yet you believe you have the right to insist on answers."

"We both know I have the right."

Sloane was facing her now, and they were only inches apart. "Get out," she said, as calmly as she could manage.

"Believe it or not, Elise, I want to know you were happy. I'd like to know I was wrong when I told you that you were throwing away your life."

She wanted nothing more than to tell him that he had been wrong. She wanted to pull out warm, happy memories to flaunt in his face. But warmth and happiness had been missing from her life. Except for her students and Amy Cargil, no one had really touched her in seventeen years.

"I'm exactly what you see, Sloane. An old maid schoolteacher living in a house that hasn't changed since you left. My mother died a bitter woman unable to reach out to anyone or appreciate anything that was done for her. I've spent my whole life giving love and not getting much in return." She lifted her head a notch.

"But there's something you can't see, too," she continued. "I've taken more risks than you'll ever take, even though I stayed in Miracle Springs and you went off to see the world. I've given love, with absolutely no guarantee of having it returned. And I don't regret one instant of it. I may be weak. I may be afraid of change. But I'm not afraid to give myself. Can you say the same?''

She had summed up the totality of his life in a few sentences, just as he had done for her. Sloane was shocked at her insight and more shocked that she would use it on him. Perhaps she didn't think that she'd changed, but this one change was obvious to him. The Elise Ramsey he had known would never have fought back so effectively. Silently he applauded her courage.

"No," he admitted, "I can't say the same. I've lived for myself."

"Has that made you a happy man?"

"Does such an animal exist?"

"I'd like to think so."

"That's always been one of the differences between us."

Elise could feel her anger melting away. For a moment Sloane's voice had lost its chill, and she could hear the echoes of the young man she had known and loved. Was it possible that Sloane was still vulnerable? That he too was searching for that elusive something that made life worth living?

"I think if you give up on happiness, you do yourself a great disservice," she said softly. Unconsciously she leaned closer to him. "I'd rather spend my life looking for it and not find it than give up the search and miss it when it's right in front of my nose."

Sloane resisted the temptation to cover the distance between them. He could smell her sweet fragrance, a faint, floral smell that reminded him of orange blossoms and night-blooming jasmine. He felt something twist inside him, something that hadn't moved in years.

He'd wanted plenty of women, but this feeling was different. It angered him, and he used his anger to keep her away.

"And if you had to reach out for this so-called happiness, Elise, could you do that now? Could you leave safety to find love?" His voice was cold again.

"You've never forgiven me, have you?" Elise took a step backward. The warmth she had begun to feel died within her. "I was young and afraid. And I felt a tremendous sense of duty to my mother. You never understood fear or duty. We were so different."

Sloane shrugged. "It was a long time ago."

"I've never forgiven you, either." Elise found his eyes and held them. "All I asked for seventeen years ago was a little time. I wanted the summer to help my mother adjust to my father's death. I'd have gone with you in the fall. Nothing would have stopped me."

"I didn't believe it then and I don't believe it now. But why are we torturing each other about an adolescent love affair?" Sloane looked at his watch. Both of them knew the gesture was a ruse. "I've kept you up long enough."

Elise wanted to protest. Now that they had begun, they needed to finish. But she didn't allow her feelings to show. "I won't say I was glad to see you," she said honestly. "I hope the next time we meet we'll have a more cordial conversation."

"I doubt that we'll be having many conversations at all. I'm working on ideas for a book while I'm here, and I'm going to be very busy."

"Then the best of luck," she said with exquisite self-control. She wanted to shout at him, rage at him for running away before they could finally, once and for all, put an end to their past. "Please tell Clay I'll be looking forward to seeing him at school.'' She turned and found her way to the hall and the front door.

Sloane's face was a mask. He followed her, trying not to notice the graceful femininity of her walk or the sensuous veil of hair that shimmered under the lights in the hallway. Why had he come? Better yet, why had he reacted so strongly to her? He always understood his own motivations, but his reasons for this visit to Elise were a mystery. Miracle Springs was already weaving its cloying spell around him. He'd be damned if he'd be its helpless victim.

''Good night, Elise,'' he said as he stood in the open doorway. Against his will he searched her face for a clue to what she was feeling. But her face was carefully blank.

''Good night, Sloane.'' She waited a split second, and then added, ''If you ever decide you'd like to finish this conversation, I'll be available.'' She smiled a little, knowing she had effectively had the last word. Even if Sloane never came back, she had made it clear that she knew he was the one who had lacked courage this time. With a small flourish she closed the door in his face.

CHAPTER FOUR

CLAY FIDDLED WITH THE STRAPS of his backpack, adjusting and readjusting it until its weight was distributed perfectly. "I guess I'm ready."

Sloane was surprised by the hesitation in his son's voice. In the months they'd been together, Clay had shown an inbred self-confidence in every new situation. Whatever his secret anxieties, he radiated a quiet composure and strength of character far beyond his years. But this morning, his first morning at Miracle Springs High, he seemed like the adolescent he really was.

Somehow, Sloane found this reassuring.

"Feeling a little worried?" he asked Clay.

Clay looked up and gave his father a tentative smile. "Yeah."

Sloane allowed himself a moment to run through his private and all too familiar litany of resentments. His son should not have to feel this apprehension. Going to school should be second nature, as natural as breathing. He ought not to have to worry about what he should do, what he should say. About now a gang of teenagers should be descending on the house, hooting on the front porch for Clay to come join them. Clay should be making some parting wiseass remark to Sloane, then standing with both thumbs hooked in the pockets of his jeans, eyes rolling while he listened to

Sloane's reprimand. His walk to school should be filled with discussions of girls and football and rock stars. The joys of adolescence.

"Miracle Springs High isn't exactly a prep school for the Ivy League," Sloane said, feeling a strong need to reassure his son, "but it's a good school with some fine teachers. After a few weeks it'll feel comfortable."

"I don't think I can sit still that long every day."

Sloane tried to imagine what it would be like for Clay to be confined to a classroom for hours after the freedom of Destiny Ranch. Clay was right; the adjustment would not be easy. "It's something you'll have to develop. This world is filled with places where you have to sit still."

"Once I was sick for three weeks. I had to stay in bed the whole time. I thought I'd go crazy." Clay fidgeted as he talked, as if to make his point more emphatically.

Three weeks in bed. Sloane swallowed, but his voice was still harsh when he spoke. "What was wrong with you?"

"Nobody ever said."

"Did anybody bother to find out?"

Clay stood very still. "They took care of me. I got better."

Sloane knew it was useless to torture either of them with more questions. Questions didn't change a thing. Questions, especially questions that were accusations, didn't bring back the little boy he would never know. "If you're ready, we ought to go now."

Outside Sloane paused by the car door and debated with himself about driving or walking. Driving would get them there faster, and Sloane had a lot to do that day. Walking would give them a chance to talk, maybe help settle Clay's fears a little. Was parenting always such a balancing act? Whose needs took priority?

"Can we walk?" Clay asked, eyeing the car warily. "I'll be sitting enough today."

"Good idea," Sloane said gruffly, the decision having been made for him. "Let's go by the springs."

They covered the blocks to the springs in silence. The route had become familiar to them both. Sloane had kept his promise to his son and in the past week they'd come every day for swimming lessons. Clay's excellent coordination and uncanny ability to concentrate completely on a task had brought quick results. His strokes were still a little awkward, he sometimes forgot to lock his knees when he kicked, but by and large, he had learned to swim.

But he hadn't learned to enjoy the water.

Sloane could see it in his son's eyes when Clay waded into the icy-cold springs each day to begin swimming the laps he felt he had to do to perfect his skills. Learning to swim was a task. He brought tremendous natural ability and wholehearted participation to it. He did not bring the abandon, the childlike release of inhibition that Sloane remembered feeling at Clay's age. Even now that Clay was safe in the water, able to cover distances without fear and able to submerge himself totally and find his way back up, he still showed no signs of liking the experience.

At the entrance to the springs they stood for a moment at the edge of the beach leading down to the water. Then they turned and continued along Hope Avenue toward Miracle Springs High.

"You've never told me why they call it Miracle Springs," Clay said, turning for one quick look before he followed his father.

"I'm surprised your Aunt Lillian hasn't told you the story."

"She probably thinks you did."

Sloane wondered why he'd never thought to explain the legend to his son. How many other things had he neglected to tell him? "Do you remember the mural in the lobby of the Inn?"

Clay nodded. "The one that needs to be repainted?"

"Either that or wallpapered over. Well, it's supposed to be a depiction of the story about the springs."

Clay tried to summon up the picture. "It had Indians on it, didn't it?"

"It's a very anglicized Indian legend. This part of Florida was inhabited by Indians as early as ten thousand years ago, and by the first century A.D. most of the peninsula was well populated."

"The Seminoles," Clay interrupted. "I studied Indian tribes one year because we had two Ind . . . Native Americans living on the ranch. They were Hopis."

"Well, you're right about Seminoles being in Florida, but not until much later. Originally the Timucuans inhabited this area. And the tribe in this county was called the Ocali. They were village and town dwellers who hunted and fished and grew corn. They were noted for being a beautiful people."

"What happened to them?"

"They got caught in the cross fire between the English and the Spanish, and they also fell prey to the Creeks, or Seminoles as they were later called, who were invading from the North. What few remained were said to have been taken back to Spain by the Spanish when Spain ceded Florida to England."

"The Timucuans named this town Miracle Springs?" Clay asked skeptically.

"No, the town fathers named the town Miracle Springs back in 1883."

"It's all clear to me now," Clay said, teasing his father.

Sloane smiled. He was enjoying himself. Somehow this conversation seemed free of the tensions that permeated most of their discussions. He wanted to prolong it. "Well good," he teased back. "Then I don't have to explain anymore."

"Go ahead if it makes you happy."

"Have you ever noticed the little island in the middle of the river, just down from the spring?"

"There's a big gnarled mass of roots and a bunch of spiky-looking plants that the water doesn't quite cover," Clay observed.

"That's where the miracle occurs."

"The miracle is that nobody's dug it up so boats can get by easier," Clay said, obviously not impressed.

"The legend says that once, hundreds of years ago when the Timucuans still called this area home, there was a beautiful Indian maiden ..."

"Let me guess. A chief's daughter."

Sloane smiled at Clay's innocent brand of cynicism. "Right. She was about to be married to a handsome young man whom she had loved since she was a child, but she grew very ill. The chief and the tribal shaman did everything they could to save her, but it was soon apparent that she was going to die."

"So they put her in the waters of the spring, and she was instantly healed," Clay finished for him.

"No. She died."

"Then they should have called it Disappointment Springs."

"Who's telling this story? Anyway, right before she died, the young maiden called her father and her young man to her side. She told them she had asked the sun—the Ocalis worshipped the sun—to spare her so that she could do good works. She said her life had been too short to do enough good for others, and she wanted a chance to do more. But the sun had withdrawn its rays in answer. Then she fell asleep and had a dream. In her dream the sun came to her and told her to ask her father to place her body on the island after her death. Then, every year on the anniversary of that day, she could return to grant wishes to those pure of heart who asked for her help."

"And does she?"

"Well, supposedly she died that afternoon and her body was taken out to the island. And every year on that day, May 13th, she comes back and grants wishes to those worthy few who ask for her help."

"Come on!"

"Variations of the story were passed down through the centuries. Some of the stories say it was a young Spanish girl, some say it was an old Seminole woman. Some say May, some say December. The version I told you is the one you'll find in the tourist brochures. Every May the town has a big celebration with festivities at the Inn. Then about an hour before midnight, anyone who wants a wish granted goes down to the beach and waits. About midnight, or a little after, the maiden is supposed to appear in a cloud of vapor. If you see her, it means your heart is pure, your wish desirable, and your chances of having it granted, one hundred percent."

"Have you ever had a wish granted?" Clay asked.

"I never tried. Not even when I was a child. I guess I figured I never qualified."

The story had carried them to the sprawling Miracle Springs High School complex. Sloane turned to face his son. "I'll take you in to meet the principal, then he'll show you where you'll need to go today."

"Thanks."

Sloane wanted to say so much more. Clay looked calm, and except for the ponytail he'd decided not to cut, he looked like any other teenager. A little less gawky, a little more reserved perhaps, but a normal teenager nonetheless. Still, he wasn't a normal teenager. He was going to school for the first time in his fifteen years. He was going to school in a strange town, in a strange state, and with only a strange man who happened to be his father to comfort him. He had shared a little, but what other feelings were hidden under that veiled demeanor?

Elise would know.

Sloane was startled by the spontaneous insight, although in the weeks since he'd come back to his hometown he'd ceased to be startled by the number of times he thought of Elise Ramsey. Elise would understand how Clay felt because her life had been spent trying to understand others, trying to walk in their shoes. If he chose to ask her, she could help him get beneath Clay's surface. Only, asking Elise for anything was a bad idea. The bond between them was already too strong.

"We'd better go," Clay said.

Sloane realized he'd been standing on the sidewalk staring right through his son. Even though they were early, the school yard was filling up fast, and curious looks were being directed at Clay.

"You're right. Let's go."

Sloane led Clay through the throng of gathering teenagers and in the wide, glass front doors of the school. The school had been new twenty years before and except for obvious wear and tear, it was exactly as Sloane remembered it. From an adult perspective, however, it seemed smaller—much, much smaller.

He hesitated at the principal's office. "I spent so much time here," he joked, "that I always thought they'd name it after me when I left town."

"Why'd you spend time here?"

Sloane realized that Clay wasn't kidding. He didn't understand a principal's function. It was going to be a hard year for him. There was so much to learn.

"I hope you never have to find out," Sloane told him, putting a hand on Clay's shoulder. "Now let's go meet Mr. Greeley."

ELISE LISTENED to Lincoln Greeley's inevitable first-day-of-school pep talk and nodded her head at the appropriate times along with everyone else in the room. The fluorescent lights in the ceiling buzzed annoyingly, and the one over Mr. Greeley's head flickered on and off making a flashing neon sign of his shiny bald head.

Bob sat next to her listening intently to Mr. Greeley's speech as if it weren't the same one they heard every year and others before them had heard every year, too. Elise fantasized generations of teachers, women in Gibson Girl hairdos, men with waxed handlebar mustaches, all of them listening to Mr. Greeley's speech.

"And so," he concluded, "it is our duty to carry on the tradition of excellence that was begun ninety years ago in that one-room schoolhouse on the Wehachee. In your hands rests the future of this town, this state and this great country."

Elise applauded politely. Mr. Greeley took out a handkerchief and wiped his forehead. Obviously he, too, was glad to have his first speech of the day out of the way. The faculty stood and filed out row by row in a fashion that would have made the fire marshal proud.

"Same classroom this year?" Bob asked as they waited their turn to exit.

"Same one. How about you?"

"Yes."

Same school, same speech, same homeroom, same boring questions. Elise wondered why she was feeling so dissatisfied. The sameness of her life had often been a comfort to her. Now it was barely tolerable.

Out in the hall she headed for her classroom, smiling and exchanging the inevitable greetings as she went. She was in one of the far wings. The school was designed to resemble a dissected spider. The administration section and auditorium were the body of the tortured insect, and the classrooms were laid out along each of six spider legs with triangles of lawn in between. A parking lot, football field and track had been laid out where the rest of the spider should have been, and there was also a small pond with a resident alligator who was the unofficial school mascot.

The unforgiving Florida sun and humidity had made a mockery of the attempt at architectural innovation. The school board had never had adequate funds to keep up with all the surfaces that needed painting and the grass that needed tending. Like many other things about Miracle Springs, the high school was a well-intentioned failure.

As she passed Mr. Greeley's office, Elise glanced through glass walls soon to be covered with the smudges of countless teenage fingers. Clay and Sloane were standing by the wide counter, obviously waiting for Mr. Greeley. She stopped, debating what to do.

Clay was in her homeroom. She had fought with herself since the night a week before when Sloane had come to her house to put their relationship in perspective. But in the end, she had requested Clay's presence in her English class and homeroom, too. Her relationship with Sloane might be a problem, but Elise knew that she had the capacity to understand Clay and the significant adjustments he would have to make at Miracle Springs High. Not everyone else on the faculty had that capacity. And no one else had the emotional investment in him that she did, as dangerous as it was.

Now she took a deep breath and pushed open the doors that led into the office.

"Good morning, Clay, Sloane."

"Hello, Elise." Sloane's smile was no more than polite, and Elise chastised herself for caring.

"Are you waiting for Mr. Greeley?"

Sloane nodded. Clay fastened his long-lashed brown eyes on her face as if she might unlock the puzzles of the day for him. Elise's heart did a flip-flop. What a beautiful young man he was. "Am I going to be in your class, Elise?"

"Miss Ramsey," Sloane corrected before Elise could answer.

"Elise will be fine outside of school," Elise said gently. "But you'll be accused of being a teacher's pet if you call me that here."

"Teacher's pet?"

"Someone who gets special favors," she explained. "And yes, you're in both my homeroom and my English class."

Clay smiled his thank-you. Elise wondered what it was about the Tyson men that made her insides run together when they gave her that certain little grin. She remembered all too well what effect that same expression had had years before when Sloane had aimed it her way.

The door wheezed open, letting in a rush of warm air from the open hallway, then shut. Lincoln Greeley came in behind the warm air, still mopping his forehead. He looked up and his pug-dog features were transformed into a mock grimace. "Sloane Tyson. Right back where you belong."

Sloane extended his hand and the two men shook warily. Elise watched as they readjusted their relationship. It was always the same. It took time for alumni who returned as adults to come to terms with their new status. Sloane wasn't immune, not even after seventeen years and two best-sellers.

"I'd like you to meet my son, Clay Tyson," Sloane said, stepping back to give Mr. Greeley a full view of the boy. "He'll be a student here this year."

"Glad to have you, son," Mr. Greeley said, extending his hand. His sharp, well-practiced eyes examined this new student for signs of trouble. "Hair's a little long, isn't it?"

"Does the school have a dress code?" Sloane asked politely.

"Not one that covers hair. We got out of that business after the sixties. Keep it clean and I can't say a word." He continued to examine Clay. "How many people have told you you look just like your dad?"

"A lot," Clay answered.

"Did your dad tell you about the time I caught him chiseling the mortar out of the bricks in the library during study hall?" He watched Clay shake his head. "Get him to tell you about it sometime. We haven't had too many like your dad in all my years as principal. He kept me on my toes. Are you going to keep me on my toes, too?"

Clay frowned a little. "Am I supposed to?"

The answer seemed to please Lincoln Greeley. He laughed and slapped Clay on the shoulder. "We've put you in Miss Ramsey's class. She asked for you specially, so you treat her right, son." He dismissed Clay and Elise with a wave. Elise opened the door and ushered Clay through without meeting Sloane's eyes. She wished he didn't know that she had asked to be Clay's teacher. She had done it for Clay, but she wondered if Sloane would see it as an excuse to be closer to him. Then she wondered why she cared.

"First days are always a little chaotic," she told Clay as they walked to the classroom. "Everybody feels strange, so don't imagine you're the only one who doesn't know exactly where he's supposed to be. If you need any help, find me and I'll see what I can do."

"All right."

Out of the corner of her eye Elise watched Clay covertly examine every aspect of his surroundings. His expression gave nothing away, and she was left with nothing but her own projections to help her understand his feelings. Two things were certain, however. It wasn't going to be an easy day for Clay Tyson. And watching him suffer wasn't going to be easy for her. She felt a stab of maternal concern so intense that for a moment it was a physical pain.

Clay Tyson might not be her son and she might not be anyone's mother, but Elise was sure that if she'd had a son, Sloane's son, the bonding could not possibly have been any stronger than what she felt at that moment.

No, it wasn't going to be an easy day. It was, in fact, going to be a very difficult year. For all of them.

ALGEBRA. Obviously, Clay thought, it was a foreign language using numbers and letters. A code, probably related to Egyptian hieroglyphics. Clay sat through his first period algebra class and wondered what the day was like back in New Mexico. Destiny Ranch was gone now, but for the fifty minutes of the class he pretended that when the bell rang, he could stand up and walk out of the school, stick his thumb out on Hope Avenue and get a ride all the way back to Destiny to find it thriving as it had been when he was a young boy. At least at Destiny he'd had some idea who he was. Here, in Miracle Springs, he wasn't even sure of his own name.

Clay Tyson. What was this Tyson bit? he wondered. Sure, he looked like the man who said he was his father. At times he even noticed similarities in the way their minds worked. But what did that mean?

Once a woman named Willow had claimed to be his mother. He remembered her only vaguely. She had been tall, but then he'd been pretty short so how would he really know? Her hair had been long, like Elise's, and dark, if his memory was correct. He remembered running to her once to be kissed and cuddled after a childhood injury. After that he only remembered her from a distance. And then she was gone.

When would Sloane leave him or make him leave? It didn't really matter. He was fifteen and he'd understood how to get along in the world for years. Oh, there might be things he didn't understand, like algebra and how to find his way around this ridiculous building. But he did understand the important things, things like not causing anybody any trouble, and teaching himself how to do what needed to be done. He didn't need Sloane. He wasn't even sure he liked Sloane. At least, once, Willow had picked him up and held him and kissed away his hurts. He couldn't imagine Sloane holding anybody.

The sound of a bell interrupted the teacher's indecipherable lecture. The school operated on bells. The kids were trained to respond, just like Pavlov's dogs. What had that experiment been called? Some kind of conditioning. Well, these kids were conditioned. Everyone jumped when the bell rang. In another week, he'd probably jump, too. Was that one of those skills Sloane had said he needed to develop?

The classroom emptied quickly. Clay followed the group of students out into the hall. His next class was American history. He recognized the teacher's name. Bob Cargil. It was the man Elise had introduced him to at the Inn. The man hadn't liked him, but then the algebra teacher hadn't looked any too pleased to see him either.

Was it the ponytail? None of the other boys had long hair; in fact few of the girls did either. Actually they all looked pretty much alike. Everyone had short asymmetrical haircuts that were molded a certain way and didn't move. They wore blue jeans or bright flowered shorts and oversize shirts. And shoes. Shoes seemed to be a big deal here. He'd watched the kids comparing brand names. High top leather sneakers seemed to have some magical allure, especially if they were made by a certain company.

He found the history classroom just as the bell rang, and slid into a desk at the back of the room.

"Tyson? Third seat on the fourth row. On the double."

Clay stood and found the seat, stooping to stow his books in the metal cavern beneath before he sat down.

"Tyson? I expect you to be on time from now on. Tyson! Did you hear me?"

Clay listened to the giggles of two girls next to him. What was he supposed to say? He shrugged, his face a careful blank. "I heard you," he said politely.

"Yes sir!"

Clay realized that something was expected of him.

"Yes sir!" the teacher repeated a little louder.

Clay returned Mr. Cargil's stare. For some reason, few adults expected someone his age to meet their eyes. He liked to show them they were wrong.

"One more chance, Tyson. Yes sir!"

Clay understood. He was expected to say "Yes sir!" back. He complied amiably. "Yes sir."

"I don't want any trouble with you, Tyson. I've got my eye on you."

Actually, Clay thought, Cargil's eyes weren't really on him at all. His eyes shifted when Clay tried to return his stare. It was funny; he acted like a man with something to hide.

"Say 'yes sir,' " a voice behind him prompted.

Clay complied. "Yes sir," he said again, as pleasantly as before.

The response seemed to mollify Mr. Cargil. He began to list supplies they would need, books they had to read and give a year's overview of assignments. Clay leaned over to retrieve his notebook from under the desk. As he did so he turned to see who had offered him help. The girl behind him was writing fast and furiously, but as Clay straightened, she stopped for a moment and gave him a tentative smile. His momentary impression was of curly golden hair and eyes so light that they were almost silver. She belonged in one of those fairy tales someone had read him as a child. A fair maiden who had rescued him from the dragon. It was a nice twist.

"Thanks," he whispered.

Her smile broadened a little showing the hint of a dimple, and she nodded.

Until that moment, Clay hadn't even realized just how lonely he was.

ELISE WATCHED the group of tenth-graders file back into her classroom for the last ten minutes of the day. Where was Clay? All day long she'd worried about him with the hysterical fear of a mother hen who knows one of her chicks is heading toward the jaws of a hungry fox. There was something so vulnerable about Clay Tyson, she reflected, for all his adult mannerisms and conversation.

She had been relieved when fourth period came and he showed up in her English class. She'd started the kids on a writing project immediately. They were to write ten pages in a journal every week, and today they were to begin with their impressions of the first day of high school.

Afterward she'd collected the journals to take a look at the writing samples. She hadn't had much time, but she had checked Clay's right away, expecting trouble.

She had worried needlessly. His handwriting was average, but his writing itself was extraordinary. His control of the language, the depth of his analysis and his unusual perspective made the simple journal entry a small masterpiece. She had seldom, if ever, seen such talent displayed.

His father had kept a journal although no teacher had required it. Elise had known about it and wondered what Sloane found to write about. And then she'd had the chance to find out. Sloane had presented it to her the day he left Miracle Springs. It had been an ironical goodbye gift. She had never opened it.

Now, instead, she was reading his son's.

The realization of Clay's potential had affected her deeply. There had been few moments in her life to daydream. But on the rare occasions when she'd had that opportunity, she'd found herself imagining a child. The child had grown in her imagination until one day she'd realized how unhealthy the fantasy was. Motherhood was never to be hers. A child would never grow inside her, never come to her for comfort or advice, never achieve adulthood because of her efforts.

But if there'd been a child ... If there'd been a child it would have had Sloane's face and her gentleness. The child would have had their love of the English language and their talent to communicate it. It would have had both Sloane's uncanny ability to analyze and her own ability not to judge too harshly.

The child would have been Clay.

Fantasies had been bad enough, but having the flesh and blood child in front of her, and knowing that she could never be more to him than an English teacher, was going to tear her apart.

"Miss Ramsey?"

Elise looked up from her desk and focused on Clay's face. She knew immediately that it hadn't been an easy day for him. He looked tired. No, he looked emotionally exhausted. She felt a wave of anger at all those who had given him trouble. "Stay after class a minute and tell me about your day," she invited.

Clay seemed surprised, as if the simple request was incomprehensible. He recovered his poise quickly. "All right."

"Do you need something right now?" she prompted him.

"I'm supposed to go to the counselor's office and take some kind of test. I got in trouble once today for not having a pass in the hall."

Elise took a packet of blue forms out of her desk drawer and filled in the necessary information. She gave the pass to Clay. "Come see if I'm still here when you're finished."

"Okay."

Elise watched him gather his books and leave. She couldn't miss the stares of the other teenagers, the laughter, the mimicking. Kids were so cruel. It was no wonder they drove each other to find ways of blotting out the pains of adolescence. Anyone who didn't understand drugs and alcohol and teenage sex hadn't been to high school in the eighties.

The final bell rang, and a spontaneous cheer echoed through the building. Elise watched her classroom clear out until, one minute later, it was a ghost town of desks.

She stood, smoothing her yellow flowered skirt around her knees and absentmindedly repinning a long strand of hair that straggled down her neck. Her eyes caught a movement in the doorway, and she realized Sloane was leaning there, arms folded, watching her.

Wouldn't it be wonderful if she could pretend, even to herself, that his presence there meant no more to her than the presence of any other parent of her students? Her hands fumbled with the hairpin and she jabbed it harder, wincing when it dug into her scalp. She waited until she'd inhaled deeply before she spoke.

"Hello again, Sloane."

"I was looking for Clay. Have you seen him?"

"He's down in the counselor's office taking a test, but he'll probably stop by here before he heads home. Would you like to wait?"

He inclined his head in a motion that could have meant anything at all. Elise decided to ignore him, turning to clean the chalkboard so that she could print the next day's assignment.

"Do you really enjoy teaching?"

His question surprised her. It seemed to be a continuation of the abortive conversation they'd had at her house. How was she to answer? Truthfully? In depth? Or just politely?

"Well, sometimes I feel pretty frustrated. I actually get kids who can't read, as impossible as that sounds. They've been pushed through the system or they've managed to fool teachers who wanted to be fooled. I have to start back at the beginning with basics and convince them how important reading is, then I have to stay with them every step of the way. I also get a lot of kids who don't want to read, and I have to spend the whole year trying to make them want to. Then, every once in a while, I get a wonderful student. Like Clay."

"Oh? You can tell after one class that he's going to be a wonderful student?"

"You teach. You should understand that."

"But I don't get as involved as you evidently do."

"No, I don't suppose you would," she said evenly. She finished wiping the chalkboard before she turned, dusting off her hands.

Sloane had moved closer. He was restless, and his energy seemed to vibrate through the small classroom. "Why did you ask to have Clay as your student?"

"Because I'm the best this school has to offer." Elise lifted her chin as she said the words. "And because he's your son, although that was almost as much a reason not to ask for him."

If Sloane was surprised by her honesty, it didn't show. "Clay will be fine. With or without your help."

"It's going to be a tough year for him, Sloane. He's not like most of these kids. He's way beyond and way behind at the same time. He needs all the help he can get."

"Elise Ramsey. Rescuer."

"Sloane Tyson. Cynic." Elise realized she was feeling the effects of a long and emotional day. She really wasn't up to trading insults with her teenage lover. And Sloane was hitting entirely too close to home.

"Don't get too involved, Elise. We'll be gone by June. The boy doesn't need one more person flitting in and out of his life."

"What the boy doesn't need," Elise said sharply, "is a hands-off policy. He's flesh and blood, unlike his father. He needs love, just like the rest of us humans do, and even if that love is short-lived, it's better than holding him at arm's length."

"You always did get overly emotional."

"And you always did put me down for it."

"Don't play games with my son!"

"Then you play games with him, Sloane. Somebody needs to. This year is going to kill him if somebody doesn't show him they care!"

They stood glaring at each other. Elise wondered if either of them really understood what their fight was about. The real fight seemed to shimmer under the surface of their angry words, just out of reach.

"I'm going to have him removed from this class. I don't want you clinging to Clay."

Elise knew the color had drained from her cheeks. Even Sloane looked pale, as if he couldn't believe he'd said what he had.

"Only you," she said finally, "would think that of me. And you most of all, should know how untrue it is."

"Me most of all?"

"I loved you once, yet I let you go. Would I do less for your son?"

Sloane passed a hand over his eyes as if to wipe away any feeling that might show at her words. He straightened. "Elise," he began.

Elise shook her head. "I'd like you to go," she said. "You can wait in the office; you can even change Clay's schedule while you're at it."

"Elise..."

"Not now, Sloane. Not ever. Please go."

She turned back to the chalkboard, effectively shutting him out. Then she began to write the next day's assignment in tiny, precise letters. When she had finished, Sloane was gone.

CHAPTER FIVE

SILENCE AGAIN. It should have been welcome after a day of noisy teenagers. But it wasn't welcome at all because the silence didn't affect the little voice inside her. As clearly as if her brain had faithfully made a videotape, Elise played and replayed her confrontation with Sloane that afternoon.

She had thought she was beyond being hurt that badly. She had been wrong.

The kitchen of the little two-story house heated unbearably as the oven cooked her frozen dinner. Halfway through the suggested time on the package, Elise turned it off and left the dinner sitting on the oven rack, still frozen inside. She wasn't hungry, and the good sense that always made her eat no matter how she felt was inoperative tonight. She settled for an ice-cold glass of lemonade and took it into the living room.

She ought to redecorate. The house still belonged to her mother; Jeanette Ramsey's mark was everywhere. Perhaps if Elise cleared out the fussy, overstuffed furniture, the frilly curtains and the knickknacks, she'd feel more like a real person.

She had the money. They had lived frugally all these years, not because they had to, but because Jeanette had been such a miser she'd refused to spend a cent she didn't have to. Elise's father had left a large life insurance policy and a pension. The untouched insurance money had sat in the local savings and loan for seventeen years collecting interest. Now it was Elise's money.

"I ought to take it and go around the world," she said, breaking the silence with her own voice. "Have an affair or two in every country in Europe." She set down her lemonade and leaned back, her hands behind her head.

What was stopping her besides the lack of inclination to do anything so ridiculous? She really was free to leave Miracle Springs; she could pack her bags and move anywhere she wanted. And Sloane was providing the impetus once again, although in a different way than he had once before. Seventeen years ago he had tempted her to follow him, even in the face of her duty to her mother. Now he was tempting her to get away from him. Sloane's purpose in life seemed to be to shake her loose from everything she held dear.

Good old Sloane. Tonight nothing seemed dear enough to make her want to stay in Miracle Springs and spend a year avoiding him. If he really did remove Clay from her classes, it would be easier. But avoiding someone in a town of three thousand was just about impossible. That was why people here treated each other as well as they did. Who wanted to come face-to-face with the enemy every day at the post office, the grocery store or the gas station? God bless small towns, thought Elise, even if Sloane had never had much respect for their rules and regulations.

The house was stifling. Elise had thrown open all the windows and there was a faint breeze stirring the humid summer air. But nothing would begin to make the mercury drop except central air-conditioning. Elise was tempted to go for a drive. She could open all the windows and feel the breeze blow through her hair. Nearby there were green rolling hills covered with thorough-bred horse farms, miles and miles of picturesque wooden fences and pastures, lush and emerald-hued. There were orange groves, too. Miracle Springs was a little too far north to be considered safe for citrus crops, although there were those who tried to grow the fruit with varying degrees of success. But just to the south, within easy driving distance, were geometrical patchwork quilts of orange trees that spread as far as anyone could see.

By the time she left Miracle Springs behind her, however, darkness would extinguish her view of any-thing except the road in front of her and the pattern of her own headlights. It was too late to take a drive, too early to sit in the frowsy living room and count the beads of perspiration forming on her forehead. Too late to find solace in the meditative motion of the car, too early to find solace in sleep.

Elise stood. She refused to be trapped by the heat and her own restlessness. There had been other nights like this one, nights when she'd felt she might go crazy from the unreleased tension that haunted her now. Miracle Springs might not have much to offer, but it did offer the source of its name. She'd put on her swimsuit and walk to the springs. There was a place farther down the Wehachee where she'd be almost guaranteed to find privacy. The cold, clear water would revive her and help wash away the humiliations of the day.

"Do you want to go for a swim?"

"I've got homework to do."

Sloane smiled sympathetically at the tone of Clay's voice. The boy sounded bewildered that he should be forced to suffer the indignities of schoolwork at home. "Do you need help?"

"It's just reading and answering questions for history. You can do the algebra for me if you want."

"I never understood algebra," Sloane admitted.

Clay shrugged. "The guidance counselor said I'll probably be moved to remedial math tomorrow anyway. Evidently no one has ever scored as low as I did on the math part of that test she gave me."

Sloane had spoken to the counselor himself. Clay wasn't kidding. Nor was he telling the whole story. The test, a basic IQ and achievement test, had indicated that Clay was going to have a tougher time than any of them had thought. His education had been so sporadic and dependent on the whims of the adults in his life that he didn't have too many of the skills of an elementary school student. The test had also indicated that the boy's intelligence was easily in the superior range. The counselor had been enthusiastic. More testing would follow, but she intended to have a conference with Clay's teachers immediately to motivate them to help this strange, gifted child achieve his potential.

The guidance counselor saw Clay as a marvelous challenge. Elise saw him as a boy badly in need of affection. Sloane saw him as a stranger with his own face, a son he didn't know how to raise. He wondered how Clay saw himself.

Tonight, watching him struggle with the homework that was so foreign to his experience, Sloane wanted to offer his son the love that Elise seemed to think he needed. He just wasn't sure how to do it. "You could do your homework when we got back."

"You go on. I'm pretty tired."

Clay did look tired. He looked as if the day had stripped something important from him. Sloane wondered if sleep alone would replace it.

Tentatively Sloane reached out to touch his son's shoulder. "All right. I won't be home late."

He changed into his swimsuit and pulled on a pair of jeans before heading toward the springs. His last vision of Clay was of the boy, head bent over his books, looking as if he wished he could be anywhere else.

In a matter of weeks an evening walk might be pleasant, with soft breezes cooling the dampness of his skin. But tonight, even with the sun gone below the horizon, the air swirled around Sloane's body like the steam from a hot shower.

It had rained earlier that afternoon, ending the drought that had curled foliage and burned grass right down to its roots. But the ground had been so dry that the water stood in puddles seeping drop by drop into the thirsty earth with a torturing slowness. And the heat was turning much of the water into humidity.

The smells of summer hung suspended in the air with the fine droplets of mist. There were the scents of jasmine and freshly cut grass, the faint tinge of sulphur water brought from deep within the earth by a droning pump to water a lawn—and the fragrances of pine, cedar and a few late roses.

Nostalgia at his age. Didn't that start later? Sloane asked himself. Wasn't he supposed to experience, not re-experience? Wasn't he too young to be so overwhelmed with memories of other summer nights when he'd headed down Hope Avenue to the springs? Nights when he'd smelled these same smells? Nights when his body had been tormented by the sensuality of a Florida summer?

There had been one place in particular where he had always gone to swim. The beach was often populated, but farther downriver had been a spot he and Elise had found together. It was a treacherous walk through palmetto and trees draped low with clinging Spanish moss, but the riverbank itself had always been clear enough with a huge fallen oak blocking the growth of underbrush and providing comfortable places to perch.

The tree would be gone, dissolved by time into the verdant Florida earth to help nourish it and begin a new life cycle. But the riverbank and that peculiar shelf of crystal sand leading out to deeper water would still be there.

And memories would be there, too. Memories of velvet nights and the smooth satin skin of his teenage lover. Memories of water so cold it left your body tinged with ice-blue tones of the water itself, water so cold and yet never cold enough to cool the passion he had felt for Elise.

The riverbank was sacred ground. Elise had lost her virginity there, and although his had been long gone before she entered his life, he had lost something there also: his aloofness, his solitude, his heart.

He had lost his good sense too. He had known from the beginning that he and Elise were two different animals. She was home and duty and kindness. He was restlessness and curiosity and hard-edged insight. They had never had a chance, but his insight had not been hard-edged enough. He had wanted to believe otherwise.

The spot on the riverbank might still be there, but Sloane knew it would not be the same. And that was as it should be. He reached the beach and his eyes drifted over the water. He could see that the springs itself had drawn others who wanted to drown the day's heat. Tonight he wanted no company.

The smells changed as Sloane walked down the beach and began to make his way through the moonlit jungle that surrounded the civilized portion of the springs. Florida had a way of reminding a person just how close to nature he still was, even if man had done his best to destroy his environment and create an illusion of civilization. Tie up so-called civilized man for a hundred years then set him free to examine his world, Sloane speculated. Florida would be a wreathing mass of vines and moss, insects and reptiles. Hurricanes would have blown away half the scenery-destroying condominiums and shopping centers that Florida builders loved to erect; humidity and heat and relentless sunshine would have taken care of the rest.

Now Sloane inhaled deeply. The smells were savage here; there was nothing civilized about them. Rotting vegetation, a fresh, unexplainable tang from the river, the occasional stark sweetness of some exotic blossom. The smells were as primal as the earth itself, and they did nothing to still the aching need of his body.

The path he followed was faint, just barely discernible in the pale light of a moon not quite full, but Sloane could tell it had recently been used. Others had discovered the special place. Sloane only hoped that on this night he would be alone.

The path took a sharp turn toward the riverbank. Seventeen years had passed, but his feet had turned before he'd even noticed the path changing direction. The river was calling to him, welcoming him home, inviting him to immerse himself in its depths far from the civilized waters of the springs.

Sloane stood at last on the sand- and bark-covered riverbank, stripping his shirt over his head with one hurried movement. Moonlight scampered over the surface of the gently flowing water, creating a pattern of sparkling diamonds and deepest ebony. Framed by the lacy shadows of moss-draped trees on the opposite bank, Sloane could almost believe that the river was inviolate. No one had ever penetrated its depths; no one had ever found its secrets.

But as he watched, the water was split by a human form. He felt a sharp stab of disappointment, like a man who has risked his life to climb an unscalable mountain only to discover a broken soft drink bottle at its peak. Sloane chastised himself for his sentimentality. The river was large enough to accommodate more than one swimmer. It did not belong to him. He had, in fact, rejected the river right along with everything else when he left Miracle Springs.

He watched the lone swimmer, debating whether to join this unknown person or vanish back into the jungle. But as he watched, he realized the person was swimming toward him.

His eyes narrowed and he concentrated on the form approaching. It was a woman. She was swimming on her back, and her body cut through the water with graceful, feminine strokes. As she reached the shallow shelf and stood, wringing the water from dark, waist-length hair, he knew immediately who she was.

Sloane realized that somewhere, deep inside him, he had wondered if Elise would be here tonight. He hadn't been able to admit it. If he had, he wouldn't have come. And yet on some level his thoughts of her had led him here to this place where they had once shared everything. Her back was still turned to him and she stood, staring up at the moon and stars as if their light provided her with a sustenance that daily living never could.

Images too poignant to bear examination flooded through Sloane's body, making him remember more than he wanted to remember. Much, much more.

A boy and a frightened girl, alone on the riverbank on a night like this one. The girl's voice was a soft plea. "Sloane, I don't know if we should. I don't know if I want to."

For once the boy had not taunted her for her lack of courage. He had understood her fears. He had kissed her gently as he explored the contours of her body through the clinging one-piece bathing suit. "I know, Elise. Just trust me, we'll stop when you want to."

He, the boy, had believed his own words; only soon there had been no hope of stopping. Even Elise's fears, the guilt inbred in her by a puritanical mother, had not been able to extinguish the innate sensuality that had flared in her that night, sensuality that had flared brighter and brighter until it had become a brilliant flame enveloping them both. Each new intimacy, each new revelation had shone in her eyes like the starlight reflecting on the crystal sand.

Undressing her had been easy. The swimsuit slid down her sleek young body inch by easy inch. Sloane had touched her breasts before, but never had he seen them. They were small and brown-tipped, and they responded to the firm pressure of his hands in a way that surprised him. Sloane had known all about male arousal, but he had never cared enough to pay attention to what happened to a woman when she wanted a man. He had been astonished when he saw the way her nipples hardened and peaked, just as a part of him was doing at the same moment. He had been astonished and oh, so proud.

Elise had made a sound somewhere between a moan of surrender and a demand for him to stop. He had soothed her, teased her by dropping small kisses all along her chin and cheeks as he continued to fondle her breasts. He had whispered words of comfort and encouragement. He had plunged his tongue into her mouth as the swimsuit slipped lower, and when he had reached the place she was protecting by crossing her legs against his intrusion, he had told her how much he loved her.

He hadn't been lying. He had loved her. At that moment with her trembling body given up to his keeping, he had meant every word. Never had he known this fierce desire to protect, to explore, to join. It was so much more than just wanting to sheath his jutting arousal in the tight warmth of her body; it was so much more than just wanting another sexual experience. This was Elise, a girl-woman who had touched him in ways no one else ever had.

The swimsuit had been stripped away along with his own, and patiently—if a seventeen-year-old male could be patient—he had run his hands over every inch of her flesh. He had taken her hardened nipples in his mouth in spite of her protest and shown her what pleasure they could give her. But he hadn't taken her as his own until, finally, she had surrendered herself to him, shown him she was ready by opening herself and clasping him to her body to give him the gift she could only give once in her life.

He had hurt her. His control had been much less than perfect in those days. But almost as if she welcomed the pain, she had clung to him, inviting him to come deeper inside her. And then there had been no pain. Only an intense pressure that had built inside both of them until his found its release in a storm of passion that left him almost senseless when it ended.

She was still shaking with need when he was finished. It was the first time in his experience with the opposite sex that he realized he had failed somehow. He had held her close and kissed her eyelids even though all he wanted was to fall asleep in the moonlight. He was shaken with guilt and with his own response to her. He wanted to help her, give her back some of the pleasure he had taken from her, but he hadn't known how.

Slowly she had calmed, as ignorant as he was about how to gain her own satisfaction. They had lain quietly together in the moonlight, and finally he had said the only thing he knew to say. "I think it'll be better next time."

She had giggled then, a musical gurgling sound that mimicked the river. "You take a lot for granted, Sloane Tyson. What makes you think there'll be a next time?"

He had expected tears, not the playful, joyous sound of her voice. His guilt had disappeared, replaced with a burning desire to discover how to make it up to her. "There are going to be many next times," he had told her cockily. "More than you can count. And you're going to love every one of them."

"It wasn't what I expected." She had sat up, pulling her long hair over her shoulders to hide her breasts from his gaze. "I knew it would hurt, but I thought after that I'd feel something else."

"What did you feel?"

She had frowned, and the moonlight had traced the lines in her forehead in molten silver. "Like I wanted to explode."

"Do you still feel that way?"

"A little," she had admitted.

"Come back here." He had pulled her next to him against her protests and settled her in the crook of his shoulder. Then his hands had begun to wander the hills and valleys of her body once more, settling at last on the place that had once been forbidden him.

They had learned together what pleasured her. It had taken time to get it right, but once they both understood, her release had come quickly. Afterwards the tears had come too, mixed with the musical sounds of her laughter.

And proud? God, he had been so proud. Prouder than he'd been the first time he'd taken a more than willing girl in the back of his uncle's pickup. Nothing he'd ever done in life had made him prouder than the pleasure he'd given Elise that night. On the banks of this river. On the crystal sand that led out to the water where Elise now stood, her face turned up to the stars. Eighteen years ago.

Sloane was so lost in memories that for a moment he wanted to call out to her, tease her as he had that night when he'd helped her slip on her bathing suit and beach robe before he walked her home.

And perhaps she wouldn't find it strange if he did. Perhaps she too was lost in her memories as the moonlight bathed her face and reminded her of another star-filled night.

Shaken with the desire to go to her and yet knowing that he should disappear back into the jungle behind him, Sloane stood on the riverbank and waited.

Elise stretched her arms to the sky and slowly twisted back and forth, her hair brushing the bare skin of her back. The stars were cascades of fire tonight, and she could feel their brilliance inside her own body. They fed the ache in the core of her being, just as the warmth of the summer breeze and the feel of her hair tickling her wet skin fed that same ache.

The icy temperature of the river had done nothing to help release the tension inside her. She knew she could swim the length of the Wehachee and she would still feel this restless energy. It promised to keep her awake for the length of one hot Florida night.

Where did you run when there was no place thought didn't follow? And memories? She had run right to the memories. Why had she chosen as refuge the place where she had first lost herself in Sloane's arms? It had been no accident. She had come here in the years that Sloane had been gone but never on a night like this one. Never to torture herself with reminiscences of the moment she had become a woman.

She had come tonight because the pain of stifling that memory was worse than giving into it. Today Sloane had destroyed what they had once had together. And so tonight she must remember, and then put the past behind her forever. It was the only way to live with his presence in the coming year. She must desensitize herself, tear down the shrine to the past that she had erected. Then, newly emptied, she could move on with her life.

But it was so hard. Tears she hadn't known she still had to cry sprang to her eyes. Until this moment she hadn't realized just how tenaciously she had clung to a memory of a boy and girl in love, making love on a riverbank of sparkling sand with cold, cold water lapping at their feet.

Sloane had been so gentle. All the things she had believed about him had been true that night. He had been sensitive to her feelings, eager to give as well as to take, lost in wonder as her secrets had unfolded to him. And she? Well she had been lost, too. Lost in doubt and uncertainty until she understood that he loved her. She had known for months that she loved him, but he had never told her until that night.

And he had loved her. She still believed it. The man, Sloane Tyson, was a creature who seemed to have forgotten the meaning of that word. But the boy, ah, that had been a different story. The words had been wrenched from deep inside him, and he had never called them back. Only when he made love to her had he been able to voice them. But she had never doubted just how much he meant those precious syllables.

Elise crossed her arms behind her head and lowered her gaze to the opposite riverbank. Life, she decided, was like swimming across the Wehachee. Even if she turned back to find a place she'd once been, it was not the same. The water flowed on, changing everything. She could remember her first night in Sloane's arms. She could remember subsequent nights. But nothing would bring them back; life and the river flowed on, and if she turned back to her past she would find that it had disappeared in the current. It was better to keep swimming and not to flounder in the cold, clear depths looking for something that wasn't there.

A single tear trailed down her cheek. She bent to splash water on her face, and her tear mingled with the river. She took a shaken deep breath and then another. Finally she turned to find her way back to the bank.

A man was standing on the sand watching her and for a moment Elise knew fear. But a moment later, even from a distance in the moon- and starlit darkness she recognized the shape of Sloane's body and the way he held his head. He had stood that way as a boy, legs spread slightly apart, hips jutting out and shoulders thrown back. It was a cocky stance, one that had always said so much about Sloane Tyson. It had been just one of the things she had loved.

How was she to forget him when he was everywhere she was? How was she to erase memories of the teenage Sloane when the adult haunted her every footstep? Elise felt a whiplike anger crackle through her body. Sloane taunted her, accused her of clinging to him through his son, and yet he stood watching her on the riverbank where he had taken her innocence. Her anger carried her through the water to stand in front of him.

"What are you doing here?" She was proud of herself for not bothering with the amenities. What was between them was too long-standing, too elemental for false politeness.

Sloane took a deep breath, forcing the air out of his lungs with measured precision. Did she know that he was so out of touch with reality at that moment that he wanted to reach out to her and pull her against him as if all those years had never existed? He knew she was angry, that his behavior earlier that day and his unannounced presence on the riverbank had fueled a fire inside her. He also knew that her anger was a good thing. It could keep them apart, keep him from mistaking her for the seventeen-year-old girl he had once made love to on this beach.

But if that was true, why couldn't he say the words that would turn her anger into a raging inferno to burn away their past and sever the bonds between them?

He stared at her. She was still so lovely. Maturity had blessed her as it blessed few women. To look at her was to know that she was no longer a girl, no longer truly young. To look at her was not to confuse her with the Elise Ramsey he had taken on this riverbank, but rather to know something else. This Elise Ramsey, the one who stood in front of him with eyes like a Florida thunderstorm, was a woman of power, a woman whose mature body could hold a man in captivity while her tongue assured him that he was free to go anytime he chose.

"Sloane, damn it, I asked you a question. Stop staring at me!" Elise slapped her hands on her hips and straightened her spine.

He could not stop himself. He reached out and touched her hair, wrapping a long strand around his hand. "I came to swim. And to remember. I think I knew you'd be here."

She recoiled as if he'd struck her. "Don't say that."

"You didn't want the truth?"

"Don't taunt me. We both know your command of the language is better than mine. You don't have to prove it."

"I wasn't taunting you." He wrapped her hair around his wrist again, like a fisherman with a prize fish on his hook. "I came here to swim. And I stood on the riverbank and remembered the first time we made love and how you felt beneath me."

She shuddered, closing her eyes. "Don't."

"Why not? Have you forgotten?" He stepped a little closer. There were beads of water on her face, and they shone in the pale light of the moon. Gently he traced them with his index finger, connecting them like a child connects dots in a magazine picture puzzle.

Elise tried to turn her head, but his hand still held her hair. "I've remembered so much about you, but until today I'd forgotten how cruel you could be."

"Until today, I was never cruel to you."

"You shut me out of your life."

"There are those who would say that was kind."

"Perhaps they'd be right." She stopped trying to pull away and waited for him to free her.

"I don't know why I tried to hurt you today. I wish I could take back my words."

She was surprised by his apology. The Sloane she knew never apologized; he was always sure he was right and that he had the right to say anything he chose. She opened her eyes to examine his face. There was an expression there that she'd never seen before. Regret. And on his face it was oddly attractive. She tried to harden her heart, to think about cold river water changing and flowing, destroying the past.

"But I wasn't trying to hurt you when I told you I stood here remembering another night," Sloane continued. "I wasn't trying to hurt you then."

"What do you remember?" she asked him softly. "A foolish girl in love giving in to a boy who had no intention of keeping his promises?"

"I promised to take you with me. I never promised to stay in Miracle Springs."

"I would have gone if you'd given me time."

"No. You wouldn't have. I understood that even if you didn't."

"Did you care? Wasn't it a relief to be free of everything—including me?" She stepped a little closer, imploring him to tell her the truth, to ease the guilt she still carried over her own lack of courage seventeen years before.

"Free?" He laughed, but the sound was bitter. "I was never free. Not for years and years. There were always other women, some who looked like you but weren't you, some, like my ex-wife, who were your opposite in every way. No, Elise. I told you before. You kept a piece of me here with you, and I never got it back. I was only free again when I learned to function without it."

"Why are you telling me this?" she asked, her eyes wide with pain.

"Because you asked. And because tonight I can't remember who I am and who you are and what year it is." His hand wound further into her hair and he pulled her closer. "Help me remember," he said, his breath warm against her cheek.

"Sloane, don't. Things are bad enough as it is."

"Or good enough." He breached the final distance between them. "It was good. Do you remember how good it was?" His lips nudged her earlobe as he whispered the words.

She jerked away from the length of his body against hers, but he stalked her, his free hand holding her still as his body found hers once more. Elise knew she was trembling, and she knew Sloane could feel it. But more than that, she knew she was no longer resisting. Past and present were united by moon and stars blending one into the other as Sloane's body blended with hers.

"So good," he whispered again. Then his lips trailed along her jawline, finding their way to her mouth. The soft brush of his mustache was different, and the feel of his body, larger, broader, was different too. But everything else about him was achingly familiar. She stood perfectly still, not breathing as his lips neared hers. Then she sighed as his mouth moved over hers, tasting her sweetness like a man who has been so long denied his desire that he isn't sure what to do.

She had expected an onslaught of passion, a skillful exhibition of his prowess. She had expected him to try and prove just how many years had passed and how much she had missed. Instead the kiss ate away all her defenses with its genuine hesitation. Elise understood instinctively that Sloane was as moved as she was by the night and by their past. The kiss was not to conquer, not to belittle. The kiss was simply a tribute, a reminder of something beautiful that was no more.

She felt herself relaxing in his arms. Her body softened against his, and her hands rested lightly on his bare back. His skin was warm and smooth, still firm and muscle-padded. His mouth was familiar, his smell, his taste, familiar too. She wanted to know more, to deepen the kiss and lose herself in the knowing. But she was hesitant, just as he was.

He pulled his mouth from hers without letting her go. His eyes searched hers in the near darkness. "Kissing you doesn't help. I feel like I never stopped."

"But you did."

"I'm trying to remember that. I'm trying to remember that we have to stop now." He untangled his hand from her hair, smoothing it back from her face. "We're not the same people we were."

"Who are you trying to convince?" Elise moved her fingertips lightly along his spine. She wanted to prolong the moment, to create another memory.

"I didn't come back to Miracle Springs to start this all over again."

"I never thought you had." Her hands traveled around his chest, smoothing a path to his shoulders where she rested them lightly. "I wasn't even sure you'd remember my name."

"I remember everything." Sloane stepped back, and Elise's hands dropped to her sides as he said, "I remember things I shouldn't."

"It was all so long ago." She tried to smile.

"Just for tonight, turn back the clock with me."

The words were a surprise, just as his presence and his kiss had been. "How?" Her question echoed with vulnerability and secret dreams.

"Swim with me, like we used to do."

"I'm tired, Sloane. I've had enough."

He extended his hand in supplication. "Please?"

"We'll never be seventeen again."

"We'll never be many things we've been, but tonight we can remember."

She could not refuse. Reluctantly she placed her hand in his. "Tonight we'll remember."

Perhaps tomorrow would be soon enough to try to forget.

CHAPTER SIX

SLOANE STOPPED in the middle of the river and waited for Elise to catch up with him. They had moved in silence through the dark water, changing their strokes to suit each other's pace. Now Elise was lagging behind, and Sloane knew that she was tired. He treaded water as she caught up with him.

"Put your hands on my shoulders and rest," he said when she was beside him.

Elise hesitated. The intimacy of swimming side by side with him, their bodies brushing, had been greater than the hesitant kiss they had shared. Here, in the middle of the river, it was harder to put their past in its proper perspective. "I think we should turn back. I don't want to be 'gator bait."

"It's too civilized for 'gators."

"You've been away too long. There are still 'gators in these waters and moccasins too. I rarely swim this far from the springs."

"Why'd you come here tonight then?" Sloane grasped Elise's hand and set it on his shoulder. Then he reached for the other one and did the same.

"I don't know."

"Do you always swim with your hair loose like that? I remember you'd always braid it in prissy little braids before you'd go in the water."

"And you'd unbraid it."

"You were my mermaid with your hair loose floating behind you as you swam." He fingered a long tendril. "I'm glad you didn't cut it."

"I've thought about it. More times than I can count."

"Some things should never change."

"A peculiar sentiment coming from you." Before she realized she'd done it, Elise reached up to trace the thick mustache, beaded now with drops of water. "How long have you had this? I don't remember seeing it in your publicity photos."

Sloane smiled. "You looked at photos of me?"

"I told you I read your books. I couldn't miss the man on the back cover."

"I grew it when I found out I was a father. I decided it would make me look more paternal. What do you think?"

"It makes you look like someone who keeps a gun under his sportcoat and a dagger strapped to his ankle." She traced the gleaming mustache once more. "I like it. Now you look as dangerous as you are."

"As dangerous as 'gators and water moccasins?"

"Infinitely more dangerous." She pulled away to begin her swim back to shore, but Sloane stopped her.

"Don't go yet. We haven't completed the ritual."

Elise knew what was coming. "Nostalgia time is over, Sloane. We're grown-ups now."

"I don't feel grown-up. Do you?" He pulled her against him until her breasts fitted perfectly against his chest and he was treading water with one hand. "Do you remember all the times we did this?"

"Sloane, don't."

"That's exactly what you always said."

"We're going to drown."

"That's what you always said next."

"I mean it, Sloane."

"So do I, Elise. Take a deep breath." He covered her mouth with his and they sank beneath the surface. Elise clung to him for support although there was no support to be had. She was dizzied with the sensation of his warm body in the cold water and his mouth drinking the breath from hers. When she thought her lungs would explode, he propelled them both to the surface.

She tore her mouth from his to gasp for air. "You could never resist that, could you?" she said when she could talk again.

"I could never resist you. Not from the first moment you turned your ladylike attentions on me." One hand cupped the back of her head and his mouth traveled over hers again as they treaded water together, their bodies moving in unison.

Elise shuddered. There was nothing hesitant about Sloane's kisses now, nothing hesitant about the hardening of his body as it brushed against hers. Immersed in the water and in memory they clung to each other. Sloane coaxed her to open her lips, demanded this further intimacy and Elise, with a sigh, complied. Her body was laced with quicksilver flashes as their tongues united, stroking, exploring, retreating only to renew their quest with more passion.

She was so hungry for this; it seemed that her body had been starved for years, denied of all satisfaction by a life led far away from this man. A few kisses in the water couldn't begin to quench the ache inside her that had grown and grown until it felt as if it might never be assuaged. Sloane was leading her somewhere she would soon be helpless to turn back from. He had always been able to do that; seventeen years of absence had changed very little.

"No more, Sloane." She turned her head from his, fighting to free herself.

He pulled her closer, forcing her to tread water with him so that their legs tangled repeatedly. "Put your arms around my neck."

"No. Let me go."

Sloane could feel the softness of her breasts press against his bare chest, and he was overcome with the desire to touch her. He wanted to slip the simple one-piece suit down and fit his hands around her breasts to feel the smooth fire of her skin and the response of her nipples. He wanted to grasp her waist, then plunge his head under the water to seek the hidden contours with his mouth. Just thinking about it turned the chill of the water into a bath of fire.

"Don't fight me," he murmured. "You're going to drown us both." He hooked one finger under the strap of her suit and began to slip it over her shoulder.

Elise jerked at the new intimacy and struggled harder. "Stop it, Sloane."

Sloane knew he should do as she asked, but he was drunk on the feel and smell and taste of her. He wanted more than he had a right to ask for. And he didn't care. "I want you," he muttered against her cheek. "Damn it, Elise. You can still make me want you."

"What are you trying to do to me?" To her chagrin, she knew her eyes were filling with tears. "I'm not seventeen anymore. I know what year it is, even if you don't." Without another word she pushed hard against his chest, and when she was free she swirled in the water and began to swim back to the shore. Once there, she grabbed her towel and clothing from a low-hanging branch and disappeared into the jungle.

Sloane remained in the middle of the river, watching her retreat.

AFTERNOON HOMEROOM was just a way to make sure the students who started the day in school also finished it. Elise checked the last name off her roll book and passed out the latest stack of mimeographed notes to her students. Announcements were still sounding over the intercom when she sat back down at her desk. It was the end of the second week of classes, and the students were beginning to settle into the routines of high school. As soon as the last announcement was finished, the room filled with the excited buzz of prisoners who knew they were about to be released.

Elise began to grade a quiz that she had surprised her classes with that day. The surprise test was a favorite technique of hers, a way to see if anyone was paying attention. The students didn't know it, but such quizzes really figured very little in their ultimate grades. By the time they realized that, however, the year was half over, and they'd learned how to listen. It was sneaky, but it was a lot less painful for them than getting a bad report card, she reasoned.

Elise divided the quizzes into two simple stacks: good and bad. She would look at the bad ones to see if there was any pattern to the way those students were seated, possibly moving them away from others who had also failed. As she worked, she kept an eye on her homeroom to make sure that the end-of-the-day horseplay didn't get out of hand.

Watching the social groupings of a roomful of teenagers was a fascinating thing. Now that a week had passed, the kids had begun to form cliques. There were the losers or the "late bloomers"—as Elise liked to think of them—who were too fat or too awkward or too shy to be friends with the popular kids, so they became friends with each other. There were the rebels, a select few who proclaimed their individuality with punk-style haircuts and angry facades. There were the neatly dressed good students wearing polo shirts with the correct emblem on the pocket and discussing student council business, and there were the popular kids who rarely wore the same outfit twice in the same month and spent their time discussing who was going to represent the sophomore class at the Get Acquainted Dance in three weeks.

And then there was Clay.

Certainly there were students who drifted from group to group; the boundaries were not yet so fixed that there wasn't room for change. But Clay was the only student in her homeroom who didn't seem to fit anywhere at all. Clay was an observer. He was the most entrenched loner that Elise had ever known to exist in a group of teenagers. He seemed totally unaffected by the commotion, the maneuverings, the joys and sorrows of adolescence.

Elise wasn't a big fan of the social climbing of the teenage animal. But neither was she stubborn or blind enough not to see the practice's value. Adolescence was a series of experiences designed to teach preadults how to get along in civilized society. Part of that was learning how to function in a group. Clay was not functioning in the group because he had separated himself from it. It wasn't just his ponytail or the fact that he was new in a school where most of the kids had attended elementary and junior high together. It was his obvious rejection of the whole experience that was causing the problem.

Elise had heard the whispers. She knew what was said about him behind his back and more and more often now to his face. He was that "different" kid, the most insulting thing one teen could say about another. The few times anyone had reached out to him in her presence he or she had been met with a polite but blank gaze. Only in his journals and in his poetry could Elise detect echoes of the pain Clay was hiding.

The bell rang and the students raced to the door. Clay was last, as if going home held no more joy for him than staying in a school where he was destined to be a perpetual stranger. Elise had avoided personal contact with him since Sloane's accusations, but today she found herself beyond caring what Sloane might think.

"Clay? Can I see you for a minute?"

He came to her desk and stood quietly, his hands clasped behind his back. Elise allowed herself the inevitable reaction to him. Yes, he was Sloane's image. Yes, it would have been wonderful it he'd been her son instead of the son of some commune member with no maternal instinct. But he wasn't. She was only his teacher and his friend. It was as the latter that she spoke.

"Clay, I'm worried about you. You don't look happy."

A new expression flickered over his face. Elise could have sworn it was amazement. Did the boy find it so strange that someone would notice how he was feeling?

Clay's face quickly resumed its careful mask. "Thank you, Miss Ramsey, but I'm fine."

"I don't believe you." Elise stood and came around to perch on the edge of her desk so that she could be closer to him. "If I were you, I wouldn't be happy. I'd be wishing I'd made some friends, or wishing I didn't have to work so hard to catch up, or even that I was back in New Mexico."

"There's nothing there to go back to."

"But you've wished you could."

His nod was slight but perceptible.

"It's hard to make so many changes at once. I'd like to help, Clay. And I'm sure all your other teachers feel that way."

"Mr. Cargil wants to help so much that he's trying to send me back to ninth grade." As soon as he'd said the words, Clay clamped his lips shut as if he wished he hadn't opened his mouth.

Elise didn't let Clay see the anger she felt at his words. "Mr. Cargil is giving you a hard time?" she asked softly.

"It's all right. I can handle it."

Elise suspected that nothing was further from the truth. Clay Tyson had entirely too much to handle in his life as it was without having to absorb the venom of a man who looked at him and saw his father. "Tell me what he's doing to you, Clay."

Clay shrugged.

She used a tactic she didn't like but knew would be effective. "Shall I ask the other students in your class? They'll be glad to tell me."

"He's just after me," Clay conceded. "I've had people after me before. I know how it feels."

"What does he do? Insult you? Pick on you? I could talk to him."

"If you talk to him, it'll only get worse. Besides, other than announcing every day that he's got my number and won't take any funny business, most of what he does is subtle."

"Like what?" Elise said, fuming at the idea of Clay being singled out as a troublemaker before he'd had a chance to prove himself one way or the other.

"He asks me questions he knows I can't answer. He sticks to the reading assignments with the other kids, but with me he hops around to other areas and quizzes me on them. He seems to love making me look stupid. Then he shakes his head and rambles on and on about my terrible education and how I shouldn't be in high school, that junior high might even be too difficult."

"In front of the other kids?"

"He calls me up to his desk, but they hear."

The terrible thing about what Clay was saying was that Elise could believe it. Bob Cargil was generally a rather harmless hypochondriac with limited understanding and sensitivity. But there was a streak of something darker inside him. If he felt threatened, he was capable of fighting back with any weapon. And for some strange reason, Bob saw Sloane and Clay Tyson as threats.

"I'll see he stops," Elise said, her mouth set and her chin tilted.

Clay's face relaxed a little, but he shook his head at her words. "Once, when I was about seven," he said, "a new kid came to live in the dome where I was staying."

"Dome?"

"Geodesic dome. Destiny had seven big ones. I lived in one of them until I was ten, then I moved into the big house. Anyway, this kid was older than I was, but he liked to pick on me. So every chance he got when nobody was looking or the person who was looking didn't care, he'd do something to me. Once he hit me with a big stick and I fell and lost a tooth. At first I just tried to stay away from him, but finally, I couldn't take it anymore. So I went to Jeff, the guy who was in charge of everything, and I told him what was going on."

Elise was amazed at the atypically long reminiscence, and she nodded, afraid to break Clay's spoken thoughts.

"Jeff got the kid who was bothering me off to one side and gave him a long lecture about how to treat people. It was a good lecture. Afterward the kid had to shake my hand and promise not to bother me anymore. And as soon as everyone's backs were turned, he redoubled his efforts. Only by then, everyone was sure it had been taken care of, so whenever I complained they told me to bug off."

Elise didn't know what to say. She wanted to cry.

"He kept after me for two more years until his parents moved off the ranch and took him with them."

Elise swallowed the lump in her throat. "And you're afraid that if I talk to Mr. Cargil, he'll pretend he's going to stop. Only then he'll make it worse for you."

Clay looked relieved that she'd understood. "It just wouldn't help me any."

"Then what can I do?" She picked up a pencil and bounced it on her knee. "You may be right about what'll happen if I interfere, at least at this point, but you can't handle this by yourself. Not with everything else you've got going on."

"I'm just studying harder, trying to catch up with everything I've missed."

"You didn't have much history at Destiny Ranch, I take it."

"The founder of Destiny, Jeff, the guy I was telling you about, didn't believe in history. He said it was all lies. He said the only truth was in the present."

"What do you think about that?"

Clay smiled a little, and for a minute he looked like a fifteen-year-old boy was supposed to look. "I'm not sure the present has much truth in it either."

Elise restrained herself from giving him the fierce hug he deserved. Why couldn't this boy have been hers to love? He needed so much, and she had so much to give. "Clay, I want you to come to me if this gets any worse. I'll have the principal interfere if he has to, but in the meantime, I have an idea. We're going to get you a history tutor."

Clay was suddenly the image of his skeptical father. "What good would that do?"

"You can read all you want, but you need somebody to help you select what's important and question you on what you've read. Another student would be best because he'd know what someone your age is expected to have learned by now." Elise was pleased with her idea. If she could get the right person to help Clay, she might be helping him find a friend too. It was certainly worth a try.

"I'd rather not."

"Will you just try it for a little while? I think it could help." Elise could see Clay struggling. He liked her, and she knew he didn't want to ignore her advice. But the idea of having someone help him was against his better judgment. Clay had received so little help in his life that the concept was as foreign as American history.

"I'll give it a try," he said finally.

"Good, I'll let you know as soon as I find someone for you."

"Are you going to tell Sloane?"

"It would be better if the news came from you. I'm sure he'll approve." Elise watched Clay leave, raising her hand in a slight wave as he vanished through the doorway. Then she stood to gather the rest of her quizzes to take home and grade.

Tell Sloane? She allowed herself a self-ridiculing grunt. No, she wouldn't tell Sloane she was trying to help his son. She hadn't seen him in the days that had passed since their moonlight swim, and she intended to continue trying to avoid him. What was it that Clay had said? History was lies and the present didn't have much truth in it either? The statement might not apply to everything, but it certainly applied to her relationship to Sloane.

Where Sloane Tyson was concerned history and memory and present experience were a curious blend that could be absolute truth or complete lies. And as Elise turned out the light and closed the classroom door behind her, she knew she was much too confused to tell the difference.

That evening Elise put the finishing touches on a chicken and artichoke casserole and popped it back into the oven. The casserole was one of Amy Cargil's favorites and one of the few things Amy's picky father would eat without complaining. Elise stepped out into the dining room and checked over the table setting. She was rearranging a display of lavender hibiscus when the doorbell rang.

"Hi, sweetie." Elise gave Amy a big hug, then stepped back to examine the striped, low-waisted knit dress that showed off Amy's nicely developed figure to perfection. "You look wonderful. We made the right choice."

"Thanks for helping me pick it out."

Elise offered her cheek for Bob to kiss and patted him on the shoulder. "I'm glad you could come," she told them both.

"We wouldn't miss it," Bob said gallantly. "Your cooking beats mine any day."

Actually they all knew that Bob seldom cooked. Either Amy made something for them or they ate out. Bob seemed to feel that domestic skills were strictly in the female domain. For Amy's sake, Elise tried to have them to dinner as often as possible.

"Well, I made something you both like," Elise said. "Bob, why don't you fix yourself a drink while Amy and I finish the salad?"

Bob settled in the living room with his eternal Scotch and water and the national news, and Amy followed Elise into the tiny kitchen. "Elise," Amy started when her father was out of earshot, "I've got a date tonight after dinner. Will you help me get out of here without a fuss?"

"Is your daddy giving you trouble about the boy you're dating?"

"No, it's Gregory Thompson, the pharmacist's son. Daddy likes him as well as he likes anybody. I think he just doesn't like me leaving him alone. He doesn't want me to go out with anyone."

Bob seemed to be becoming more rigid, more irritable all the time. Elise thought of her conversation with Clay earlier in the week, and she thought of her own mother. Jeanette Ramsey had got worse as she'd grown older. Whatever positive qualities she'd had seemed to disappear with the passing of the years. Elise had taken the brunt of her moods. She was determined not to let the same thing happen to Amy.

"I'm on your side, sweetie. I'll keep him entertained while you're gone. I might even let him beat me at Scrabble."

"Thanks, Elise. I knew I could count on you."

"Can I count on you for something?" Elise asked, turning to face the girl who was like a daughter.

"Anything!" Amy said with heartfelt enthusiasm. "Always!"

"I need to find a history tutor for Clay Tyson. He's not doing well in one of your daddy's classes, and I think a tutor is just what he needs."

"Clay Tyson?"

"Do you know him? I know you're not in my English class together."

"Actually I'm in his history class. He sits right in front of me."

Elise tried to read the tone of Amy's voice, but she was unsuccessful. "His father and I were friends many years ago," she explained carefully. "I like Clay a lot, and I want him to do well in school. He's very intelligent."

"My father can't stand him. He's picking on him in class."

There had been a part of Elise that had wondered if Clay was imagining Bob's harassment. Now she felt a return of the anger she had experienced when Clay had described Bob's behavior. She tried to be fair. "Does Clay give your dad a reason to pick on him?"

Amy shook her head. "Not that I can tell. He's a quiet kid, hardly says a word. He acts like he's from another planet." She picked up a carrot and took a sizable bite, crunching it with small, pearly teeth. "But he doesn't do anything that would bother anybody. Just listens and tries to answer when he's called on. I've helped him a few times when he doesn't seem to know what to do."

"Thank you, Amy. Clay needs friends."

"Oh, I'm not his friend. I don't think he wants friends. And he's not shy or anything, because he always meets your eyes. He's just . . . just off by himself. You know what I mean?"

"Only too well."

"It's too bad, too, because he's cute." Amy punctuated her sentence with another crunch.

So Amy thought Clay was cute. Elise couldn't believe she hadn't thought of Amy as a tutor for Clay. Who better to work with the boy than the daughter of the man teaching his history class? Certainly Amy would know exactly what information Clay should have. Elise broached the subject with all the caution her enthusiasm would let her muster.

"Amy, I just had a brilliant idea. There's only one person who's right for this job. And I happen to know that person would like to earn a little extra spending money so she could buy a certain designer dress for the Get Acquainted Dance."

"Me?"

"Got it." Elise opened the oven door and bent to lift out the casserole. "What do you think?"

"He's cute, but he's so strange, I don't know if I can help him."

"Are you afraid of what your friends will say?"

Amy crunched the last of her carrot. "Sure. A little."

Elise appreciated her honesty. "Is 'a little' too much to keep you from doing it?"

"He'll pay me?"

Elise nodded.

Amy visibly struggled with her answer. She wasn't as much a victim of the high school herd mentality as some, but peer pressure had its effect on her, too. Finally she nodded. "I'll give it a try. But not at my house. I probably won't even tell my dad unless he asks where I'm going."

"If you think it's going to be a problem with your dad ..."

Amy giggled. "He's always telling me how important hard work is and how I've got to earn my way in the world. If he finds out and says anything, I'll tell him I did it for him."

Elise tried to stifle a smile. "I'm never going to have to worry about you. You're going to be all right, aren't you?"

"Sure am," Amy agreed blithely.

"WHEN'S YOUR FRIEND coming, honey?"

Clay met his great-aunt's eyes and shrugged. "Sometime around four."

"I baked brownies. It's not often I get to have two young people in my house for the afternoon. I'm glad your father's over in Gainesville on Wednesdays doing his research." Lillian Tyson dropped an affectionate kiss on Clay's head. "I'm glad you're going to be studying here."

Of all the adjustments in his life, Clay decided that the most pleasant one was getting to know this great-aunt who seemed to care about him no matter what he did or didn't do. It was so strange knowing that in her eyes he was accepted just because he was a Tyson. Certainly she was the only person he could ever remember who had felt that way.

No, that wasn't quite true. Elise Ramsey seemed to care about him, too. For some unknown reason Elise seemed to understand his feelings and want to help him. And her concern didn't seem to be based on how he did in her class or whether he told her what she wanted to hear. She just seemed to care. Period.

He supposed that on some level Sloane cared, too. Once he was over the shock of being presented with a son who was obviously going to be a problem, he had tried to do his duty. That was caring in action as they would have called it at Destiny. Love was what you did for others, not what you felt. If you clothed or fed someone, that was caring.

Sloane did those things for him, and he didn't have to. He could have denied paternity, relinquished any rights over this stranger who was said to be his son. No one would have blamed him. He supposed he was really lucky that Sloane had saved him from the foster home where he'd had to stay until the child welfare people untangled his background. But at least in the foster home someone had been paid to take care of him. He wondered what reward, if any, Sloane was getting.

"Clay? You were staring into space like a zombie."

Clay pulled himself back into the present. "Sorry." He wondered if he dared ask his great-aunt if she knew what he could do to make his presence a little easier on Sloane. There must be something he could do to soften the grim expression that so often crossed Sloane's face when he looked at him.

"Don't be sorry, boy. Tell me what you were thinking."

Clay shook his head. "Just about my homework."

The doorbell chimed. "Well, that'll be your friend," Lillian said cheerfully. "Why don't you get it?"

Clay rose obediently and crossed the room. Amy Cargil was standing on the front porch, her books clasped in front of her. She was wearing a pale-yellow shirt and shorts to match. Clay thought she was just as pretty on the front porch as she had been the first day of school when she rescued him from her dragon-father.

"Hi, Clay. Am I late?"

Clay shook his head. "No, come on in." He waited until Amy was inside, then introduced her to his aunt.

"Glad to have you help Clay here," Lillian's voice boomed. "Now I'll leave you two youngsters alone. There are brownies in the kitchen when you get hungry. And soda pop."

"I didn't think I was going to be fed, too," Amy said after Lillian had left the room.

"Lillian . . . Aunt Lillian," Clay corrected himself, "likes to feed people till they burst."

"Do you live with your aunt?" Amy asked curiously.

Clay shook his head. "No, I live with Sloane, down the street a ways."

"Is he your brother or something?"

"My father."

"You call your father by his first name? My dad would eat me alive if I tried that."

"What do you call your father?"

"Daddy, or Dad sometimes now that I'm older."

Clay tried to imagine calling Sloane either of those things. He smiled a little.

"Do you think that's funny?" Amy asked with an edge to her voice.

Clay realized she thought he'd been making fun of her. "No. Not at all." He didn't know what else to say.

"Maybe we'd better get started," Amy said. "Where do you want to work?"

Clay pointed to the table where his books were all spread out.

"Good grief! You've got the whole library there."

"Just the history section." Clay sat down and motioned for Amy to take a seat.

"You don't have to read all these books, Clay. If you do you'll know more than my dad, and he'll dislike you even more." Amy bit her lip as she realized what she'd said. "I'm sorry," she said softly. "That was awful."

Clay frowned. "What was?"

"Saying that thing about Daddy."

"It wasn't awful. It was the truth. He does dislike me."

Amy was quiet for a moment as if she had to adjust to his words. "Well, doesn't it bother you?" she probed.

"Sure. Nobody likes to be picked on. Not even that 'strange kid from New Mexico.'"

Amy winced at the direct quote. It was a title for Clay that she'd heard more than once from more than one person. "I wish people wouldn't say things like that. They don't really mean it."

"Sure they do." Clay looked up from the table where he'd been clearing a space for them to work. "People almost never say things they don't mean. They may not tell the whole truth, but when they say something they're telling part of it.''

Amy was becoming increasingly uncomfortable with Clay's unflinching gaze and his direct words. She was used to her friends hedging when a subject was controversial and to boys who rarely met her eyes for any length of time. Clay was so different. Already their conversation had been more honest and more serious than any conversation she'd ever had with anyone under twenty. "Do you always say whatever's on your mind like that?" she asked. "It's kind of unsettling."

"Why? I always think it's unsettling not to know what someone is thinking." He thought of Sloane. "In fact, I hate it when people play games with me."

"What kind of games?" In spite of her discomfort, Amy wanted to find out what he meant.

"If somebody's feeling something about someone else, he ought to tell the other person. That's the only way that person is ever going to understand. At school it's so different. Everybody plays games. They pretend they like somebody and then they talk about them behind their backs. Or even if they do like somebody and nobody else does, they won't talk to that person because they're afraid of what other people will think. It's weird." Clay examined Amy's face as he talked. She looked utterly flabbergasted. Maybe Amy wasn't really any different from everybody else.

"We'd better get to work," she said finally.

Clay shrugged. "All right. Where do you want to start?'

Amy wished she had the nerve to tell Clay where she really wanted to start: with a full explanation of where he had come up with these ideas and more importantly, where he had got the courage to talk about them. Why was he so different? Most boys couldn't manage a sentence unless it was about football or their favorite rock group or what kind of skateboard they were getting. Clay really was "that strange kid from new Mexico," and at that moment, Amy didn't know if she liked him or not. But one thing was certain, he was sure more interesting to talk to than anyone she'd ever met.

Clay watched Amy stare at him, and he wondered if he ought to tell her she could go. Obviously they weren't going to be able to get anything important done. But as he watched, she smiled a little and seemed to pull herself together.

Amy sat down and opened her book. Then she lifted her eyes to his. "Clay, you're a very different kind of person." She gave him a wide, brilliant smile that did funny things to the muscles in his chest. "But you know something? This may turn out to be an education for both of us."

CHAPTER SEVEN

ELISE SAT OUTSIDE on the rusty front porch glider and waited for Bob's arrival. The early October air was mixed with a gray drizzle that promised to get heavier as the evening wore on. She shut her eyes and pictured all the Miracle Springs High School girls who were at that moment trying to figure out how to keep their hairdos intact on their journey to school. It was the night of the Get Acquainted Dance, an annual event that was already old when Elise herself had been at Miracle Springs High, and along with Bob, she had agreed to be a chaperone.

It was traditional for the weather to be bad this time of year. Summer was officially over, but the air had not yet begun to turn cool with autumn's arrival. The drizzle presaged the change. It would probably go on for weeks as the thermometer dropped one degree at a time until the temperature was bearable.

The bad weather didn't matter to Elise. It matched her spirits. As the weeks had passed, she had sunk into a depression so utterly foreign to her that she had no idea how to pull herself out of it. She had been unhappy before, but rarely had she felt this listlessness, this apathy toward what life had to offer.

Maybe it was her mother's death catching up with her. Maybe it was the fact that she was thirty-five with little to show for all her years. Or maybe it was the fact that she was starving for the feel of a man's arms around her—Sloane's arms.

The last thought didn't even shock her out of her malaise. She had grown so used to the realization that she needed what only Sloane had ever given her that she was no longer surprised when the thought resurfaced. She was starving, starving for the feel of his arms, the touch of his mouth and the moment when they became one. Sex was a natural part of life; Sloane had taught her that. Years of abstinence were unnatural, and those years were taking their toll on her spirit.

Of course Sloane wasn't the only man in the world. There were probably plenty of men who would be glad to oblige her. But she remembered only too well what it was like to slip into lovemaking with a man she didn't really want. She had tried so many times to find pleasure with Bob, and had rarely succeeded. She had only felt gratitude when that part of their relationship had died a natural death, and she had been in no hurry to try again with another man.

But Sloane was back now, reminding her every time she saw him of what was missing in her life. Oh, he didn't say anything provocative; in fact he rarely said anything at all. He just looked at her as if he saw straight through to her soul—and nodded his head in greeting.

The simple gesture was enough. She was so aware of him, of the masculine strength of his body and the enormous attraction she felt that she froze each time she encountered him. The night in the river had destroyed the part of her that could pretend the year could be got through safely. Her defenses were toppling and now all her energies went toward making sure they didn't tumble to the ground. If she was depressed, that was why. She had absolutely no energy left over for daily living. Her entire body, mind and spirit were caught up in the battle that was going on inside her.

She pictured a hundred miniature Elises shoring up stone after stone of a wall that was being steadily shaken by earthquakes. No wonder she was emotionally exhausted. If the rest of the year continued with this output of energy, she'd be a true mental case by the time Sloane left town.

The sound of a car stopping in front of her house alerted her to Bob's arrival. She stood and peered through the drizzle. She could see Amy's silhouette in the back seat and as she watched, Bob's door opened and a big black umbrella pointed toward the darkening sky. She straightened the skirt of the black and white dress that made her look properly imposing as a chaperone and waited for him.

"All ready?" Bob temporarily closed the umbrella and shook the water off it, then turned to Elise. "You look very nice in that dress."

"And you look nice in that suit." She smiled a little and stepped forward to straighten his tie. "Ready to face a gym full of cavorting adolescents?"

Bob grimaced. "How'd we get into this?"

"By being responsible, dedicated teachers. And by being in the wrong place when Lincoln asked for volunteers."

"Next time he gets that certain look on his face, let's head for the hills."

"Let's." For a moment Elise tried to imagine what it would be like if she tried once again to have a relationship with Bob. They did have things in common. They were both lifetime residents of Miracle Springs, they both enjoyed teaching, they both loved Amy. And in their own ways, they both needed someone. Good relationships were built on much less, she mused. With difficulty, she tried to concentrate on what Bob was saying.

"I wish you'd talk to Amy. I don't know what's getting into her, but she's gone all the time lately." Bob's tone was whiny, and it snapped Elise out of her speculations immediately. *I must really be lonely and repressed,* she thought, *to consider a life taking care of Bob Cargil.*

"She's a teenager, Bob," she said, trying hard to control the rise of temper she had felt at his words. "She's not your caretaker."

"What's that supposed to mean?"

Elise sighed. "I'm sorry. I'm edgy tonight. We'd better get going."

"You've been edgy for weeks," Bob said huffily. "Does Sloane Tyson coming back to town have anything to do with your behavior?"

The pointed remark was so close to the truth that Elise couldn't even summon up the energy to tell Bob to mind his own business. She just shrugged. "I don't intend to stand on my front porch and pass the time talking about my feelings."

Bob's expression was the same as a child who's just discovered that throwing a temper tantrum doesn't get him another cookie. "You really have changed, Elise."

"If so, it's the first time in thirty-five years," she said heavily. "Come on. Amy's waiting."

The rock band made up of students from a nearby community college was still setting up when they arrived. Amy, wearing the new dress she had bought herself, left to repair her damp curls, and Bob went to help the band haul in more equipment. Elise wandered around the crêpe-paper-bedecked gymnasium talking to the students who were already there and commiserating with the chaperoning parents. More students arrived until the huge gym floor no longer looked empty, and finally the band, after numerous sound checks, began to play.

Elise watched from the sidelines as the students selected partners and immediately began to gyrate around the gym. Amy was dancing with Greg Thompson, and to Elise's jaded eye, she was the prettiest girl there. Her pale-golden curls set off her clear skin and light-gray eyes, and she had a smile that most girls her age would die for. Just four weeks into the first term, Amy showed signs of being one of the most popular girls in her class. She hadn't been chosen to represent the sophomores tonight, but Elise had been there when the votes were counted. She knew just how close the totals had been.

Bob came to Elise's side and stood with her watching the teenagers dull the finish on the handsome maple floor. "We're supposed to let them dance for a while, then I'm going to announce a ladies' choice."

"That's hopelessly old-fashioned. The girls are already choosing the boys." Elise pointed to the other side of the room where a girl was leading a boy onto the dance floor where they were waiting for the music to start again.

"I'd better not see Amy do that."

Elise couldn't tell if Bob was kidding. She wasn't sure if he knew, either. But just as she opened her mouth to comment, she saw Amy cross the room and disappear into a cluster of boys who were standing by the gym door. She reappeared holding Clay Tyson's hand.

Elise wasn't sure what surprised her most, the fact that Amy would ask Clay to dance or that Clay would even be there. She knew that the tutoring sessions were going well. Every once in a while Amy let slip some remark about Clay, although most of the time she seemed to be guarding her comments about him. Elise knew that Clay was rapidly outdistancing his tutor and that Amy couldn't believe how smart he was or how much he remembered. She even knew that Amy was now spending three afternoons a week with Clay rather than the two they had originally agreed upon. What she didn't know was how the tutoring sessions were affecting their personal relationship. Obviously she was going to find out tonight.

"Who is Amy dancing with now?" Bob asked, squinting across the room.

"Clay Tyson," Elise answered, preparing to do battle.

"He's got nerve asking my daughter to dance."

Elise's vision clouded with anger. "For your information, your daughter asked him to dance."

Bob's answer was a growl that was easily interpreted. "Why would she do that?"

"Because she can see what a nice kid he is, even if her father can't."

"What are you talking about?"

"I know you're picking on him in class, Bob. I've heard it from more than one source. I can't imagine a teacher doing that to a student, but obviously Amy doesn't share your prejudices."

Bob ignored everything but her last comment. "I don't want her hanging around with some hippie troublemaker."

Elise replied as calmly as she could. "He's not a hippie, and he's not a troublemaker. He's a kid who's having a confusing year and needs a friend. How can you object if Amy shows him the kindness you've taught her?"

"I still don't like it."

"It's one dance, Bob. They aren't eloping."

But it was more than once dance. Seemingly oblivious to the angry stares of her father, Amy danced with Clay so many times that eventually most of the rest of the boys stopped asking her. She chose him whenever she could, and Clay, obviously reticent at first, began to ask her to dance whenever she was free.

Clay was a marvelous dancer. The fact surprised Elise, but she supposed that dancing was one of the things he had picked up at Destiny just like he had picked up wonderful writing skills and a knowledge of poetry that was outstanding. His education might have been unbalanced, but he hadn't spent his fifteen years doing nothing. And apparently he had spent some portion of them dancing.

Someone dimmed the lights, and then the band chose a slow tune. Students who had begun the evening acting shy cuddled up to each other and swayed in time to the music. Elise hummed along; it was an old Beatles tune, a surprise in the midst of a set of songs with questionable lyrics and a driving beat the folk song hero John Henry could have laid a railroad track to. But this song was dreamy and much too familiar.

"Yesterday," she whispered, as she remembered the song's title. The last time she had really listened to the song she had been locked in Sloane's arms and they had been drifting dreamily around this same floor. Then, interested only in tomorrow, the song had been nothing but a lovely melody with words she could sing along with. Now it forced her to remember her own yesterdays.

Elise caught sight of Amy and Clay. Amy's head came just to the bottom of Clay's ear, and she was leaning against him, arms wrapped loosely around his neck as they moved around the room. They were a good-looking couple. Clay looked particularly handsome dressed in dark-brown slacks and a yellow oxford shirt with a dark tie; Amy's pale-rose dress set off her lovely coloring. But nothing they wore compared with the smiles on their faces. They were happy to be together, obviously thinking about their tomorrows just as she and Clay's father had done. Elise wanted to go to them, to tell them to step carefully, to cherish this time in their lives. Young love was so fragile; tomorrow was so fragile.

Elise blinked back tears, ashamed of her own sentimentality. She was standing at a high school dance letting the past drain all that had once been satisfying out of her. If she didn't take care, she would find herself doing something stupid just to feel alive again.

The band seemed to sense the mellow mood of the crowd and swung into another chorus of the song to give the boys a chance to pull their partners a little closer. Elise's gaze followed Amy and Clay. They didn't seem upset that they would have to dance a little longer. Someone else did seem to be upset, however.

As Elise watched, Bob strode on to the dance floor and clamped his hand on Amy's shoulder. Even though she was across the darkened room, Elise could tell that

Bob's expression was angry. He said something to Amy and Clay, and Clay said something back to him. Amy's hand flew to her mouth and she turned and fled across the room and out the wide gym doors.

Clay started to follow, but another sophomore boy who had been dancing nearby and had obviously heard the whole thing grabbed his arm to detain him. Bob said something else to Clay and then melted into the crowd of spectators on the sidelines.

Elise knew where her duty lay. She wanted to confront Bob and find out what he had said to cause such a commotion; she wanted to question Clay, who was now the center of attention. Most of all, she wanted to comfort Amy who was somewhere outside in the gray drizzle. She turned and followed Amy's path, calling her name.

"Amy?"

Amy was nowhere in sight. Had she decided to walk home? It was unlikely, since her house was a good three miles away. Elise tried to imagine what she would do under the same circumstances. Where could you go to sit and be alone at Miracle Springs High? Elise tried the parking lot, peering into Bob's car, and when that didn't bear fruit, she walked to the portico behind the school where students waited for buses. There, on one of the stone benches, she found Amy in a forlorn huddle.

Without a word, Elise sat down and put her arms around her. Amy sighed, wiping tears off her cheeks. She leaned her head against Elise's shoulder.

Elise brushed Amy's curls back from her forehead. "Do you want to tell me what happened?"

Amy sniffed. "My father behaved like an ass."

Elise let the small lapse in vocabulary pass unnoticed. "I saw him stop you and Clay while you were dancing."

"He's been glaring at me all evening, but I never thought he'd do something so dumb."

"Did he tell you to stop dancing with Clay?"

"Worse! He pulled us apart and told Clay to get his hands off me, that I wasn't some kind of floozy for him to maul."

Unfortunately Elise could imagine Bob saying just that, archaic language and all. What was the right thing to do now—explain Bob's feelings? Should she attempt to patch up this quarrel between father and daughter to the best of her ability? Or should she simply tell the truth, that she too thought Bob had behaved like an ass?

Elise finally compromised. "Your dad was wrong to say anything to you, but he did it because he was worried."

"He wasn't worried!" Amy sat up straight and glared at Elise. "He was furious! He doesn't want his little girl to have a life of her own, especially one that includes Clay Tyson. He hates Clay. I don't know why; I wish I did."

"I'm afraid that's my fault," Elise said softly.

"What's your fault?"

"My fault he hates Clay."

"Why?" Despite herself, Amy's voice lost some of its angry edge.

"It's a long story, but it involves Clay's father. In a strange way, I think your father is jealous of something that happened years ago. Clay looks like his father and so he's a constant reminder to your dad of the past."

"He calls him that 'hippie kid.' I don't even know what he really means by that, but if it's true, I like hippies!"

Elise smiled. "I didn't know you and Clay were such good friends. Didn't that happen kind of suddenly?"

"I don't know." Amy dug her teeth into her lower lip. "I guess," she admitted finally. "At first I thought he was really strange. He's not like anybody else I've ever met. But after I got used to him, I decided I liked him. We've been eating lunch together, and I've been tutoring him. Last Saturday I met him at the springs, and we went swimming with some other people."

"So he is your boyfriend?"

"No. Nothing like that. We're just friends," Amy protested.

Now Elise understood why Clay had been looking happier. He no longer seemed to be as haunted, as detached. He still didn't take part in the horseplay going on around him at school, but he no longer seemed to be so completely alone either. Once or twice Elise had seem him exchange words with other students, and once, after she'd read one of his poems aloud in English class, she'd seen two or three other kids stop to praise him before they left for their next period. Amy's acceptance of Clay had made him more acceptable to the others.

Faced with Bob's bullheadedness, Elise tried to decide what to do. She didn't want to make the situation any worse, but neither did she want to keep Amy from facing the truth. Silently she damned Bob Cargil for causing this trouble. Then she spoke. "Your father isn't ever going to approve of Clay, Amy. Not even if you remain 'just friends.'"

"I don't care! Clay's my friend. I'm going to keep seeing him whether Dad approves or not."

"That could be pretty tough," Elise cautioned. "On both you and Clay."

"If he keeps bothering Clay, I'll go to Mr. Greeley myself," Amy vowed. "I'll tell him my own father is picking on a student!"

They both knew she wouldn't visit the principal, but Elise was still pleased by Amy's spunk. Amy would never fall victim to her father as Elise had fallen victim to her mother. When the time came for Amy to make the break from Bob, she would.

"Well, before it gets to that point," Elise said, "let me talk to your dad. I'll try and straighten him out for you."

"Could you?"

"I can try."

Amy put her arms around Elise's neck and gave her a hug. "Thanks."

"Now, let's get back inside. I'll say something gentle to your father like," she cleared her throat and made her tone menacing, "Bob, if you cause another scene Amy and I together will pull every remaining hair out of your head." Elise smiled at Amy's giggle. "And in the meantime, until I can really talk to him, no more slow dances with Clay unless you stand a good foot apart. Deal?"

"Deal," Amy said with a sigh. "I just wish my dad didn't teach here. I wish he laid bricks, or worked on the *Banner*, or raised racehorses."

"We'll do what we can to make it easier."

After another quick hug they both rose to their feet and began their walk back to the gym.

Inside, Elise skirted the edge of the floor until she was standing beside Bob. She watched as Amy defiantly sought out Clay to ask him to dance with her. Elise could feel Bob stiffen next to her. She didn't even look at him. "Bob," she said under her breath, "if you so much as move one foot in Amy's direction I'll follow you and make a scene like none this school has ever known."

"Stay out of this, Elise."

"I won't. I'm the closest thing to a mother that girl has ever had, and as such, I'm telling you that if you keep this up, you're going to lose her for sure. She likes Clay; he's not doing anything he shouldn't; and the more you make of it the more they'll make of it." She faced him. "You're picking on Clay because once, a long time ago, his father and I were lovers."

"That's ridiculous!"

"It's the truth." Elise turned back to the dance floor. "Sloane may be back in town, but he has nothing to do with you and me. And Clay has nothing to do with you and me. Don't make him a scapegoat."

Bob was silent, and Elise imagined she could feel the tension emanating from his body. But the evening passed without another confrontation, even when Clay and Amy danced the last slow dance together.

Finally the long night ended. Kids streamed out to the parking lot to find their cars or to wait for their parents. Amy and Clay stood by the door saying goodbye, and Elise demanded that Bob help her thank the chaperoning parents until she saw that Clay had gone.

With obvious reluctance, Amy joined them. "I'm ready to go," she told Elise, refusing to acknowledge her father.

To his credit, Bob looked a little sheepish. Faced with Amy's withdrawal, he seemed to reconsider what he'd done. "Let's go out for ice cream," he said with false joviality.

"No thank you," Amy answered coldly. "I want to go home."

"Elise, how about you? Wouldn't you like some ice cream?"

Elise was tired. The emotional scene with Amy had taken its toll. She felt unstrung. She could not face being the buffer between father and daughter anymore that night. They would have to be left alone eventually; it might as well be now. "No. In fact, I think I'm going to walk home. You two go on without me."

"But it's raining," Bob objected.

Suddenly Elise didn't care about anything except getting away from everyone who made demands on her. "I like the rain."

"Your dress . . ."

"Is cotton and will wash nicely," Elise finished for him. "Thanks for the ride over." She bent and kissed Amy's cheek. "I'll see you on Monday," she told her. "Have a good weekend." Without another word to either of them she headed for the gym doors.

SLOANE WAITED while Clay slid into the front seat of the car and slammed his door. Then he pulled out into the steady stream of cars heading down Hope Avenue. "How was the dance?"

"All right."

Sloane searched for a way to prolong the conversation. "Got your eye on anyone in particular?"

"No."

Sloane wondered if Clay had danced at all. It had surprised him that the boy had wanted to go. He had showed no interest in any other aspect of high school social life. Other than his tutoring sessions, he seemed to have no contact with any of the teenagers in town. According to Aunt Lillian, however, Clay's relationship with Amy Cargil was progressing nicely enough to make up for whatever other friends he lacked. Perhaps Amy was the reason that Clay had attended tonight's dance, even if he wouldn't admit it.

"Look! There's Miss Ramsey." Clay pointed ahead of them. Sloane realized his son was correct. Elise, with neither umbrella nor raincoat, was hiking along through the light rain.

"What on earth is she doing out in this?" Sloane passed Elise, then slowed down and pulled over to the side of the road just ahead of her. He opened his door and stood beside the car. "Elise, get in. You're getting soaked."

"I want to get soaked," she muttered, without so much as a glance in his direction.

Sloane caught up with her, getting splashed by a passing car as he did. "Elise, this is crazy." He caught her arm. "Are you all right?"

"No, I'm not all right." Elise pulled her arm from his grasping fingers. "I'm not all right at all." She faced him, raindrops beaded on her forehead and in her eyelashes like tiny diamonds. "I'm going to do what *I* want to do for once. I'm going to walk home even if the heavens open any moment and drop hail as big as golf balls. Then I'm going inside and I'm going to fix the world's largest hot toddy and drink myself witless. And then, if I haven't had too much to put me out for the night, I'm going to lie awake until dawn and fantasize about what my life would be like now if I'd left this god-awful place years ago when I should have!'' Without another word she turned and continued down Hope Avenue.

Sloane watched Elise go, torn between picking her up and putting her in his car and following her to try and talk some sense into her. In the end he did neither. He walked back to the car and slid under the steering wheel.

''She doesn't want a ride?'' Clay asked, a worried expression on his face.

''I think she needs to be alone, son,'' Sloane said. ''Something's upset her.''

Clay wondered if Sloane realized he'd just called him son. The word had sounded so strange, almost like an endearment. An endearment from Sloane? It was just one more puzzling thing in a puzzling night. He sat back as Sloane started the car and pulled carefully back on to the avenue.

ELISE TOOK HER TIME getting home. The heavens did open, although it was sheets of silver rain that deluged her, not hail. She hadn't gone walking in the rain for more years than she could remember.

Her father had been the one to introduce her to the pleasures of rain and splashing in puddles. He had been a true outdoorsman, happy in any kind of weather, as much—and Elise had known it even then—to get away from his nagging wife as for any other reason. He had taken Elise with him whenever he could, although he'd never had the energy to stand up to Jeanette Ramsey when she refused to let Elise go. But Elise had treasured their few times together. She had loved her father, even with his weaknesses, and it had devastated her when he had been killed right before her high school graduation.

The accident had been senseless. Her father had been fishing; someone else had been poaching alligators. Her father had got in the way. The poacher had never been found, but there had been no suspicion of foul play. It had just been one of those freak things that happened. One stray bullet—one life had ended and others had changed. Her own life had never been set right again.

Sloane had understood her sorrow, but he had not understood her need to help her mother by staying in Miracle Springs for the summer. Perhaps he had seen the truth more clearly than she. Perhaps he had realized that she was going to end up with all the life sucked out of her and all her dreams buried too deeply to retrieve. Perhaps it was fear of watching her slow disintegration, rather than his own restlessness, that had made him jettison his birthplace the moment he was free to go.

At her house, Elise stepped on to the front porch and shook herself like a Labrador retriever coming out of a lake. Drops of water flew and the wet skirt of her dress clung to her knees. She slipped out of her shoes and flung the door open, leaving it that way as she walked through the house. She wanted to hear the rain.

In the kitchen, she opened the back door too, oblivious to the threat of mosquitoes and flies. As she warmed up milk she stood staring at the backyard. Her fingers found the pins that were holding her hair in a restrained chignon, and she pulled them out, tossing them on a counter. The wet length of her hair blanketed her back as she turned to the stove and tested the milk. She poured it in a cup and completed the toddy with a dollop of honey and a double shot of Jack Daniels.

Without changing into dry clothes she found her way to the front porch glider and rocked, listening to the rain, as she sipped the warm drink.

The night and her walk home had done one thing for her. They had shaken her out of her depression. Depression was an absence of feeling, a blue-gray haze that dulled all of life's glories. No, she was no longer depressed. She was sad. She was angry. She was bone-deep lonely. She was so many things that they were all tied up inside her trying to fight their way loose. Elise wasn't sure which was worse, depression or this writhing, jumbled mass of emotions. She took another sip of the toddy and closed her eyes.

She had no idea how long she'd been sitting that way before she heard footsteps on the porch and the sound of a man's voice in front of her.

"You didn't even change your clothes."

Without opening her eyes, she knew who was there. "Go away, Sloane. Even I'm entitled to be miserable once in a while." Elise felt his warmth beside her and the heaviness of the glider with two bodies on it. She ignored him, taking another long swallow of the toddy.

"You always did have a temper, only it was so well hidden I was one of the few who ever got to see it."

"You deserved to see it. You were rotten, selfish and totally unforgiving." She drained the rest of the toddy with one big gulp.

"I was all those things. I was also madly in love with you."

Elise snorted.

"You doubt that?"

"My memory doesn't extend back that far." She opened her eyes. "Why are you here?"

"I was worried about you."

"That's a first."

"I thought you didn't remember back that far."

"Go away, Sloane."

"You're not all right, are you?"

She turned her face up to his. "No, I'm not all right. I haven't been all right since our friendly little moonlight swim, and I probably won't be all right until you leave town. There, do you feel happier knowing that?" She stood, opening her arms for his examination. "What you have here, Sloane, is a sexually frustrated middle-aged woman pining for a fantasy lover. It's a nasty situation. Truly nasty." She spun around and stalked back into the house, ending up in the kitchen where she poured more milk in the pan to warm.

"Why are you frustrated? Are the men in this town blind?" Sloane was standing behind her, but Elise didn't turn at his words. "I can't believe all of them, single and married, aren't beating a path to your door."

"Did you see a path?" Elise put her hands on the edge of the stove and leaned against it, staring at the burner. "Do you want the truth? You'll find it hysterically funny. It's been years since I've made love to a man, and there's only been one since you left town."

"Cargil?"

"Does it matter? I'm just a dried-up, unhappy old maid. I'm just what you said I'd be if I stayed in this town. You've been vindicated, Sloane. You were right; I was wrong."

"Elise." Sloane didn't know what to say. He was shocked and sick at this waste of a wonderful woman.

He was furious that she'd given herself to that oaf, Cargil, and more furious that she hadn't found someone worthy to love her. He put his hands on her arms and felt her stiffen, but he didn't move away. "Why, when you have so much to give?"

"Nobody but you ever saw that," she said, her words punctuated by peculiar little gulping sounds.

"I'm sure that's not true."

"Sloane, the comforter. This is hard to believe."

Sloane rubbed his hands up and down her arms in a soothing gesture. "What happened tonight to upset you?"

"Nothing that should make me act like such a fool." Elise watched the milk bubble around the edges of the pan. It was time to turn it off, but she couldn't make herself move.

"You're not acting like a fool. You're upset. Hurt."

"Let's not forget lonely. Do you know what that word means? Do you know what it feels like to be a tiny little part of lots of lives but not important to anyone?"

Sloane reached around in front of her and switched off the burner. Then he put his hands on her shoulders and turned her to face him. "You're tired, cold, wet. Look, you're shivering. Go upstairs and change. I'll make you another hot toddy. Then we can talk."

"I don't need talk."

Sloane felt Elise's words burn right through him. Her eyes were wide with emotion and her control seemed to have completely vanished. "What do you need?" But even before she spoke, he felt his body stir in response to the inevitable answer.

"I need to be loved. Right now. Will you love me, Sloane?"

CHAPTER EIGHT

ELISE SEARCHED SLOANE'S FACE until she could find no undiscovered clues. She dropped her gaze to the ground and suffered waves of humiliation as she turned back to the stove. She wanted to ask him to leave, but her mouth was so dry she was afraid she wouldn't be able to enunciate the words. She picked up the milk with a shaking hand and poured it into her cup. This time the whiskey flowed without prior measurement. She just poured until the cup couldn't hold another drop, and she didn't even bother adding honey.

"I don't know what to say," Sloane said from behind her.

"I got my answer. Please go."

It took two hands to lift the cup to her mouth. Her first sip was straight Jack Daniels since she hadn't bothered to stir the drink. It burned a fiery path down her throat and through her chest, and she swallowed convulsively to keep from coughing. She waited for the sound of Sloane's retreat, but the house remained silent.

She felt his hand on her back, stroking her hair, and as if he'd given a signal, her eyes overflowed. Now, in addition to pleading for lovemaking from a man who obviously didn't want her, she was crying. She wondered what she could do to bring herself any lower.

"I don't need your sympathy," she snapped at him, her voice unsteady.

"You've never had it. My anger, my passion, yes, but never my sympathy."

"If you're not feeling sympathy, it must be pity. God, I've sunk so low!"

"Stop it, Elise." Sloane's fingers gripped her shoulders, and he shook her lightly.

"Get out of here!" Elise slammed the half-filled cup on the stove top and turned to face him. Her fists beat on Sloane's chest. "Get out of my house!"

He stopped her assault by pulling her tightly against him and crushing her to his chest. Elise cried out, trying desperately to pull away, but he wrapped his arms around her and bent her backward, muffling her mouth against his cheek. Elise struggled, flailing her arms uselessly at her sides where Sloane had them pinned. Whatever was happening was something she had driven him to, not something he had chosen. She wanted no sacrifices, no concessions.

"Stop fighting me." Sloane held her imprisoned as his mouth bathed her face in kisses. "Calm down and stop fighting me."

Elise knew she was beyond self-control. She continued to struggle, hoping that he would grow tired and release her. She lifted a knee and aimed it where it would do the most good, but Sloane was too quick for her, thrusting his own leg between hers and clamping it tightly to block her. His arms tightened around her and his mouth continued to soothe her heated face. She managed to inch her hands up to his chest to push against him, but it was like pushing at a wall. She pulled at his clothes, trying ineffectually to scratch him, but her hands were too tightly pressed to his body.

Even in the hysteria that gripped her, Elise realized that Sloane was not going to release her until she stopped fighting. She continued to struggle against him, but the hopelessness of it was apparent to them both. When she was finally exhausted she relaxed against him, her tears soaking the collar of his shirt.

He held her as she cried until there were no tears left. His hands slipped under her hair and covered the length of her back, kneading and stroking it as she leaned against him, her breath coming in dry sobs until the sobs were gone, too.

"How many years have you needed to cry that way?" Sloane rested his cheek against her hair. "How many years have you needed someone to hold you while you did?"

Her anger was gone. She was empty of emotion, and Sloane's quiet caresses had completed the purge. "Forever," she whispered, not even sure if the words were loud enough for him to hear.

"Lise, you turn yourself inside out giving to everybody else, and you never take anything for yourself. Not even a good cry. I had to wrestle it out of you."

She was startled at the nickname; it had been seventeen years since she had heard it.

"I'm all right now." She pulled away and Sloane let her go. Elise turned to look for something to repair the damage to her tear-streaked face, but Sloane beat her to the sink, soaking the edge of a dish towel with cold water.

"Come here."

She shook her head, but he ignored her, reaching out to pull her closer. Gently, beginning with her forehead, he rubbed the wet towel over her face. Elise shut her eyes, letting him do as he wished. She could imagine what she looked like, although she was much too drained to care. She could feel the rough terry cloth slide over her nose and around her eyes. He mopped at her cheeks and her chin and then started all over again.

"You can go," she said when he seemed to have finished. She commanded her voice to be steady and rational even if inside she felt anything but. "I'm sorry I caused such a scene, but I really am all right now."

"I'm not going anywhere." Sloane leaned back against the sink and crossed his arms in front of his chest. "I was issued an invitation, and I haven't heard a withdrawal."

Elise hadn't met Sloane's gaze since she had asked him to make love to her. Now her eyes shot up to his face in surprise. "Consider it withdrawn."

"I don't think so."

Elise forced a bitter laugh. "Wouldn't that be something? You'd make love to me, and I'd be so pathetically grateful it would make you feel like God. It would be an experience to remember."

"It would be an experience to remember."

"Look, Sloane, I don't know what got into me to ask you such a thing, but whatever it was is gone now."

"Is it?" He reached out, and before she could object he grasped her hand. "Funny, I want you more than I ever have."

"You didn't want me. You made that obvious. Do tears and tantrums turn you on?" She tried to pull her hand from his but he wouldn't let her.

"Didn't want you?" He laughed softly. "I can't remember not wanting you. Are you talking about the night at the river? Didn't I want you then? Or how about the night I came here to settle our past and you greeted me in a sheer white robe with your hair streaming down your back? Didn't I want you then so badly that I had to get out of here before I lost whatever sense I had?"

"Sloane..."

He brought their clasped hands to her mouth to silence her. "Or tonight? Spitting at me like a drowning cat, that dress clinging to every curve of your body until my insides went liquid. Didn't I want you then?"

She turned her head. "Don't."

"Is that what you really want to say, Lise?"

"I practically threw myself at your feet, and you didn't say a word!" Elise felt a resurgence of anger, but it died quickly when she looked in Sloane's eyes.

"I felt like someone was choking the words out of me. Here you were offering me exactly what I wanted, and I knew you were only doing it because you were distraught. What could I say?"

"Yes."

Sloane shook his head. "Do I want you hating me when you wake up tomorrow? You don't give yourself to a man easily. What would it have done to you to give yourself like that?"

Was he handing her a good line or was the concern she saw in his eyes genuine? "Well, now you won't have to worry."

"You're right. Because now when I make love to you, you'll know it's my idea, too. It's what I want." He pulled her inexorably closer. "Not that you're not going to want it."

Elise could feel her heart stop, then begin to pound so fast that the beats merged into one rolling crescendo. "No. Not like this. Not because you know it's what I need."

"Have you ever known me to be charitable? I need it, too. I've never forgotten what it feels like to sink inside you and feel your life pulse around me." He dropped her hand and dug his fingers gently into her waist, pulling her ever closer. "We owe each other this night."

Only this night? Did she need to be loved that badly? "We don't owe each other anything."

"You're right. 'Owe' is the wrong word. It's not a debt; it's a gift freely given. I give myself to you, taking what I need in return. You do the same."

Elise reached up to touch Sloane's cheeks. She smoothed trembling fingertips over the faint roughness of his skin and down over the luxuriant mustache. Could she let Sloane feed this ache inside her until once more she sated herself on the only taste of heaven she'd ever known? Would one night be enough to help her get on with her life?

"Lise?"

"No one but you has ever called me that." Elise traced the fine lines around Sloane's eyes, her fingers memorizing the new additions to a face that was still very much the same. She stroked her thumbs over his eyelids when he closed them. His eyebrows were wiry, and she smoothed them, watching them spring back to life immediately. His hair was of a wiry texture, too. Her fingers fanned out to tangle in it. It was not quite curly, not quite straight. It had a resiliency that wouldn't change, not even, she suspected, when the few silver strands giving it character turned to many.

It would be so easy to forget everything....

Sloane's fingers swept up and down her spine. When the rain-cooled wind from the open back door whipped through the kitchen he opened his eyes. "You're shivering. You need to get out of those wet clothes."

Elise debated what to do. He was offering her solace, warmth, pleasure. She was an adult and perfectly free to take him up on his offer; she had in fact begged him for this night of loving. So why the hesitancy? Why the doubts?

"I'm all right," she said, shivering again.

"You're asking for pneumonia."

There was not one rational reason to say no. She needed this, and Sloane said he needed it too. They were two consenting adults who—at least on some level—cared about each other. She knew Sloane would be a magnificent lover. She had spent her whole life being afraid to take what she wanted. Tonight, just for this night, she would.

She shivered again, and then laughed a little at the warning in Sloane's eyes. She felt suddenly much too shy just to invite him to her bedroom. And yet her decision seemed to have been made. They were going to make love. Even saying the words to herself increased the throbbing inside her. What should she do? Go upstairs and change into something dry, then come downstairs only to go back up again later with Sloane? She wasn't very good at this. She and Sloane had only made love outdoors or in the back seat of his mother's car. The times she had made love to Bob had been at his house when Amy was away with friends. What was the protocol now?

"I'll tell you what we'll do," Sloane said softly, as if responding to spoken words instead of thoughts. He brushed his index finger over her cheek and around her ear. "I'm going to take you upstairs and find your bathroom. Then I'm going to run a hot bath for you."

"And then?" Her eyes focused somewhere right below his.

"And then I'm going to make love to you. And it's going to be very slow and very gentle and very, very right." His finger lodged beneath her chin and lifted it a little so that she was looking right at him. "For both of us."

Elise wasn't sure that slow and gentle was what she needed. Already she could feel her body's response to his words. Her nipples tightened against the wet fabric of her dress and bra, and she felt a heated rush in the very core of her. If he could do that with only a few words...

"But first I'm going to kiss you, just the way I've wanted to kiss you all evening." His fingers spread into her hair, and he tugged gently at her chin until her mouth was close to his. She could feel his warm breath against her lips, then his lips hovering against hers, not quite making contact. The first brush of his mouth was so soft, she wasn't sure it had even happened. Inadvertently she sighed, parting her lips a little as she sought more pressure.

He pulled back to slow their pace and brushed his mouth against hers again. "Do you want more?" he asked.

"You always were an awful tease." Elise opened her eyes without moving away. "An awful tease and an awful flirt."

"And you always were so easy to do both with. How could I help myself?"

She smiled a little, aware that Sloane's words were having just the effect he had clearly intended. She was already less anxious. "You could do anything you wanted with me. I never knew how to stop you. I never wanted to stop you.''

Sloane bent toward her. ''I was always too out of control to take it slowly for long.'' This time his mouth found hers with more passion. He wet her lips with his tongue then slid it into her mouth to trace the straight line of her teeth.

Elise clung to him, parting her lips to give him easy access. Up against the full length of his body she could feel him stir to life as one kiss melted into another. Any doubts she'd had about his involvement, his desire, were put to rest. Sloane wanted her; this was not charity. Their lovemaking might be slow and gentle, but it wouldn't be passionless.

He sucked lightly on her full bottom lip, then took it between his teeth and tugged gently. Elise could feel the tugging deep inside her as if everything was connected, one part of her a conduit of sensation for another.

''What are you smiling about?'' Sloane asked, pushing away from the sink so that they were standing straight but still touching.

Elise slipped her arms around his neck and pulled his head back down to hers. ''I was wondering how anyone could top the miracle of the human body.''

Sloane laughed and scooped her into his arms, swinging her feet off the ground as he did. ''Even soaking wet you don't weigh as much as you did when you were eighteen.''

''You're just stronger.''

''Let's go upstairs.''

He held her off the ground, walking to the steps where he set her down. Obediently Elise turned and began her climb, then returned to the bottom to grasp

Sloane's hand and pull him up with her. "After telling me we were coming up here, were you waiting for an invitation?"

"Exactly."

She realized he'd been giving her one more chance to back out. She was surprised at his patience. Sloane had never been patient, and she was grateful for this new sensitivity. It strengthened her resolve and heightened her desire. "I only issue one invitation," she said, her voice provocative.

"But that one wasn't specifically for your bed."

Elise squeezed his hand. "You're right. I'd intended to knock you to the kitchen floor and have my way with you between the sink and the refrigerator."

In the second-floor hallway she paused outside the bathroom door. The idea of a hot bath was a good one, but she wondered if the time away from Sloane would give the doubts she was suppressing a chance to reassert themselves. "I'm warmer now," she said hesitantly. "I don't think I need a bath. I just need to get out of these clothes."

"We're going to do both."

She shivered at the promise in his voice, but she pushed on. "I don't want to leave you right now."

"I'm not going to leave you, I'm going to get in with you." Sloane entered the bathroom, still holding her hand. His eyes took in the old-fashioned claw-footed bathtub. "Perfect."

Elise had to remind herself to breathe. She watched as he bent and pushed the rubber stopper into place, then turned on the water and adjusted its temperature. He straightened and faced her. Even though they weren't touching now, Elise felt as if Sloane were stroking her body. Her hand went to the top button of the bodice of her dress and froze there. She looked down at her own long fingers wrapped around the dainty mother-of-pearl button. She couldn't move.

Sloane's hands covered hers. He pried her fingers from the button and unfastened it himself.

"What would your mother say if she knew what we were about to do in her bathtub?" Sloane whispered in her ear.

It was the last thing in the world Elise had expected him to say. She felt a surge of laughter start at the tips of her toes and progress up her body. She couldn't speak, she couldn't do anything except give in to it. How had Sloane known that the same thought had crossed her mind?

"I've never even kissed a man in this house," she told him when she could.

He unfastened the next button and caressed the newly revealed skin with his thumbs. He smiled at the noise she made deep in her throat. "I could never understand how you could be such a perfectly proper daughter and still have a streak of sensuality as deep as the Wehachee running through you."

She trembled with anticipation as the third button was undone. She was grateful for Sloane's conversation. He had sensed her fears, and his voice was soothing. He was talking to her like the old friend he was as he undressed her like the ex-lover he was. The combination was irresistible. She lowered her eyes and watched his hands as she answered him.

"Split personality. I learned to cut one off from the other, at least when I was around you. I never needed to do it any other time."

He unbuttoned two more; now the dress was open down to her waist. His fingers brushed the soft skin of

her stomach as he reached behind her under the dress
and unhooked her bra. "Such a waste." He stepped
closer and his mouth nuzzled her neck. "All these
years, when I allowed myself to think about you, I'd
imagine you married to some lucky Miracle Springs
businessman who didn't deserve you. I pictured you
having your mama over for Sunday dinner and running over here every night to be sure she'd taken her
pills or tucked herself into bed properly. Then I pictured you going home to your husband and shedding
your clothes and your inhibitions in his arms." Reluctantly he abandoned the smoothness of her back and
his hands came out of the dress to settle on the dainty
linen collar. Slowly he pulled the fabric down over her
shoulders, over her arms, until it was free to her waist.
"I never thought of you alone. Why did you let that
happen?"

"You spoiled me for anyone else." Elise reached
behind him and locked her fingers in his hair. "I tried.
With Bob."

Sloane snorted against her ear.

"I dated others. Every time a man would get close,
I'd realize he wasn't you."

"I'm surprised you didn't think that was a recommendation."

"For a while I did. But when it got to the point
where it was either full steam ahead or breaking away,
I broke away. In my own naive fashion, I think I was
being faithful to you."

Sloane was shaken by her admission. His hands
tightened spasmodically, and he pulled her closer
against him. "Lise, did you think I was coming back?"

She sighed, and her head dropped against his shoulder. "No. But I had this dream of coming after you."

"Why didn't you?"

Elise wondered what there was about standing almost naked against a man that loosened her tongue so. "I almost did once."

"What stopped you?" he asked harshly.

"Fear. I knew you were in college by then, at Goddard. I bought a ticket to fly to Boston. But when the time came for me to get on the plane, I couldn't do it." She pulled her hands from his hair and placed them lightly on his shoulders. "What would you have done if I'd showed up at your door?"

Sloane truly didn't know. He shook his head in response.

"I knew it was too late for us," she said, her hands falling to her side. "But I should have come anyway. Then I would have known. I could have got on with my life."

Sloane reached around behind her to hook his fingers under the scrap of lace that had bound her breasts. The bra fell to the floor.

His eyes closed for a moment, but watching him, Elise knew it was not disappointment that held him in its grip. A curious strain seemed to settle over him. "You should have come." He opened his eyes once more. Almost hesitantly he reached up and stroked one breast with his fingertips. Elise could feel her flesh tighten. "How can you still be so beautiful? And so responsive?" He shook his head.

Elise unhooked the black leather belt that held the dress at her waist and felt the fabric billow around her feet. She slid her fingers under the elastic of her half slip and pants as Sloane watched her, and pulled them down over her hips until they were lying with the dress. Bending slightly she rolled down the tops of her thigh-high stockings until they were off, too. She straightened to face him, her hair falling over her shoulders like a veil.

She knew she had changed. Years didn't pass without changes. She had neither borne nor suckled children to mark her body with those wonderful signs of transition, but age had still left its imprint on her. Nothing was as firm or as smooth as it had once been. The straight planes of her body were softer now; she was rounder in the hips and thighs, her breasts no longer tilted perkily to the sky. She was thirty-five, not seventeen, but she was curiously undisturbed that Sloane would see her this way. She was still the same woman, even more of one than the teenage lover he remembered.

Sloane reached behind him to turn off the water, but his eyes never stopped traveling the length of her body. He drew a deep breath as she lifted her arms to twist her hair and sweep it into a thick knot on top of her head, fastening it with a barrette that had lain on the counter over the sink.

He stepped forward and settled his hands at her waist, then lifted her and turned to place her in the tub. She gasped as the heated water stung her skin, but she settled down into it and turned to watch him undress.

Elise had seen Sloane clad only in swimming trunks, and she had tried to ignore the response of her body to the firm, hair-roughened skin and the broad expanse of his shoulders. But now there was no reason to ignore anything. She let her eyes drift slowly over each part of his body as it was revealed to her. Sloane was older too, and yet the changes in his body were good ones. He was broader, more padded, but the padding was muscle and firm, supple flesh. He was stronger, more solid. If possible he was more desirable. She felt a wave of internal heat at the realization.

"Feeling warmer?" Sloane asked, one corner of his mouth lifting in a smile as if he could read the response of her body in her eyes.

Elise could feel the heat travel to her cheeks and she knew she was blushing. Thirty-five and she still blushed like a virgin under his gaze. "Not warm enough," she said, holding out her arms to him to counteract her response.

If he was surprised by her invitation, he didn't show it. He stepped over the edge of the tub and slid into the water behind her. Then he slipped a leg around each side of her and cradled her body between his muscular thighs. The intimacy, the sheer luxury of being surrounded by a man, by Sloane, destroyed whatever shyness she'd felt. She was too alive with feeling, too suffused with waves of desire to feel anything else. Elise leaned back against Sloane's chest and moaned softly as his hands settled at her breasts.

"You fit my hands so perfectly. You always did," Sloane murmured in her ear. He cupped the warm water and drizzled it slowly over her breasts, then smiled at the small noise Elise made in response. "When I was seventeen I thought that was no accident. I fantasized an understanding being somewhere in the skies who'd created us to fit together so well."

Elise leaned more fully against him and began to stroke the tops of his legs with her palms. The hair-covered skin against the smoothness of her hands was a homecoming. How well she remembered this feeling. How she had longed for the special freedom of exploring a man, knowing every inch of his body intimately. Even as she thought the words, she knew it was not just any man she had longed for. Only this one.

The tips of her fingers sank lower in the water to discover the sleek softness of his inner thighs. His response was immediate.

Sloane's hands tightened on her breasts and his thumbs brushed against her nipples. Elise's breath caught in her throat.

She felt Sloane's lips against her shoulder. Slowly he nuzzled his way up to her ear. His teeth caught her earlobe and tugged lightly on it. Then his tongue traced the graceful whorls, dipping inside to send sparks through a body that was already on fire.

As he played with her ear, his hands slid lower, skimming the taut satin skin of her abdomen to rest at the juncture of her legs. With a measured cadence he began to stroke the soft black curls he found.

It was only then that Elise realized how great was her need. She caught her breath and held it, fighting back the instant response to his touch. Her hunger embarrassed her, humiliated her. What would Sloane think? They'd only just begun.

She turned a little so that her side was against him and she could see his face. She felt she had to explain, to apologize. "Do you know what this is doing to me?"

Sloane suspected. He nodded his head in response.

She was ashamed of her needs, ashamed that she had let them build until they were driving her to rush something she'd wanted for years. "I feel like I'm coming apart inside," she mourned.

"That's what it's supposed to feel like." He bent his head and found her lips, turning her around with his hands at her waist until she was lying across him, her breasts rubbing against his chest. "Has it been that long, Lise?"

"Too long. God, much too long."

There was no more reason to talk, to rehash a past that had cheated them both. They were starved for each other and for forgetfulness. Sloane explored her water-slick body as he explored the tastes and textures of her mouth. Elise pressed against him, forgetting to be careful, to be afraid. Sloane was hers for this evening. That was more of him than she'd ever dreamed of having again.

She tried to know each inch of his body. She wanted to remember it all, to be able to pull out and cherish the sensation of his skin against her fingers, her lips, her breasts. Frantically she drove herself to make memories. If this was to be a reprieve from her loneliness, let it be complete, she prayed. Let it be a moment caught in time.

Sloane's response was immediate, although he seemed to hold himself back as if he were afraid to give in to the depth of his desire. "Lise, I want to be gentle," he said finally. "If it's been such a long time for you it might hurt ..." He tried to push her away, to slow down the passion that had ignited so fully.

Elise ignored him, seeking the probing evidence of his desire for her. She'd done little to excite him directly, yet he was completely ready for her, hot and hard and more than willing. She couldn't believe he really wanted to wait. Grasping his hardened flesh with her fingers she lowered herself over him, bringing him home where he belonged. Her cry was exultant. Sloane was truly hers once more.

He shut his eyes and clasped her against his chest. He could feel the shudders run through her body. He knew it would take very little to turn them into full-blown quakes. "We never had any control," he apologized as she moved against him again.

"I don't need control. I need you." The ecstasy she felt at his presence inside her was so overwhelming that it surprised even her. Her body, set free to pursue its goal of pleasure, ignored all the warning signals from her brain. It carried her along like the tumult of a rising river, and she could only go with it. Each time she moved, each time Sloane moved, she experienced such an intense agony of sensation that she knew she was going to explode.

Yet she didn't. Sloane was holding back as if he were afraid his own passion would hurt her. He had promised her slow and gentle lovemaking. He seemed determined to uphold that promise no matter what it cost him.

"Don't you want me?" she asked him finally, her words as heated as the sensations flooding her. "Have you forgotten what it's like to want me?"

Suddenly she could feel his control slip. His fingers dug into her and he turned her slightly so that he could plunge deeper into her flesh. "I never forgot. Never."

She gasped at his words and at the increase of pressure. She felt herself spinning away from him even as he held her closer. He thrust once more and she came apart against him, crying out his name. He thrust once more and joined her.

Afterward they lay in the cooling bath, their breath mingled and slower. Elise rubbed her hand over Sloane's chest to spread the beaded droplets of water and watch them condense. She was strangely embarrassed to meet his eyes. She had orchestrated this, rushed them to a conclusion that should have taken much longer. But she had needed him, wanted him so badly. And that need and desire had been communicated to him. She felt painfully vulnerable.

"Let's get out of here before you get chilled again," Sloane said finally. He sat up straighter, bringing her with him. Elise pushed away to stand and step out of the tub. She was numb with uncertainty. Did she dress again? Did he? She turned to see if she could read an answer in his eyes. She saw in them a duplication of her own doubts.

She turned and took a bath towel off the rack on the door and began to dry herself, carefully avoiding any more direct glances at Sloane. She wanted only to maintain whatever dignity was left to her. She heard Sloane get out of the tub and then felt him tug the towel from her fingers. He dried her, using long, gentle strokes. Then he unpinned her hair and used the towel to blot the moisture from the long strands. When he was finished, he dried himself, then lifted her chin and forced her eyes to his.

"I don't know what to do," he told her. "I want to stay the night. Will you let me?"

Elise wondered if she had misread Sloane's feelings. Or perhaps she hadn't, and he was being kind. She had certainly made her needs clear enough. They were needs most men would be glad to oblige for a night, Sloane included.

"What do you want, Sloane?"

"This night. With you," he said, stroking the soft skin under her chin.

Elise knew a clearer statement of his intentions would never be issued. He would give her this night, even enjoy the giving, but he was warning her that it was all she could expect, no matter how powerful her own needs. It was what she had known all along and what she had feared.

"Lise?"

"What about Clay?" she hedged.

"Clay's staying at Aunt Lillian's for the night because I have to get up early tomorrow and head over to Gainesville. No one will know if I spend the night here."

"That's not exactly true, not with your car parked outside. The whole town will know."

Sloane stiffened and drew away. "That would be a problem, wouldn't it?"

It would be a problem. Short affairs in a small town were grist for the gossip mill. Elise could imagine the speculations of her neighbors. They would know just exactly what she had given Sloane. They would also know how little it had mattered to him.

"I have to live here," she countered quietly. "What people think matters to me."

"How about what I think?"

Elise lowered her eyes. "I know what you think."

"What's that supposed to mean?"

The humiliation she had successfully suppressed came rising to the surface. "I threw myself at you tonight. Completely. I imagine it was flattering and scary as hell at the same time. But you don't have to be scared, Sloane. I know what tonight was, and I know what it wasn't. I just don't want the whole population of Miracle Springs to know the same things."

"What do you mean, what it was and what it wasn't? It hasn't had time to be anything compared to what it could be."

"Tonight was a one-night stand. I'd rather not share that piece of news."

"Fine." Sloane reached for his clothes and began to dress. "In other words, now that I've served my purpose, I can get the hell out of your house before your neighbors begin to speculate that you're really flesh and blood."

She wanted to protest, but Sloane was turning toward the door, one hand buttoning his shirt as he did. "I won't be back," he said, "even if you get all charged up again and invite me. I won't be used like some kind of gigolo to relieve your sexual discomfort. I thought we could have something different, but I was a fool. You're no different than you ever were. You put everybody else's needs and opinions before your own because then you don't have to make decisions. You're a coward, plain and simple."

"What do you mean?" she asked, suddenly afraid that she had misjudged him. "Tell me what you mean!"

"Figure it out by yourself. I've got to go move my car!" Sloane slammed the bathroom door and the explosion resounded through the silent house. Elise leaned against the sink with her eyes closed and listened to the angry sound of his retreating footsteps.

CHAPTER NINE

AMY TURNED UP THE COLLAR on her gray wool jacket to cover the back of her neck and pulled the front zipper a little higher. It was hard to believe that only a few weeks ago she'd been wearing shorts to school. The change in temperature that had begun the night of the Get Acquainted Dance was now firmly established. It was truly autumn. She could only be grateful she didn't live farther north, where blizzards had already been reported.

Amy tucked each of her hands under the opposite arm and stomped from foot to foot to keep warm. Kids streamed past her on their way home to seek shelter. Amy nodded her head in response to their comments, barely registering what was said to her.

The first wave of students had come and gone before she saw Clay appear in a cluster of boys walking in her direction. Yes, it was definitely Clay, deep in conversation with some of the kids in his homeroom. So deep in fact that he almost missed seeing her. Just as Amy was beginning to feel irritated at his lack of interest, his head lifted, and he looked directly at her and smiled.

That smile. She could forgive him anything for that smile. Why had it taken her so long to notice Clay? Really notice him, that is. Sure, she'd noticed—in passing—that Clay was cute the first time she'd seen him. But lots of guys were cute and worth noticing. Only a few guys were worth paying serious attention to. Clay was one of them, and it still bothered her that it had taken her so long to realize it.

"Amy!" Clay lifted his hand in greeting, then turned back to his friends. "Catch you later." In a moment he was at her side.

The November sun spilled over everything, refusing perversely to warm the earth with its rays. It glinted merrily off the golden highlights in Clay's hair, and Amy reached up to smooth a short strand that had fallen over his forehead.

Clay made an approving noise low in his throat. "If I'd known how often you were going to do that, I'd have cut my hair weeks ago."

Amy giggled, dropping her hand immediately. "If anyone had suggested you cut your hair weeks ago you would have looked at them like this." She stared at him without expression for a long moment, then giggled.

The corners of Clay's mouth lifted in a smile. "Well, weeks ago, you probably weren't available to cut it."

"When I was finished with you last Friday, you wished I hadn't been available." Amy started down the sidewalk.

"As a barber, you're a great history tutor." Clay walked beside her.

"What did you expect? You were my first customer."

"And your last. The real barber told me if I ever came in with such a mutilated mess again, he'd toss me out on my ear."

"I thought you looked like a British rock star."

"Wouldn't your father have loved that?"

The teasing comment had the effect of sobering them both. In the two months of their friendship, they had covered almost every possible subject. The one subject that was still difficult for both of them was Amy's father.

"You never did tell me what your father said about your hair," Amy said, trying to change the subject.

"Nothing much."

"Does he ever say much to you?"

"No. He stares at me a lot when he thinks I'm not paying attention. I think he wishes I'd tell him it's all a mistake, and I'm really someone else's son."

Amy was beginning to distinguish the fine gradations in Clay's tone of voice that expressed pain. Clay would never admit it, but the distant relationship he had with Sloane made him unhappy.

She tried to lighten the heavy mood they were falling into. "Maybe he just doesn't know what to say. Besides, you could be lucky. Most of the time I wish my father wouldn't say anything. What if Sloane starts talking to you and you find out he's a nerd?"

Clay rested his arm on Amy's shoulders and moved closer so that their hips brushed as they walked. "The world needs people like you, Amy."

"It needs people like you and me," she amended. "But I'm not sure it needs people like our fathers."

As if to punctuate the end of her sentence, a horn blasted on the road beside them. Amy turned to see her father beckoning to her from the front seat of his car. "I thought Daddy had a faculty meeting," she said forlornly, "or I'd have just met you at your aunt's." She waved back. "I'd better get this over with."

Clay stood on the sidewalk and watched Amy walk slowly to the car as if she already knew just what was going to occur and her feet were protesting the inevitable.

"Hi, Daddy." Amy opened the door but didn't move to sit down on the seat.

"Get in."

"Daddy, I'm going over to Clay's aunt's house to help him with his history homework. Mrs. Tyson will be there the whole time, and she'll drive me home when we're finished."

"Get in. You're not doing any such thing."

Amy's normally amiable expression vanished. Her jaw clenched and her eyes narrowed until she was glaring at her father. "Why not?"

"Don't question me, young lady. Get in!"

Amy took a deep breath. "No."

"What!"

"I said no. I'm not doing anything wrong. I'm helping a friend with his homework. When I'm finished, I'll be home. In plenty of time, I might add, to do the cooking and all the chores I do every day of my life. Without fuss," she added for good measure.

"How dare you talk to me like that!"

"I'm sorry, Daddy, but I'm right this time, and you've always told me to do what I know is right."

"Who do you think you are?" Bob slid toward her, as if to haul her down to the seat beside him.

Amy backed away. "Your daughter. A very good daughter who never gives you trouble. But I am going to Mrs. Tyson's house. I've been going three times a week for months now and I'll keep on going!" Amy straightened and turned to walk back to Clay.

"Three times a week for months?" Bob's voice was apoplectic. "Whose idea was this?"

"Elise's." Immediately, Amy wished she hadn't revealed the truth. There was little question what her father would do next. Elise was in for it.

"I should have known!"

With her back still turned, Amy heard the revving of the car engine and the squeal of tires. She had a sick feeling in the pit of her stomach, and she wasn't sure exactly why. Was it because she'd stood up to her father at long last? Because she had just condemned Elise to suffer her father's wrath? Or was it knowing that she and Clay might never be allowed to be together again after this afternoon?

Clay seemed to understand immediately what she was going through. He put down the books that hadn't fit in his backpack and reached for her when she joined him again. "It's going to be all right, Amy," he reassured her. "You were in the right. You didn't do anything wrong."

Amy leaned against Clay, and she knew immediately what bothered her most. She didn't want to be separated from him. More than anything, she didn't want that. "He's going to make sure you never see me again," she whispered against Clay's navy-blue jacket.

"We won't let him do that," Clay said evenly. Hesitantly he smoothed his fingers under her chin and lifted it slowly so that Amy was staring at him. Then he lowered his mouth to hers and took it with firm, steady pressure. For a first kiss, it was wonderfully effortless.

Amy blinked back tears, and her eyes shone with something else when Clay finally drew away. "If that's the way you say goodbye," she said breathlessly, "I could get to like going away."

"That's the way I say hello," he said with a shy smile. He kissed her again, an exuberant, quick kiss. "Hello, Amy."

"Hello, Clay." Amy raised her hand and let her fingers trail lightly through his hair. Then she stepped away from him, turned and began to run. "I'll beat you to your aunt's."

Clay watched Amy sprint down the sidewalk, and he suspected she was right. She was going to beat him. Amy might be able to run, but his feet felt strangely unattached to his legs. He would just float to his aunt's house. With a grin he followed her path.

ELISE RARELY DROVE her car to school. Unless she had an errand to do she walked the mile or so each way. Other women might do aerobic dancing or take up tennis to keep their weight down, but Elise walked everywhere she could with the same results.

This day was one of those rare occasions when she had reluctantly been forced to drive. She was so low on groceries that she had been compelled to eat freezer-burned waffles for her dinner the night before. Malnutrition had less appeal than eating—although neither appealed to her much. She had sat over her tasteless meal making a grocery list.

Now, one canceled faculty meeting behind her, Elise packed her little car with three bags of nutritious food and turned toward home. She had brought enough groceries to feed a family of four. She supposed her shopping spree reflected a secret desire to do just that. She liked cooking; she hated cooking for one person. On the occasions that she had a guest over for a meal, she lavished attention on her menu and cooked difficult dishes with only the freshest ingredients. When she cooked for herself she could hardly be bothered warming up fish sticks.

It said something basic about her life. She was a giver. As long as there was somebody to give to, she was happy. Of course, she was happiest if that person appreciated what he was getting. She hadn't been happy giving to a mother who had always found fault with her efforts. And she wasn't happy giving to Bob, who seemed to feel it was somehow his due. But on the occasions in her life when she had been given credit for what she did, she had been filled with happiness.

As if her mind had to take this latest realization to its obvious conclusion, she thought of Sloane. Sloane had always appreciated what she did for him. As arrogant, as impatient as he could be, Sloane had always been grateful for whatever she chose to give him, whether it was the gift of her body or something more trivial.

Sloane had always been the one to point out how little she asked for herself. He had been right. It was his biggest failing. He was almost always right. He had been right about her lack of courage. He had been right about her attempts to get approval from the wrong people. He had been right about her inability to make demands on others. Only about her reasons for rejecting him he had been wrong.

She was beyond caring what anyone in town thought of her virtue. Miracle Springs could be damned. If Sloane truly wanted her and claimed her for his own in front of the whole town, she wouldn't give anyone else's opinion a second thought. She would give him her hand and go with him gladly.

What she hadn't wanted was to suffer the humiliation of knowing he didn't want her and knowing that the town knew the same thing. She knew she had been suitable for a one-night stand, but there had been no indication on Sloane's part that he wanted anything more, not until he had blasted her with the ice-cold anger that made the weather outside today look like blazing summer. He had not understood her fear of being left high and dry, of seeing him day in and day out and longing for him with this newly awakened desire that was gnawing away her insides.

And now he would not understand her other fears. Sloane moved through life without looking anywhere except straight ahead. Not for Sloane the long reminiscences and emotional replays of the past. He had left her once without so much as a glance backward. Then he had probably put her out of his mind like a little boy's forgotten teddy bear, traded in for baseballs and roller skates. He would do the same thing the day he left Miracle Springs again. And what would she be left with? Memories?

She already had enough of those to last a lifetime. Memories were fine...if you enjoyed tormenting yourself. What joy would there be in remembering a year of love when she had to live the rest of her life without it?

Immediately, another part of Elise's mind accused her of being too careful, too controlled. It was caution mixed with a sense of duty that had kept her in Miracle Springs in the first place. Other women could abandon themselves to the future and take what came their way. Not Elise Ramsey. She opted for the secure, the known.

And with them had come a life of servitude.

Elise stopped unloading her groceries from the trunk of her car and realized just where her thoughts were leading. Being careful, taking no chances, she realized, had led her exactly to her present situation. She was a lonely spinster, unloading three bags of groceries she would never finish eating, spending every spare ounce of energy trying to convince herself that she'd made the right decisions.

If her decisions had been good ones, she'd know it. She'd feel it inside her and neither Sloane nor any other human being would be able to shake her faith in her own judgment. But she didn't feel that way. She felt bereft and angry at her own cowardice. She felt used, used by everyone in her life except Sloane Tyson and the children she had taught and loved.

"Elise!"

She had been so caught up in her self-discovery that she hadn't heard Bob's car pull in behind her.

She turned and wearily waited for him to come to her side. She put her emotions on hold; with a touch of self-pity she realized she'd been doing just that for years.

"Elise, I want to talk to you."

She sensed Bob's anger immediately. His words were clipped, and he was standing straighter than usual as if his anger had literally carried him to new heights. Irreverently Elise decided that whatever was enraging him had made him forget his affected stoop.

"Go ahead, Bob," she said calmly. "Here, make yourself useful." She balanced a bag of groceries in front of him and waited for him to grab it. When he did, she handed him another one. Since she never asked him to do anything for her, the gesture momentarily disconcerted him. Elise saw him blink. She wondered if it would be enough to make him forget whatever was bothering him.

Inside, she got her answer. He moved through the hallway and into the kitchen with a purposeful stride she hadn't seen him use for a long time. Elise decided that anger agreed with him somehow. Maybe Bob's life had been too settled to be good for him. Like hers.

"Just what do you mean by setting Amy up with Clay Tyson?"

"You must be talking about their tutoring sessions." Elise took the bags of groceries from his arms and set them on the counter. She unpacked as they talked.

"Tutoring sessions. Is that what you're calling it?"

"Yes." She stopped and studied him, her eyebrows lifted. "What are you calling it?"

"I just found out about it, so I—unlike you—haven't had time to give it a name."

"Try calling it tutoring sessions, then," she said lightly. "It fits beautifully. Amy helps Clay with his history, Clay pays her for her time, and they both benefit. It's the American way."

"This is serious. You don't have to be flippant!"

"And you don't have to be angry. There's nothing wrong with what's going on. In fact, if you hadn't taken out your prejudices on poor Clay in the first place, the sessions wouldn't have been necessary." Elise shoved a bag of sugar in Bob's direction. "Here, fill that canister behind you."

"How dare you blame this on me!"

"Who should I blame it on? Frankly, I didn't even know you were still in the dark about the sessions. What did you think Amy was doing all this time?"

"She said she was studying."

"So she was. I bet her history grades will reflect the work they've been doing."

Bob continued to clutch the bag of sugar. "You knew I didn't want her associating with that Tyson kid. You saw what happened at the dance."

Elise could feel her temper rise. It didn't take much these days to make her angry. Just one request too many, one criticism she didn't deserve, one blow to the underdog. *Midlife crisis,* she decided. *Premenopausal syndrome, if there is such a thing.*

"The only thing I saw at the dance," she said, enunciating every word distinctly, "was a man so wrapped up in his own selfishness that he couldn't even let the daughter he purports to love dance with a harmless boy she was attracted to."

"Harmless!"

She faced him, clasping her hands to steady their trembling. "The only reason you don't like Clay Tyson is that he looks exactly like Sloane. And you don't like Sloane because he had me first. Not that you want me! Not really! But what I felt for Sloane might affect your plans for my life. God forbid, I might stop taking care of you!" Elise knew she was shouting, but she couldn't make herself lower her voice.

"Calm down. You're screaming like a crazy woman!"

"I am a crazy woman. I've been crazy for years. Crazier than anyone I know to put up with you and your demands and your hypochondria. No more! And it has nothing to do with Sloane Tyson, so leave Clay out of it!"

"He's a troublemaker. I'm going to make sure he never goes near my daughter again if I have to call in every favor anyone's ever owed me!" Now Bob was shouting. "I'll have him put back in ninth grade. I can do it, too! And I'll make life so miserable for him that he'll leave Amy alone just to get me off his back!''

"You couldn't make his life that miserable because Clay's not a self-serving sniveling bastard like you are!'' Elise drew a deep breath and clamped her lips shut. She couldn't believe the words that had just come out of her mouth. And she had meant every one of them.

They both stood in shock, staring at each other. They were two people who had never known any kind of passion together. Neither had any idea how to handle the storm that had just passed over them.

"I shouldn't have said that,'' Elise said finally. It was the best apology she could manage.

"Why not? You meant what you said.''

"I did when I said it. And if you carry out your threats, Bob, I'll mean those words again. You have no right to interfere in Clay's life.''

"Amy is my daughter. I have a right to do what's best for her,'' he said coldly.

"Then do what's best. Leave her alone.''

"We disagree.'' Bob turned to go, dropping the sugar on the counter as he did. He was almost at the door before Elise's words stopped him.

"If you make trouble for them, Bob, you should know two things.''

"What?''

Elise sounded regretful. It wasn't difficult. If her words failed to move Bob, she would regret them always. "I'll step out of your life and Amy's life totally. I won't be a party to this injustice, and I won't pretend to Amy that I think you're doing the best thing. You can raise Amy by yourself. You can pick out her clothes, answer her questions about her body, help her try new hairstyles, give her advice about how to act on dates. You can do it all. If you shut me out of this decision, she's yours to raise. Alone, Bob.''

''You love her too much to do that to her.''

''I love her, yes. But I'm not going to help you with her unless I have some say in her life. I won't be your yes-man, I won't be the person who carries your load with none of the responsibility for what's really important.'' Finally, she played her trump card. ''And Bob, if you do one thing to Clay, I'll go to Lincoln and tell him you're harassing a student because you're jealous of his father.''

''You might as well run your dirty linen right up the school flagpole!''

''That wouldn't bother me at all.'' Elise realized she was telling the truth. She really didn't care what people knew about her and Sloane. Years ago most of them had suspected their love affair anyway. She imagined there would be a few raised eyebrows and more than a few yawns. People would watch her and Sloane carefully to see what was going on now. They would give the sleepy little town something to talk about. She would be doing Miracle Springs a favor.

Bob was silent, but Elise could almost hear his brain whirring. She knew she must let him save face if she was to get him to agree to leave Clay and Amy alone. By now he probably wanted to, considering the consequences. But even Bob had his pride. She swallowed her own.

''You know I don't want to hurt you. We're both upset, and we've both said things we regret. I care about Amy, and I care about you. That's why I don't want to see you make a mistake. I know you'll realize I'm right if you just think about this a little.''

His answer was a grunt.

"Will you think about it?"

This time his answer was a shrug. Elise realized the gesture was Bob's way of telling her she had won. She would never get a clearer message, but she suspected that the vendetta against Clay Tyson was over. Bob would probably lecture Amy, ground her for not telling him about the tutoring sessions, but in the end, he would allow the two teenagers to see each other, and he would not persecute Clay.

Elise realized that she would never know if it had been her threats or her logic that had been the deciding factor. But she would always have her suspicions. "Will you tell Amy I'm still planning on our trip into Ocala on Saturday?"

Bob left without giving her an answer.

ON THANKSGIVING MORNING Sloane stretched his arms out high, and then folded them under his head. He listened for the sounds of Clay's stirring, but the house was quiet. More and more Clay's life was beginning to take on the rhythms and patterns of a normal teenage boy's.

Sloane remembered their first months together. Clay had risen at dawn to prowl Sloane's Cambridge apartment with restless energy. He slept little, always alert and curiously tensed as if he were waiting for some signal that his life was going to change yet again. The city itself had simultaneously fascinated and frightened him. Sloane, who was so used to urban living that he scarcely gave its problems a second thought, had begun to realize that Boston and Cambridge were producing a sensory overload in the impressionable young man who was his son.

Miracle Springs had been a much better choice for Clay's first year away from Destiny Ranch. Yet even here it had taken a long time for Clay to begin to feel secure. Now Sloane could see that Clay was beginning to make friends at school, beginning to fit in. He mentioned names, told an occasional story. Sometimes the neighbor boys dropped by to get homework assignments or to play video games on the home computer Sloane used as a word processor.

Clay slept better now. He allowed himself to get tired. He didn't seem to worry that something was going to happen to change his life if he gave in to sleep. The prowling restlessness of before had been tempered and with it some of the boy's watchful intensity that had so worried Sloane. Clay had even cut off his ponytail. And to Sloane, there was no clearer symbol of his son's adjustment than that.

Clay was not yet an all-American boy, nor did Sloane care if he ever became one. But slowly, slowly, Clay was adjusting to life outside Destiny Community. His own intelligence and strength of character would carry him through this difficult time and on into adulthood.

Sloane wished he could be of more help. He wanted to reach out to his son, but he didn't know how. Other than providing the proper environment, the proper equipment, he was at a loss. They never discussed anything personal. When they did talk, Sloane spoke and Clay listened. The boy rarely volunteered anything and when he did, some internal mechanism seemed to stop him after a sentence or two. He seemed convinced that Sloane didn't really want to hear what he had to say, and no probing on Sloane's part could change that.

Sloane knew he would just have to be patient. He'd been cheated out of fifteen years of Clay's life; he would not ruin his chances of getting to know his son by pushing too hard. He would take it slow and easy. Eventually they would become closer.

He wished there was somebody to talk to about Clay, somebody who could understand and sympathize with what he was going through. He'd never needed a sounding board before. Even during his divorce he had felt no need to bend anyone's ear. The divorce had made sense, for both him and his ex-wife. The marriage had been wrong from the beginning; ending it had been right. His lawyer had been the only person he'd wanted to talk to. But now he needed someone to confide in.

Elise. He hated it, but he needed Elise. She was the only person he knew who would understand, the only person with both common sense and sensitivity. She was drawn to Clay, seemed to understand his struggles. In many ways, Sloane could see that Elise and his son were very much alike. She would be able to help him understand Clay.

But even as a confidante, he couldn't have her; the problems between them were legion. Elise kept a part of herself walled off and she didn't want him to break through that wall because then she might have to confront the problems in her own life. And she didn't have the courage to do that.

As he lay in bed, hands still folded behind his head, Sloane heard noises from downstairs. It was Thanksgiving Day. He and Clay would be going to Aunt Lillian's house along with the other Tysons from around the county. It would be Clay's very first family holiday and Sloane's first in a long time. He must be getting old; the idea of a family reunion was actually appealing. He liked the thought of people he was connected to all sitting down together for a turkey feast. The bird itself would have been shot by one of his cousins, the pumpkins grown in a family pumpkin patch. It was a shame that the family was short on teenagers now; Clay was the only one in the whole group. But there would be younger cousins and married cousins. The gathering would give Clay a sense of belonging and continuity. And in some strange way, Sloane realized it would give him the same thing, even though he's spent most of his thirty-five years refusing to believe he needed it.

He showered and dressed to go downstairs and eat breakfast with Clay. He found his son in front of the television set watching the Macy's Thanksgiving parade. Sloane settled beside him with a bowl of the granola Clay faithfully made once a week. "This is good," Sloane complimented him. "It tastes different than usual."

"I used cashews instead of peanuts. It costs more, but I like to vary it."

"What do you think about the parade?" Sloane asked between crunches.

"I'd like to see it in person."

"Maybe we could someday. I never have."

"Yeah."

Sloane tried again. "Are you looking forward to Thanksgiving dinner?"

"I always liked Thanksgiving best of all the holidays at Destiny. We'd have a huge feast with every kind of food you can imagine, except meat, of course. Then afterwards someone would light a bonfire and there'd be dancing until everyone was too tired to dance anymore." Clay's nostalgia for the familiar celebration was evident.

For once, Sloane could listen to the memory of Destiny Ranch and not be mute with anger. The boy had a right to his memories; they were sacred to him. Sloane put aside his own sense of loss for all the holidays he had missed with his son. "I was at the Destiny farm in Vermont one year for Thanksgiving," he recalled. "We did pretty much the same thing except that there was no bonfire. Only a fire in the fireplace. But we danced."

Clay's ears seemed to perk up. "I forget sometimes that you used to be part of Destiny."

"I never was, not really," Sloane said gently. "I was an observer. I always knew I'd move on."

"Did Willow know you were going to move on?"

Sloane was surprised by the question. He and Clay had never discussed Clay's mother except in the most cursory of ways. "Yes," he said honestly. "I think that's why she chose me to father you."

"And you didn't know."

"Not until I got the phone call six months ago."

"I asked Jeff once who my father was. He said my father was Destiny."

Sloane swallowed more than his granola. He could barely speak for a moment. Then he cleared his throat. "In some ways he was right, but only because I was never given the chance to be your father, Clay. I never would have left you there if I'd known."

Clay inclined his head and shrugged. "I was happy."

"Were you?" Sloane set his bowl on the coffee table in front of him. "I have dreams sometimes about a little boy who needed a daddy and a daddy who needed a son but didn't know it. In my dreams the little boy isn't happy."

Clay looked away. "I was happy at Destiny."

Sloane knew better than to push. Clay was not ready to repudiate the only home he had known for fifteen years. "Are you happy here, Clay?" he asked instead.

Clay focused his eyes on a spot across the room. "Yeah."

"Really?"

Clay realized he could be more honest than he had originally thought. Sloane was surprisingly mellow this morning. "I'm getting happier," he amended. "Some things are working out real well."

Sloane settled back against the sofa cushions. "Like what?"

"School. I've made some friends."

"I understand from your aunt that Amy Cargil has become a good friend."

Clay smiled a little and turned back to his father. "Don't they call this the third degree or something?"

"You're catching on."

"Yeah, Amy's a friend, especially now that her dad is . . ."

"Her dad is what?"

Clay considered whether to tell Sloane but surprisingly, Sloane seemed genuinely interested. He filed that fact away to consider more deeply at another time. "Well, her dad was picking on me. Amy says it's because I look like you and Mr. Cargil doesn't like you because of Elise."

Sloane frowned. "What does Elise have to do with anything?"

"I don't know. That's just what Amy said. But it doesn't matter because Mr. Cargil isn't bothering me anymore."

"What changed his mind?"

"Amy says Elise talked to him. He's been leaving me alone in class ever since. Amy's allowed to see me after school, too. Things are a lot better than they were."

"Why didn't you tell me this before?" Sloane asked.

"What could you have done?"

"Talked to Cargil myself. I won't have anyone picking on my son." Sloane stood and picked up his bowl to take it into the kitchen.

"Would you really have talked to him?" Clay sounded surprised, and the tone of his voice made Sloane turn to look at him.

"Of course I would have. That's one of the things fathers do. I think I could have managed that much. Don't you?"

"I never thought about it before."

"Think about it, son." Sloane disappeared into the kitchen.

Clay turned back to the television set and watched a giant helium balloon of Garfield the cat float down a New York avenue. He wondered if there was more to this father-son business than met the eye.

CHAPTER TEN

ELISE STRIPPED OFF her gloves and unzipped her short coat. Anyone who thought Florida was sunny and warm all year around should be in Miracle Springs on this particular Thanksgiving Day, she reflected. The sun was shining. That part was correct. But it was anything except warm outside. Fall had only just arrived, but already it felt like winter. Elise had just completed an errand in record time, anxious to stay indoors for the rest of the day.

With her winter garb carefully stowed in the closet, she walked through the hallway into the kitchen. The room looked just like a kitchen was supposed to look on Thanksgiving. There were pots and pans that needed washing, dinner ingredients that needed to be put away, leftovers that needed to be wrapped. It was funny, really. Here were the remnants of a Thanksgiving feast, and she hadn't eaten a bite all day.

At this moment two elderly widows who lived out on Mercy Road were enjoying her cooking, as they had every year for as long as Elise had known how to cook. It was one of those acts of conscience that Elise truly enjoyed performing. Mrs. Waid and Mrs. Furman counted on her to make the holiday special, and she never disappointed them. In return, they served her peach brandy and regaled her with tales of Miracle

Springs sixty years ago. It was an hour of folklore that Elise wouldn't miss for anything.

Usually she came home to put the finishing touches on the rest of the meal so that when Amy and Bob came for dinner late in the afternoon she could just sit and enjoy being with them. This Thanksgiving, for the first time in ten years, Amy and Bob were eating at home, alone. Elise was eating alone, too.

She supposed it was for the best. She had invited Bob as usual, and he had stiffly declined. There was no question why. He was still angry with her for interfering in his handling of Clay and Amy. She didn't regret her interference, not one little bit. But today, faced with the remnants of a Thanksgiving feast that she would have to eat by herself, she did regret the change it had made in all their lives.

What was lonelier than a banquet for one? She knew she was responsible for her own loneliness. Whatever she was, it was because of choices she'd made. Whatever she became would be because of the choices that were left to her. Her life probably wasn't even half over. She could turn it around, fling her arms open wide and embrace opportunity. She deserved happiness—and could make it happen.

So why was she staring at the holiday dinner like a lost little waif? Elise smiled wryly at her own vulnerability. She had great intentions, but today even a little thing like a kitchen filled with uneaten turkey and dressing could bring her down quickly. She was going to have to learn how to be courageous. It was going to take time.

Halfway through repackaging the turkey into freezer bag-sized portions, she heard the knock on her front door. "I hope it's somebody who'll take some of these leftovers,'' she muttered to herself, wiping her hands on a dish towel.

Sloane stood at the front door, dressed in a wool jacket the color of his eyes. He was the last person she had expected to see. ''May I come in?''

Elise stepped back, and Sloane brushed against her, bringing the smell of autumn air and wood smoke with him as he stepped into the hallway.

The fragrance of turkey and Thanksgiving greeted him. Sloane sniffed appreciatively. ''Obviously I'm interrupting dinner.''

''Not really.''

''You've eaten already?''

Elise shook her head.

''Then I have interrupted.''

''Actually, I was just putting it away.''

''Without eating?''

''It's a long story.'' Elise turned back to the kitchen. ''Do you mind if we talk while I finish up?''

Sloane watched the gentle sway of her hips as she moved away from him. Elise had a natural grace to her movements that sometimes haunted him when he was away from her. He wouldn't be thinking of her; she would be the furthest thing from his mind, and then suddenly, he'd be struck by a memory of her body in gentle motion. It was disconcerting when he saw such mental images, for it was as if his unconscious mind was waiting for exactly the right moment to surprise him, the moment when he least expected it and his defenses were down.

He followed her, hopelessly entranced. He had not come to renew a relationship that could never be renewed; he had not come for intimacy. He had tried that once, and it had only led to a new distance between them. No, today he had only come to say thank-you.

So why hadn't he said it and left?

In the kitchen Sloane looked around and his eyes narrowed. "There's enough food here to feed the world's hungry."

"I know. I guess I got carried away."

"Who's coming to dinner?"

"Nobody. I cooked for a couple of ladies from my church and this was left over." Elise waited for Sloane's lecture. He would put her down for her unselfishness, ask her what she got from performing these endless acts of charity, and condemn her with a look that neatly said it all.

"Well, they were lucky ladies," he said instead. "This looks fabulous. If I hadn't just eaten at Aunt Lillian's, I'd tackle some of this meal myself."

Like a dog who's expecting a kick and gets a pat on the head instead, Elise didn't know how to react. Sloane had missed a chance to give her a hard time. "Yes, well ..."

"Lise, you ought to eat some of this before it gets cold. I'll sit with you while you do."

Too surprised to respond, Elise watched as Sloane opened the cabinet, got a plate and began to dish up the food for her. He piled the plate with turkey, then stuck a finger in the dressing and shook his head. "It's cold. Will this dinnerware go in your oven?" He turned the oven dial as he asked the question.

He had taken over so quickly that Elise hadn't made a move to stop him. She wanted to tell him to forget about her dinner, but suddenly she realized just how hungry she was. She nodded, and was treated to the full power of one of Sloane's disarming grins. For a moment she wondered exactly what she was hungry for.

Sloane finished dishing up and then held out the plate for her approval. "Good enough?"

"Fine." Elise watched as he slipped it inside her oven and adjusted the temperature. Then he straightened. "Now, how about a drink while we wait?"

"You really don't have to stay to make sure I eat."

"I want to stay. May I?"

Elise could have worked up the courage to send him away if he'd been belligerent or arrogant. But this concerned man was someone she couldn't be rude to. "What would you like to drink?"

"Something light."

"White wine?"

"Perfect." Sloane watched as Elise poured them both a glass and took his when she was finished. Then he followed her out of the kitchen and into the living room. "I could help you finish putting everything away," he offered.

"I'll do it later, after I've eaten." Elise sat on the sofa and took a sip of her wine. It hit her empty stomach like an icy blast of autumn air.

Sloane sat beside her. "How have you been?"

Elise set her glass on the coffee table and folded her hands primly in her lap. "You didn't come here to ask me how I've been," she said, more sharply than she had intended.

"No, I didn't," he agreed easily. "But I'd still like to know."

"I've been fine."

"If you've been fine then why are you having Thanksgiving dinner alone?" he countered gently. "Where are Cargil and his daughter?"

"At home." She lifted her eyes to glare at him. "If it's any of your business."

"Evidently it is my business. Clay told me today that you stood up for him with Cargil."

"That's right."

"Obviously it's had an effect on your relationship with him."

Elise shrugged.

"Cargil's a fool."

"Now you're talking like the Sloane I know." Elise reached for her wine again and swirled it around in the glass for something to do.

"I mean he's a fool for letting this come between you. You're the best thing in his life." Sloane put his hand on Elise's shoulder. "But I didn't come to insult him. I came to thank you for what you did for Clay. I had no idea what was going on until he told me this morning."

"I'm surprised he never mentioned it." Elise remembered what had happened at Destiny Ranch the one time Clay had asked an adult to help him. She sighed a little at the memory. "I guess I'm not surprised," she amended. "Clay doesn't believe that adults will really do anything for him. I'm sure he felt if he mentioned Bob's persecution to you, you either wouldn't help him or your help would make things worse."

"He must have trusted you or he never would have told you."

Elise was surprised by the hurt hidden in Sloane's words. "The truth slipped out with me," she assured him. "He didn't want to tell me, and then afterward he insisted that I stay out of it. The only thing I was allowed to do was arrange to have Amy tutor him. Even after the scene at the dance he..."

"What scene?"

Apparently Clay had not told his father everything. Elise found herself feeling sorry for Sloane. "Bob got angry because Clay and Amy were dancing together. I had to...to straighten Bob out. But even after that, Clay refused to let me do more. Actually, Bob was the one who finally brought things to a head, and when he did, I was able to say what needed to be said to him."

"What did you say?" Sloane sat back and took his hand from her shoulder.

"I just told him if he didn't leave Clay alone, I'd make life difficult for him." Elise took another sip of her wine and then set it down. She had to eat.

"You threatened him?"

Elise smiled a little at the memory. "Sort of."

Sloane watched her and he didn't miss the smile. Elise might be sad that Cargil was angry, but she wasn't sad that she'd stood up to him. He felt a rush of pleasure at her reaction.

"I won't ask you exactly what transpired." Sloane stroked the smooth sides of his glass, and he watched Elise relax at his words. He'd seen that she was gearing up to tell him to mind his own business. He waited until she appeared completely relaxed again before he continued. "But I will ask why Cargil's been picking on Clay. Clay says it has something to do with us."

So far they had managed to keep their conversation fairly impersonal. Elise didn't want that to change. "Clay's different, and Bob doesn't like people to be different. I think it frightens him."

"And?"

"And what?"

"And what do you and I have to do with it?"

She realized Sloane wasn't going to let the subject drop easily. Her best defense was to answer quickly and simply. "Bob's jealous because he knows you were my first lover."

"Well, well." Sloane drained the contents of his glass. "Territory. Is he afraid I'm back to take you for my own?"

Elise was surprised how much Sloane's words hurt. He made the possibility sound ridiculous. "I suppose," she said, hiding her hurt feelings. "Silly, isn't it?"

"Silly, considering how clear you've made it that you wouldn't consider such a thing." Sloane stood. "I'm going to check on your dinner."

He was in the doorway before Elise's words stopped him. "Would *you* consider such a thing, Sloane?"

"What are you asking?" He faced her, leaning casually against the doorframe.

Elise had known Sloane wouldn't make this easy for her. She'd thought if she ever had the chance again to put things right between them, she'd do it with courage, ignoring his scorn. Instead she stood, nervously smoothing the folds of her plaid wool skirt. "I'm not sure."

"Then how can I answer?"

She reminded herself that it was Sloane who had come to her. She remembered their angry words weeks before, but she also remembered the distinct impression she'd had when he stormed out of her house—the impression that she'd made a terrible mistake. She knew this was her last chance to reach out for what she wanted and to hold fast to it.

She put her hands in her pockets to still their nervous movement. She lifted her chin. "Sloane, I know you didn't come back to claim me as your own—that's Bob's little fairy tale. I know you'll be leaving town in June, and I won't be. But is it so silly to believe that you might want me while you're here? Was he wrong about that?"

"I answered that question the last time I was in this house," Sloane said, almost hissing the final word. Suddenly politeness and gratitude were forgotten and weeks of repressed anger poured out. "You knew I wanted you that night. The signs were unmistakable. You were too worried about what Miracle Springs would think to consider more than a quick screw."

"You're wrong about that."

He was at her side in a moment, her dinner forgotten. "What am I wrong about?" he demanded.

"I was scared." Elise saw her own hand leave its shelter and reach out to touch Sloane's cheek. It surprised her.

"Scared? Of what?"

"Of doing just what I wanted, without worrying about the consequences. Can you understand that?"

He shook his head, but he reached up to cover her hand with his to keep her from withdrawing it. "Explain it to me."

"I thought you only wanted me for that night. Afterward, I couldn't bear the thought that I'd be seeing you day after day, continuing to want you and knowing that I couldn't have you again."

"You thought I wanted to make love to you once just to get you out of my system?" Sloane's laughter was harsh. "How little regard you have for either of us." His hand dropped to his side, and Elise withdrew hers.

"What did you want, Sloane?"

"Believe it or not, I hadn't drawn up a contract with exact terms. I wanted you. I knew that feeling well enough to know it wasn't going to go away after one night together. And I knew us both well enough to know that when June came, I'd leave, and you'd stay behind. Beyond that, I didn't know anything."

"And now?"

"Now there's nothing left to know. You made it clear to me that you didn't want me in your orderly existence. I bowed out as gracefully as I could."

"There was nothing graceful about it. You ranted and raved."

"That was as graceful as I could be!"

He looked so fierce, and yet, once again, Elise could sense the pain behind his words. She swayed toward him and her body was heavy with longing. She had been convinced it was too late, or perhaps she had convinced herself because she was always afraid to go after what she wanted. But now she was faced with a chance. It was a small one. Sloane looked as if he'd like to pick her up and shake her. He was fed up with her cowardice, her excuses. She could feel him slipping away from her as she stood in front of him, trying to put her doubts behind her.

"Sloane..."

"Don't apologize. I don't need your apologies."

She focused her eyes resolutely on his. This was the man she had loved so long ago. Inside of him was the boy who had taught her all she knew about her own body. It was to that boy that she spoke.

"Make love to me, Sloane. Now, and for as long as you desire me. I won't be afraid anymore."

He shut his eyes, and suddenly he looked tired. "Don't, Elise."

She understood his response. She had offered herself before, and then afterward she had sent him away. The miracle was that he was in her house again. She reached up to stroke his cheek once more. Even with his eyes shut, he flinched at her touch.

"I want you, Sloane. And you want me. We care too much about each other to want to inflict any more pain than we already have. Love me now. When it's time for you to leave, I'll let you go. And I'll cherish the months we had together."

Sloane felt the gentle slide of Elise's fingers over his cheek. Until that moment, he hadn't realized just how much he'd wanted to know her touch again or hear the words she had just spoken. He could feel the floodgate of his desire that he had so carefully locked burst open.

"What about the town?" he asked.

"What about it?" Elise smoothed her fingers around each of his eyes and then into his hair. "I won't lose my job if we're the slightest bit discreet. Beyond that, I don't care what people know or think they know. I want this for myself. For me. Just for me."

Sloane opened his eyes and gathered her close in a painfully tight hug. "This is crazy," he whispered against her hair. "I'm crazy. You're crazy."

"It's crazy to resist," Elise whispered. She could feel Sloane's body stir to life against her. She had months of wonderful closeness, this anticipatory pleasure ahead of her. It would be enough. It would have to be.

"Can we make it to your bed this time?"

"If you promise to ignore the rug on the landing."

"That's going to be hard."

Elise broke away from Sloane's arms and took his hand. The trip to her room was a blur. Later she would remember only the steady pressure of his fingers wrapped around hers and the moment when he scooped her up and fell on the bed with her.

He undressed her slowly, one piece of clothing at a time, covering each inch of her body with his hands and mouth. There was nothing patient in the way he touched her. His need was powerful, and he focused it on each movement, each caress, building their excitement into excruciating mutual arousal.

Elise was no less needy than she had been weeks before, but this time she knew Sloane would not disappear. She let him fan the flames of her desire, knowing well where it would end. She trusted his passion. She knew he would take and take and give in the taking.

She arched against him, crying out as his mouth fitted itself over her breast and tugged at it. She dug her fingers into his flesh, first pushing him away, then pulling him toward her. Her body was no longer under her control. Her legs wrapped around him, urging him on. Their skin heated and became slick; she felt the boundaries between them soften and disappear until she was no longer sure where she began or ended.

This time Sloane held her back from premature completion. When they were naked together he lay half on top of her, cherishing the smoothness of her skin and the ripe softness of her breasts. They didn't talk, but there was no need for conversation. Everything they would have to say for the next months had already been said. They had only to feel, to know, to accept.

Elise met each of his movements with one of her own. There was nothing obscure about the gift she was giving him. She was giving herself, her softness, her warmth, the very center of her being. That gift was apparent in every stroke of her hand, every sweep of her lips and tongue, every twist of her body. They melded together, changing forever what they had been before.

Finally Sloane pulled her under him, sliding deeply inside her. Elise wanted more. She strained to gather all of him within herself, the indefinable essence of him, the whole person. She loved him, had never stopped and never would. Sloane Tyson, her teenage lover, now a man. Her love was ageless and without boundaries. Sloane set her free, and in her freedom she could turn back to him and give him everything.

She did. She vibrated to the rhythm he set, meeting each of his thrusts with one of her own. Each time she gave, her own pleasure increased. Wasn't that the way it was supposed to be? Always?

Elise squeezed her eyes shut and let the rhythm accelerate, let the faster tempo eat into her control until what little had been left vanished altogether in a wild burst of heat and color and primitive sensation. She could feel him explode too, his release part of her own and yet different. She wrapped trembling arms around his back and pulled him to rest against her.

Sated and content, they lay entwined, exploring each other's bodies without haste and with more control. Elise lazily traced the ridges of Sloane's muscles, the curve of his ribs, the tapering curls. She leaned over him and the black silk of her hair, which he had unpinned, fell over his chest. She watched his eyes widen in pleasure, and she bent forward to kiss him. "That was spectacular," she congratulated him. "Amazing what a few years did for your skills."

Sloane laughed and affectionately patted her rump. "Two can play that game. Shall I tell you what a few years did for yours?"

Secure in the pleasure she had given him, Elise nodded, then kissed his nose. "Tell me."

"Absolutely nothing. You were always the best lover a man could want. That hasn't changed at all."

She was surprised by the tears that sprang unbidden to her eyes at the compliment. "That's lovely," she said huskily.

"It's true." Sloane pulled her to rest on top of him with her head cradled on his shoulder. "I've never met anyone who had your capacity to give and receive love. That's true in bed, too."

"Just how many people have you met in bed, young man?" she asked in her best schoolmarm voice.

Sloane laughed and hugged her tight. "Enough to know."

Elise lay against him and basked in the warmth of his embrace. There were few times in her life when she'd felt she was exactly where she was supposed to be. This was one of them.

"After you left," she said softly, "sometimes I'd lie in bed and remember just exactly what this felt like. Then I'd pretend that wherever you were, you were remembering, too. There were times when I actually felt like I was communicating with you, that somewhere, you were listening."

Sloane slipped his hand under her hair and kneaded a path along her spine with the palm of his hand. "Sometimes," he admitted, "I'd be in the middle of something—important, or not important, it didn't matter—and out of nowhere I'd start thinking about you. Other times I wouldn't even have you on my mind—not consciously anyway—and the next thing I knew I was turning around, expecting you to be there.''

"I probably was there, at least a part of me was.''

"It wasn't enough for me,'' Sloane said with a trace of bitterness.

"Hush.'' Elise lifted her head to look at him and she put one finger on his lips. "We can't change the past. And if we could, who knows where it would have led? Were you really ready for a wife at eighteen? You had wild oats to sow. I would have held you back. Wasn't there relief mixed with regret when I told you I wouldn't come with you? Wasn't part of your rush to get out of town because you were afraid I might change my mind after all?''

Sloane opened his mouth to protest, then closed it abruptly. He had sometimes wondered the same thing. "We were both immature,'' he said finally. "I was a volatile mixture of emotions I can't identify now. Neither of us can.''

"And neither of us will ever know what would have become of our relationship if we'd left here together. Perhaps we wouldn't have this much left of it.'' Elise smoothed Sloane's hair back from his face and kissed him. "I'm through with regrets. Tell me you are too.''

"I'm through with regrets,'' he repeated. Then his eyes warmed, smoldering with new heat. "But I'm not through with you.'' With one quick twist he turned her over onto her back and covered her body with his own. Elise gave herself up totally to the present. There was no more past and no future. She had the man she wanted. Time was no longer important.

"TURKEY TASTES BEST as leftovers,'' Elise said later. She and Sloane were sitting on the living-room rug, feeding each other bits of Thanksgiving dinner with their fingers. Elise wasn't sure which she liked best, the food—the first food she'd put in her stomach that day—or Sloane's fingers, when she got to lick them clean. "But didn't I hear a rumor that you already ate your dinner?"

"I think I worked off enough calories to deserve this," Sloane said, swallowing a morsel of dressing that Elise had dropped into his mouth.

"More than enough," she agreed.

"You should have a family of ten children to cook for," Sloane said, refusing another bite. "I can just see you stuffing their little bodies until somebody would have to roll them to school."

Elise laughed, and then she realized that Sloane was frowning at his own words. "What's wrong?" she teased him. "Did the mashed turnips catch up with you?"

"Elise, are you using birth control?"

She licked her own fingers and wondered at the stab of pain his words had given her. Obviously he was hoping her answer was yes. But then, of course he would. He was still trying to adjust to one surprise son. He was a man who said quite frankly that he'd never expected to have any children.

"I don't need to, Sloane. Didn't you ever wonder why I didn't get pregnant when I was seventeen? It wasn't those condoms you occasionally remembered to use. I rarely ovulate. Without medical intervention— fertility pills, hormones—my chances of conceiving a child are infinitesimal."

To Sloane's credit, he didn't breathe an audible sigh of relief. "When did you find that out?"

"Years ago. Bob asked me to marry him, and frankly, I'd wondered for years why I'd never got pregnant when you and I were together. So I went to my gynecologist for tests. He explained my problem, and when I told Bob, he was overjoyed. Turns out he didn't want another child—my child—anyway."

"And that was the reason you didn't marry him?"

"I'd like to think I wouldn't have anyway. But honestly, I don't know. If I could have had children with him, I might have felt it was worth it."

Sloane surprised her by putting his arms around her and pulling her close. "You'd be a wonderful mother."

"I know. But I've devoted all that maternal instinct to my students. It's made me a better teacher. I have the satisfaction of knowing I've changed lives."

"Clay certainly thinks the world of you."

"He's a beautiful young man. I love him."

"So do I."

Sloane's voice was so full of emotion that Elise turned in his arms and put her hands on his shoulders. "Of course you do," she soothed him.

"I don't know how it happened," Sloane said, almost as if he were detailing a crime he had committed.

Elise smiled a little. "Hadn't you ever thought you could love a child?"

"Not this way. I feel like I could lay down my life for him. I have nightmares of something happening to him and not being able to help. I wake up feeling like I'm fighting my way out of a black pit."

Elise understood. "You have to tell yourself that you're there for him now. That you'll always be there for him as long as you live."

"How do I make him understand that?"

Elise tilted her head and drew a line from his brow to the tip of his nose. There was so much that Sloane understood about the world and so little he understood about human emotions. Especially his own and Clay's. "Have you told him?"

"Not in so many words. What would they mean to him? He's never been loved before. A parent's love is as foreign to him as white bread and roast beef."

Elise smiled a little. "Well, he eats white bread and roast beef now—even if he was probably healthier without them. What makes you think he won't get used to the idea of being loved by you, too?"

Sloane shrugged in answer.

"I think you're afraid."

Sloane stiffened, but Elise's fingers massaged his shoulders until he had to relax again. "I don't know," he finally admitted. "Maybe."

"Don't be afraid, Sloane. He'll love you back. You need each other."

Elise let Sloane pull her down to the rug, and she nestled against him as he began to cover her face with kisses. Clay wasn't the only one who needed what Sloane had to give. But if there was a small part of her that envied Clay the love of his father, she pushed it resolutely away. She had as much of Sloane this moment as she would ever have. She could not begrudge the boy she also loved having more.

Afternoon turned into evening, and Sloane reluctantly dressed to go pick up his son. Elise stood in the doorway to watch him walk to his car. He stopped and turned, lifting his hand in farewell. She saw him touch his fingers to his lips in an unusual gesture of affection. Then he was gone.

For the first time in seventeen years she knew he would be back. As she closed the door behind her, she reminded herself that it was more than she had ever hoped to have. It would have to be enough.

CHAPTER ELEVEN

"I DON'T BELIEVE what you're humming." Sloane stood in the doorway between Elise's kitchen and living room, a glass of eggnog in his hand. He was watching Elise and Clay put the finishing touches on a Christmas tree.

"I can wish, can't I?" she said, stretching on tiptoe to rearrange one of the god's-eye decorations Clay had made for her.

"'I'm dreaming of a white Christmas'?" Sloane taunted her.

"Are you?" She turned a little and shot him a smile. "You're so sentimental."

Sloane laughed and watched as the two of them completed the task they so obviously loved. Everything seemed so natural, so right, that it was hard to believe only a month had passed since he and Elise had become lovers again. It seemed like a lifetime. "The tree's crooked," he pointed out, after the last ornament had been hung.

"Have you no sense of tradition? It's not supposed to be straight. If there was a Christmas tree in Bethlehem, it was crooked." Elise came to stand beside him and Sloane pulled her close. They examined the tree together. "Actually," she admitted, "it's a little more than crooked. Horizontal might be a better word." She poked her elbow in Sloane's ribs when he laughed at her. "It's just like you to wait until the tree has been decorated before you point out its problems."

"Actually, I like it," Sloane said, finishing his eggnog. "I'm thinking of starting a pool. The person who comes closest to guessing the exact minute when that tree hits the dust wins a dinner for two at the Miracle Springs Inn."

"Ebenezer Scrooge. Making profit off the misery of the world."

Sloane's arm tightened around her. "You do realize where you're standing, don't you?"

Elise smiled. She had wondered how long it would take Sloane to get around to the obvious. "No. Where?"

"In the crook of my arm with my fingers dangerously near your armpit." He tickled her a little to make his point.

"Such a romantic!" Elise squealed. "You'd rather tickle me than kiss me?"

"Kiss you? Why would I want to do that?"

"Because I'm standing under mistletoe and so are you!"

"I've been meaning to discuss that with you." Sloane brought his face down to hers. They were a scant inch apart. Elise shut her eyes. "Are you a druid?" he asked.

Elise opened her eyes and glared at him. "What?"

"A druid. That tree, the mistletoe, the holly on your dining-room table. All druid traditions."

"No, I'm just a crazy woman who invited you and your son for Christmas Eve dinner." She shut her eyes again. "Kiss me if you're planning to be fed "

"Such bribery." Sloane met her lips for a kiss that lasted as long as propriety would allow. Then he straightened. "You don't taste like a druid."

"How does a druid taste?"

"Different." Sloane lifted his hand and tucked a long strand of hair into the braid that trailed down to Elise's waist. "Very, very different."

"That's reassuring." She gave him a bright smile, then turned back to Clay who was staring at the tree. "What do you think, Clay? Other than the angle, don't you think we did a great job?"

The Scotch pine was covered with dozens of small god's-eye ornaments. Each ornament consisted of two crossed branches wrapped in an intricate design of different-colored yarns. To go with them Elise had wired hangers on small glitter-dipped pine cones and hung them beside the god's-eyes. At the last minute, she and Clay had examined their attempt at decoration and then run out to the store to buy strings of miniature flickering lights. Sloane had taken one look at the resulting mixture of technology and homespun charm and disappeared to buy a bright gold star for the top.

"It's interesting," Clay answered tactfully. "Unique."

"My son has a way with words," Sloane said proudly.

Clay looked at his father and grinned. Elise thought her heart would burst. For tonight, the peculiar tension that seemed to hover in the air between Clay and Sloane had dissolved. They seemed to have forgotten about roles and expectations, and they were thoroughly enjoying each other. During the past month Elise had seen this absence of tension very rarely.

"Ignore him," Elise counseled Clay. "Come help me check the pie."

"Actually, if you don't mind, it's past time for Amy to get here. I told her I'd wait outside for her."

"Better hurry then. She might beat you." Elise and Sloane together watched Clay spring for the front door.

"Remember?" they said together, then stopped.

"You first," Sloane said, playing with her braid.

"Remember the Christmas Eve I waited for you out on the front porch after my parents went to bed?"

"That's what I was going to say." Sloane tossed the long braid over his shoulder and wrapped his arms loosely around her. "You were blue by the time I got there."

"You were always late."

"I never wanted you to know how anxious I was to see you." He kissed her forehead.

"We gave each other presents."

"I gave you a Beatles album."

Elise smiled in remembrance. "I still have it."

"You gave me a pocket watch."

"Who says I'm not practical?"

Sloane put his cheek on her hair. "I still have it. It stopped ticking years ago, but I never did throw it away."

"Such an old softie." She put her arms around his waist and leaned against him, wrapped in memory. "You kissed me out on the front porch, and your lips were ice-cold."

Sloane was still remembering the watch, silent for so many years. "I ought to take it to the jeweler's and see if it can be fixed."

That possibility gave Elise a surge of pleasure, although she didn't know why. "I wonder what Clay and Amy will give each other."

"They're younger than we were. Not as serious."

"They're both older than they should be. That's one of the things they share. And they're just as serious as we were."

"If that's true, we'd better keep our eye on them. I'm still adjusting to having a son. A grandson would be too much."

"Bob's got his eyes open, believe me. Amy's so well chaperoned that she'll never have a chance to get into trouble." Reluctantly Elise pulled away and turned toward the kitchen. "About that pie."

"Why do you suppose Cargil let Amy come to dinner over here?" Sloane asked.

"I'll bet he has a date."

Sloane grabbed her arm and stopped her. "A date?"

Elise laughed and slapped Sloane's hand away. "Do you want this pie to burn?"

Sloane followed her, standing with his arms crossed as Elise lifted the pie from the oven. The sudden heat brought roses to her cheeks, and wisps of hair around her face curled delicately. He admired the softening effect for a moment before he spoke. "Who's he dating?"

"You're playing Miracle Springs's favorite sport. I'll warn you, professor, you may leave here with a small-town mentality." Elise set the pie on top of the stove and wiped her forehead with the back of her hand.

"Who?"

"Carol Groves. She's a widow. Lives down by the railroad crossing. They've known each other for years."

"And she mellowed him enough to let Amy come here?"

"More likely Carol invited Bob to dinner by himself. It's hard to carry on a romance with a teenager staring you down."

"We're managing nicely," Sloane said, putting his arms around Elise's waist and pulling her back to lean against him for a moment.

Elise understood the difference, even if Sloane didn't. Bob and Carol had all the time in the world. She and Sloane had to make memories to last a lifetime. She relaxed against him and moaned softly as his hands crept up to her breasts. A month had slipped by. More months would come after it, each one taking on the frantic pace of a river nearing its destination. In no time Sloane and Clay would be gone. She dismissed the thought. This month had been the best in her life. There were more coming. That was what she had to think about—that and each precious moment as she lived it.

A HALF MOON lit the tropical winter landscape, resplendent with poinsettia in full bloom and tall evergreens that screened Elise's house from those of her neighbors. Clay watched Amy, her arms filled with packages, climb out of her father's car and shout goodbye as he drove off. Then the boy stepped off the porch and joined her on the sidewalk. She set down her packages, and as naturally as if they'd always been together, they melted into each other's arms.

Clay lowered his mouth to Amy's and greeted her with a kiss. She wrapped her arms around his neck and stood on tiptoe to kiss him back. For a minute they were oblivious to everything else.

"Merry Christmas," Amy said, when she could talk again.

"Merry Christmas."

"I've missed you."

"I'm glad you're here." Clay watched as Amy retrieved her presents, then he put his arm around her waist and they began their walk to the house. "I was surprised your father said yes."

"I think he was glad I had a place to go. He's having dinner with Carol."

"Again?"

"Yeah. That makes three times since school let out." Amy giggled a little. "I think he'd marry her if he thought he could talk her out of keeping her Pekingese."

"Maybe he'll get used to it."

"Maybe. Carol's a good cook, and she loves to wait on him. He always comes back looking relaxed and happy."

"Do you like her?"

"She's okay. She tries to be nice to me, but she talks to me like she talks to her dog." Amy raised her voice three octaves. "Amy sweetie pie, have just one more bite of your pork chop. There's a good girl. It's so-o-o-o good for you. Do you want me to warm it up? Cool it down? Chop it up? Put it back together?" Amy giggled and resumed her normal tone. "She's perfect for Daddy."

They reached the porch and Clay leaned against a pillar, pulling Amy against him to delay their entrance into the house. "Why didn't your father discover her sooner?"

"Elise. I think he's been hoping for years that..." her voice trailed off.

"That she'd marry him?"

Amy nodded. "I hoped the same thing. She already feels like my mother."

"I don't know what a mother feels like," Clay said with a tiny smile, "but I suppose if Elise married my father, I'd find out."

"Are they going to get married?"

"I don't know. They never say anything about it."

"Are you still leaving in June?" Amy transferred her packages to one arm and smoothed back an errant lock of Clay's hair.

"Sloane has to go back to Boston. I guess I'm going too. If he still wants me."

"He's your father. Of course he wants you," Amy said indignantly.

"Amy, just because he fathered me doesn't mean he wants me. Haven't you figured that out yet? How many kids do you know who actually live with both their parents?"

"But that's divorce, not . . . not this!"

Clay kissed her forehead. "Sloane thought he was doing the right thing by bringing me to live with him, but he's not getting anything out of it. Eventually, when people don't get something out of whatever they're doing, they stop doing it. He's playing father now, but he'll get tired of it. Then he'll find another place for me."

"But he's your father!" she repeated.

"That doesn't mean anything," he explained patiently. "The only person you can ever really count on, Amy, is yourself."

"You can count on me."

Clay laced his fingers through Amy's short curls. "I hope we'll always be friends."

"But you don't think we will be."

"People change."

"You sure were raised funny." Amy stood on tiptoe once again and kissed Clay's nose. "You've got a lot to learn."

The front door opened, and Elise stepped out on the porch. "Are you two ready for dinner?"

"I'm always ready for dinner," Clay told her, pushing away from the pillar and catching Amy's hand.

Inside, the house was fragrant with the smells of pine and baked ham, cinnamon and bayberry candles. Amy took a deep breath. "Now this is what Christmas is supposed to smell like. Elise, you never had a tree before, did you?"

"No. My mother thought they were much too messy. If we put up anything, it was always one of those ten-inch ceramic trees with blinking lights."

"I like this better."

"So do I," Elise said fervently.

"I haven't had a tree since I left home," Sloane said, coming to stand next to her. "I'd forgotten how sentimental it can make you feel."

"We always have a tree," Amy said. "An artificial one. One year I sprayed it with pine air freshener to make it smell real and Daddy sneezed every time he walked by. I guess I overdid it."

Clay laughed and squeezed Amy's hand. "We always had a tree at Destiny. Not pine, usually—they were scarce—but whatever we could get. Everybody made decorations—paper chains, popcorn and cranberries. Then, on Christmas night, we'd stand around it and sing carols."

"Sounds like you had the most authentic celebration," Elise said, laying her hand on Clay's shoulder.

"And I'll bet you made god's-eyes for the tree, didn't you?"

Clay nodded. "It was always beautiful."

Elise looked at Sloane and saw the regret in his eyes. She shook her head in warning. One thing she was sure of, Clay would not understand Sloane's sadness and it was better for Sloane to keep his feelings to himself. Clay had his good memories; they were important to him. It was better that he didn't know the effect they had on his father.

Dinner was a festive affair. Elise was in her glory cooking for the people she loved most in the world. She had planned the menu for weeks, like a new bride serving dinner for the first time to her in-laws. There were baked ham and sweet potatoes rich with butter, brown sugar and spices. There were green beans, over-cooked the long, slow Southern way and delicate yeast rolls. There were mincemeat pie and a *bûche de Noël* made from sponge cake and mocha cream frosting with marzipan mushrooms to make it look like a real Yule log. And finally there were groans from everyone and protests that they could not eat one more bite.

Afterward, Elise and Sloane relaxed together on the sofa while Amy and Clay did the dinner dishes to the loud strains of rock music interspersed with an occasional carol.

"Nothing could point out how unusual those two are more than the fact that they offered to do the dishes," Elise told Sloane.

"I never washed dishes," Sloane admitted. "Not once in all the years I was at home."

"You were a rotten teenager. You should have had one just like you were as punishment."

"Clay's too good to be true. It's like he's always aware of what adults want from him, and he goes out of his way to give it to them." Sloane pulled Elise to rest in the crook of his arm. He stroked her hair. "I'd be happy if he'd argue with me once in a while or yell at me or throw things."

"I'm sure he thinks if he did, you'd toss him out on his ear."

"I wouldn't."

Elise turned a little so that she could brush Sloane's cheek with her fingertips. "Then tell him. Tell him you love him and plan to keep him no matter what he does. It would relieve his mind enormously."

"It's not that simple."

"It's a start."

"I'm not sure I understand love, but I understand what it's not. It's not pretty words. It's what you do for somebody."

Elise thought about Sloane's comment. She traced a line down his nose and smoothed her finger over his mustache. Finally she brushed his lips lightly. "I'll bet that in fifteen years, no one has ever told that boy he's loved. You should be the first."

"The last time I told someone I loved them was seventeen years ago." Sloane caught Elise's finger between his teeth and bit it lightly. Elise withdrew it. "I believe I was in the throes of passion at the time."

Elise was shocked at Sloane's statement. "What about your wife?" she asked.

"I didn't love her."

"Why did you marry her then?"

"She was pregnant. She lost the baby right after the wedding."

"I'm sorry."

"I wasn't. She would have made a lousy mother, and I had no desire to be a father. We were both relieved, as awful as that sounds."

Elise tried to understand. "But you married her? You must have felt something."

"Duty. And just barely that. Neither of us had any illusions about the potential our marriage had. It was strictly to give the baby a name. I resented her for being careless about taking her pills; she resented me for being in the right place at the wrong time."

"You love Clay. You would have loved the baby, too." For some reason, Elise wanted to believe her assertion was true.

"Lise, haven't you noticed? This is not top-notch parent material you're sitting next to. Clay snuck up on me, grabbed me by the gut when I least expected it. But a baby? I don't think so. As much as I regret the years I lost with Clay, I can't be sure it wasn't for the best. If I'd had him with me all that time, maybe I wouldn't love him now."

Elise wanted to believe that Sloane was just being hard on himself. She knew he was still adjusting to parenthood, trying to come to grips with the sudden onslaught of emotion he felt for his stranger-son. But there was something that rang true in his words. She couldn't imagine him tenderly holding an infant, walking the floor at night while the baby teethed or screamed from an earache. Clay was a real person with ideas. But a baby? What was a baby other than a mass of nerves and sensations it couldn't interpret? A baby took patience, endless unqualified love and faith that your efforts would be rewarded with a healthy, happy human being farther down the line. Elise wasn't sure that Sloane had those qualities. But she wasn't sure he didn't, either. Sloane was always a puzzle.

"It's funny we should be having this talk now," she mused. "Tomorrow is all about birth and hope and love."

"And miracles."

"Sometimes the biggest miracle is finding out that we have more inside us than we thought."

"Always the optimist."

"Always the pessimist." Elise leaned over and covered Sloane's lips with her own, then she drew back. "You loved me seventeen years ago because I saw more in you than anyone else did. Maybe I still do. And maybe I see more than you do."

"What do you see?"

What did she see? A man who for all his academic titles and success still didn't truly believe in his own value as a human being? A man who was afraid to reach out, a man who wanted to share himself with his son but didn't know how? A man who for seventeen years had not uttered the three most precious words in the English language to anyone?

"I see Sloane Tyson. A man who has so much to give that those of us who love him would never be able to take it all if we had a millennium to try."

"Lise . . ."

She put her finger against his lips to stop him. "I love you, Sloane. I'm not ashamed of it, and I'm not trying to bind you to me. I just want you to know I still do. I don't think I ever stopped, and I don't think I ever will." She rested her head on his shoulder.

"And what happens when I leave?"

"I go on loving you." There was a commendable lack of self-pity in her voice. "And we both go on with our lives, glad for the time we did have together."

Amy and Clay came out of the kitchen, arm in arm. "All clean," they said together as if they'd rehearsed it.

"Terrific." Elise tried to sit up and fell back groaning. "I can't move."

Sloane gave her a push and watched as she finally got to her feet. It amazed him that she could act so naturally after what she had just said to him. She had told him she loved him as if it were the most normal, everyday kind of thing to tell someone. He wondered what it said about the depth of her feelings. He wondered what it said about his own reluctance to say the same words.

"It's time to open presents," Elise announced. "Under the Christmas tree." She turned back to Sloane and extended her hand to help him off the sofa.

"Can you lower me to the rug under the tree or shall I call for a crane?" he asked, laughing.

Sloane let her pull him off the sofa. He filed away her words and his thoughts about them to examine another time. He had always been good at living for the moment.

When everyone was sprawled around the tree, Elise passed out packages. "Amy, you go first."

Amy opened Elise's gift, exclaiming over the blue and gray sweater she had once admired when they shopped together. Clay was next, opening one of Sloane's gifts. He was genuinely thrilled with a beautifully bound book from a multivolume encyclopedia that was waiting for him at home. Elise would have throttled Sloane, who had been stubbornly determined to give his son something so impersonal and academic, except that she knew that along with the encyclopedia there was also going to be a new stereo for Clay on Christmas morning.

Elise went next, opening a monogrammed leather wallet from Amy, and Sloane followed with a large volume of e.e. cummings's poetry from his son. Then they began again. Amy rattled Clay's present, frowning. "I can't tell what it is."

"You're not supposed to be able to tell," Clay said helpfully. "If you could tell, I wouldn't have had to wrap it at all."

Amy stuck out her tongue at him and began to rip off the wrapping. Inside the small box was a silver and turquoise pin in the shape of a tiny bird. "It's beautiful." She leaned over and kissed Clay on the cheek. "Thank you."

Clay just smiled. Amy handed him his present next, and he performed the rattling ritual before he opened it. It was a colorful plastic watch, exactly like the ones every other student at Miracle Springs High had. "Because you're usually late," Amy informed him.

"Is he?" Elise asked with interest as Clay kissed Amy in thanks. "It's obviously in the Tyson genes."

Sloane grunted in protest as he handed Elise her present. She unwrapped it slowly, sadly aware that it was the last Christmas they would spend together. She wanted to draw out each moment. She opened up the box from an expensive boutique in nearby Ocala and shook out the burgundy silk that lay inside. It was a blouse, richly detailed with cutwork and lace and Victorian in style. "It's beautiful. Thank you."

Sloane stole his own thank-you kiss and then reached for his present. He opened it with no ceremony, just ripped open the wrappings and stared at the contents of the box. "Where did you get this?" he asked finally.

"Don't you remember?"

Sloane shook his head.

Elise covered his hand with hers. "You gave it to me seventeen years ago. Right before you left town. I've kept it all these years. I'm glad I did."

"What is it, Sloane?" Clay asked curiously.

Sloane held up his old journal. The cover was smudged with ink and the corners were torn away. Even with the smell of Christmas dinner hanging heavily in the air, the journal gave off the pleasant, musty scent of the past. "I kept this from the time I was your age until I turned eighteen," he told Clay. "I guess it has every feeling I felt in it, every single thing I did."

"And you gave it to Elise?" Clay asked. It was obvious he wanted to know why.

"Did you ever read it?" Sloane asked, turning to her.

"No. I couldn't."

Elise was sure Sloane understood. He had thrown it at her in anger the day he had come to say goodbye to her. "Read this if you ever get lonely," he'd said. "It's all you're ever going to have of me if I leave tomorrow and you don't."

And she had been lonely for him. So lonely sometimes that she'd picked up the journal just to feel his presence. But she'd never read it. She'd never wanted to suffer that much. And the day she'd decided not to fly to Vermont to see him once more, she had packed the journal in the attic and never looked at it again.

Not until yesterday when she had unpacked it and wrapped it in Christmas paper.

"I'm not sure I'll be able to read it either," Sloane admitted, staring blankly at the cover.

"It's the past," she reminded him. "And now is now. That's why I'm giving it back to you."

"Thank you." Sloane's eyes caught hers and held her gaze.

Amy and Clay got to their feet. "I'm going to walk Amy home," Clay informed them.

"She lives a long way from here. I'll drive you," Sloane said, still looking at Elise.

"We're walking." Clay took Amy's hand. "I'll be home late."

Elise smiled at Clay's show of spirit. She could see that Sloane appreciated it, too. "Fine," he said, giving in gracefully. "I'll see you later."

There was a flurry of goodbyes and thank-yous, then the two teenagers departed. Elise stood at the living-room window and watched them disappear down the street. She felt Sloane's arms slide around her waist, and she leaned against him.

"Two gifts, Lise. You gave me two gifts."

She knew immediately what he meant. "My love and our past," she said.

Sloane was silent, but he pulled her closer.

"Both were freely given," Elise told him. "No strings."

"You're coming over tomorrow?" he asked after a long silence.

"I still have to give Clay the book I bought for him."

"Come early. I'll make us brunch." Sloane's hands worked their way up her sides to her shoulders. Slowly, he turned her around. "Are you in a hurry to get rid of me now?"

Elise shook her head.

"How do soft carols, another glass of eggnog and me under the Christmas tree sound?"

"Like the best Christmas present of all." Elise lifted her hands to the top button of his shirt. "But let's save the carols and eggnog for later."

"Much later," he agreed, bending his head until his lips were a fraction of an inch from hers. He began to tug her blouse out of her skirt until his fingers grazed the soft skin of her stomach.

"Much later," they said together. And then they didn't say anything for a long, long time.

CHAPTER TWELVE

ELISE TUCKED THE PLAID NAPKIN over the basket of food she was carrying and swung it to the crook of her left arm. She opened the front door of Sloane's house and poked her head inside. "Sloane? Are you up? If you aren't I'm coming to get you!"

Sloane stepped out of the kitchen, wiping his hands on a dish towel. "If I'd known that, I'd have stayed in bed. Want me to go upstairs and pretend?"

"Is Clay here?"

Sloane pointed to the ceiling. "He's getting dressed."

"Then no, we'd better stay down here," Elise answered regretfully. She stepped over the threshold and into Sloane's arms. They had made leisurely love the night before, but they kissed as if they were starving for each other and had been for years. Finally Elise pulled away. "Are you sure Clay's here?"

Sloane smiled. "He's been moping around the house all morning because he can't see Amy until lunchtime. Her father's making her clean house."

"Bob's been in a foul mood ever since Carol started dating the man who owns the male Pekingese she bred hers to. He's not speaking to anybody."

"Obviously he's speaking to Amy." Sloane guided Elise into the kitchen and settled her at his table. "Coffee?"

She nodded and Sloane fixed it just the way she liked it. There was something wonderfully intimate about watching him add cream and sugar to the cup without having to give it a second thought. For a moment, she let herself pretend that this kind of familiar sharing wasn't going to end soon.

"I can't believe you're going to the celebration with me today," Elise said after half a cup was finished in comfortable silence.

"I can't believe it either. I have written proof up-stairs that I once vowed I would never do this."

"You said you'd never come back here, period," Elise reminded him. Without thinking she reached out and stroked his smoothly shaven jaw. "You've been reading your journal, haven't you?"

"Last night. What a passionate creature I was."

"Passionate. Sensitive. Intelligent." Elise lowered her voice to a whisper. "Obnoxious."

Sloane grinned at her. "You won't get an argument from me on that. I was worse than obnoxious. I was prejudiced, small-minded, totally set in my ways. All the things I accused this town of being. How did you stand me?"

"Well, I never saw you that way. I guess I saw a boy whose feelings ran deeper than anyone I'd ever known. That was the part of you I fell in love with."

It was the first time in months that they had mentioned their past. With Christmas Day as a new begin-ning they had lived only in the present. They had spent every spare minute together, laughing, loving, build-ing onto a friendship that had begun so many years before. Their time together had to be carefully orches-trated. Sloane had Clay to worry about, and Elise had her reputation in the community. But they had seen those obstacles as challenges, and they had found ways around them.

January had included a weekend in Miami where Sloane was supposed to be researching his next book but instead, had thoroughly researched Elise. February, a month too short on days, had been long on leisurely evenings by Sloane's fireplace while Clay studied or slept upstairs. In March, over Easter break, they had explored nearby Disney World. There Sloane had immediately scrapped the nebulous ideas for his next book and begun an impassioned sociological study of what Mickey Mouse had and hadn't done for Central Florida. And in April, more than once, they had visited the riverbank to wade in the icy Wehachee and watch it awaken to the glories of spring.

Now it was May. In a month, Elise knew that Sloane would be gone.

"I got a letter from the couple subletting my apartment in Cambridge today," Sloane said, as if he were reading her thoughts. "They're moving out two weeks earlier than they'd intended. It means I can leave a little sooner than I'd planned."

"When will you be going?" Elise forced herself to meet his gaze.

"Right after school ends. There's a summer program for gifted high school students at Boston University. I talked to a friend who teaches there and he wants Clay to attend. He'll meet some kids in the city, and it'll help him get ready for school next year."

Elise kept her tone neutral. "That sounds like a good idea. I'll send a recommendation if you need one. I know he's still struggling with math, but he's absolutely brilliant in English."

"Science is a puzzle for him. He told me yesterday that his biology teacher says he knows more biology than any student he's ever had. Then he told me that until he was twelve, he didn't know that man had ever been in space. He can identify all the stars in the heavens, put a car engine together with his eyes closed and explain Darwin's theories better than Darwin could. But he's never heard of an ion, a proton, or a neutron."

Elise wondered why they were talking about the peculiarities of Clay's education when what they really needed to talk about was the fact that Sloane was leaving in less than a month. But the reason for the evasion wasn't too mystifying. She suspected that Sloane, like herself, didn't want to face their parting.

She chose to continue talking about Clay, too. "Clay's going to miss the friends he's made here. I hope you'll let him come visit Lillian from time to time."

"Actually, he wants to stay and finish school here." Sloane's voice was emotionless.

Elise imagined the hurt behind Sloane's carefully guarded expression. She wanted to comfort him, but she knew there was little she could say. Even though Sloane and Clay had lived together for almost a year, they were still strangers in the most important ways. Sloane rarely discussed it, but Elise knew how much he yearned for his son's love.

"Have you considered letting him stay?" she asked, reaching out to cover Sloane's hand with hers. "He could live with me if Lillian isn't up to it."

"I want him with me."

Elise nodded, relieved at his answer. Sloane wanted to continue trying to be a good father. He had no intention of giving up. "Good."

"Maybe I'm wrong."

"Maybe you're not." She laced her fingers with his and brought them to her cheek. "He needs you more than he needs to stay here."

"I'm not sure Clay needs anybody. Except Amy, maybe."

"Didn't you need a father when you were Clay's age?" she asked gently.

"I always needed a father."

"Clay's no different. He just doesn't know how to let you know."

"Sometimes I think I'd know what to do better if my own father had lived and I'd grown up with him." It was a rare moment of vulnerability for Sloane, and Elise squeezed his hand in tribute.

"Hi, Elise." Clay's entrance was heralded by the clatter of his topsiders on the stairs. He headed straight for his father. "Can we pick Amy up on our way to the Inn? Mr. Cargil said she could leave at noon if she was finished, and she is."

"I don't know how she finished, considering the two of you spent most of the morning on the telephone," Sloane observed. "But I think we're about ready to go."

"I packed a picnic lunch." Elise patted the basket, which she'd set on the table. "We can avoid the food at the Inn."

Clay peeked under the napkin. "You made your own bread!"

"Just for you. I used your recipe."

"And it made enough for an army," Sloane guessed out loud. "It took Clay three months before he figured out how to cut down his granola recipe for the two of us. We were eating it for breakfast, lunch and dinner. I gained three pounds."

"If I flunk out of that fancy New England prep school you're planning to send me to, I can always get a job as a cook in a health food restaurant," Clay said nonchalantly.

"What's this about a prep school?" Elise asked Clay.

"Sloane's got his eye on the Ivy League."

"Sloane?"

"You know," Sloane teased, "one of those places where Clay'll have to wear a coat and tie all day except when he's out on the field in his rugby uniform."

"You wouldn't!" Elise slapped the table in front of her.

"Actually it's a military academy."

"Sloane!"

"How about a private coed Quaker school that concentrates on small classes and individual learning?"

Elise smiled and relaxed. "That sounds wonderful."

"Convince my son, then."

"Don't you want to go, Clay?" she asked, turning back to the teenager who was rummaging through the picnic basket approvingly.

"I don't know."

Elise recognized Clay's answer for what it was. An attempt to avoid telling the truth. Pretending indecision was better than saying yes when he didn't mean it and not as good as saying no. As much as she wanted to ease the strain between father and son by getting them to talk to one another she decided not to push. "Well, I know a certain man—a man who is sitting at this table in fact—who would have loved to go to such an institution at your age. Correct?" she asked Sloane.

"At Clay's age I didn't know such a place existed. But yes, I would have loved it. I think Clay will, too. If not, we'll find something he likes better."

Clay abandoned the basket and faced his father. "Really?"

Sloane's voice showed his surprise. "Really. Did you think I was going to stick you somewhere and leave you? You'll be living at home; we'll talk. If you hate it you can tell me."

"And you'd listen?" Clay sounded as if he wanted to make sure he understood.

"Don't I listen now?"

Father and son were staring at each other. Elise wanted to disappear under the table and leave them alone. All she could do was remain perfectly still.

"I don't know if you listen because I don't say much," Clay said finally. Then he turned to leave the kitchen. "I'm going to call Amy and tell her we'll be over in a few minutes." He was gone before Sloane could say another word.

THE INN HAD ENDURED its yearly sprucing up for the Festival of the Miracle. The grounds were as neat as the proverbial pin with all the shrubs trimmed to immaculate perfection and the grass cut so that each blade was identical. Summer annuals bordered the Inn's front porch and hanging baskets of shocking-pink petunias and lilac lantana decorated the rafters. Even the

Spanish moss on the trees seemed to have been arranged in lacier designs.

Church groups and local entrepreneurs had set up booths and tables all over the grounds. Behind the Inn where the long yard sloped down to the Wehachee, blankets were spread and family groups sat at makeshift picnic tables enjoying the late spring sunshine.

The temperature was a not-so-subtle reminder of the blistering heat that would follow in the months to come, but everyone had dressed accordingly in shorts and cool summer dresses. The air was redolent with the smells of spring and coconut sunscreen.

Elise and Sloane, followed in the distance by Amy and Clay, spread two quilts side by side and began to unpack the picnic basket. Sloane inventoried out loud as he set the food on the quilt. "Deviled eggs. Chicken sandwiches. Celery stuffed with cream cheese. Brie. Brie? The Piggly Wiggly is carrying Brie these days?"

"I bought it in Ocala. Keep going. I'm starving."

"Homemade bread." Sloane sniffed the bread. "Raisin bread." He looked up and grinned. "How much is at home in your freezer?"

"Six loaves. That's why we're having chicken sandwiches. I had to take out two chickens to make room for it."

"You have to cut all of Clay's recipes in half."

"I did." Elise pushed Sloane playfully to one side and finished unpacking the basket herself. "Marinated mushrooms. Artichoke salad. And," she waved the last item in front of Sloane's nose, "fresh blackberries."

"My sweet little yuppie Florida cracker," Sloane crooned, planting a big kiss on her willing mouth. "You can pack a picnic for me anytime."

"Just remember to order well in advance so I can drive into Ocala." She picked up a stalk of celery and stuck it in Sloane's mouth. "Do you know how many people just saw you kiss me?"

Sloane crunched on the celery thoughtfully. "What happens if I do it again?"

"They'll read the banns next Sunday at church."

"Everyone knows we're sleeping together."

"Everyone suspects," she corrected him. "They're just looking for a shred of firm evidence."

"Has anyone said anything to you?"

Actually she had been innundated with tactless queries, but Elise didn't want to burden Sloane with that knowledge. She had become adept at evading questions. She would evade this one, too. "Well, sure. Mrs. Barlow said hello this morning, and Marion, the cashier at the grocery store, asked me how I was when I bought mayonnaise for the sandwiches."

"Is your job in jeopardy?" Sloane asked, cutting through to the heart of the matter.

"No."

"You could find a job in Boston."

Elise met his eyes. "I could find a job anywhere."

"Do you want to leave this place?"

Elise had no idea why Sloane had asked the question. A part of her leapt in hope that it was his way of asking her to go with him. Another part drowned in despair because the question seemed so casual. He might as well have asked her to pass another piece of celery.

"Sometimes leaving here is the only thing on my mind," she said carefully. "And sometimes I realize I'm lucky to live somewhere where I'm held in high esteem. Teachers in big cities are just part of the scenery. In a town like this one, we're part of people's lives."

Sloane seemed contented with her answer. "I could never live here. Even now, with my departure right around the corner, I feel so constrained and hemmed in that I think I'm going to explode."

"I haven't sensed that." Elise felt a surge of pain at his words.

"I don't feel it when I'm with you," Sloane reassured her. "I've never felt it with you. I'm going to miss you, Lise."

"I'm going to miss you, too." More than you could ever imagine, she thought as she leaned over for the second forbidden kiss. Probably more than she could imagine herself.

Clay and Amy joined them a few minutes later and the afternoon became the makings of a bittersweet memory. Each of them knew that the time for finding simple joy in each other was coming to a close. They took the time remaining to them and colored it with laughter and kisses and poignant conversation.

After stuffing themselves with Elise's picnic, they strolled to the front of the Inn and visited the festively decorated booths. Elise and Amy had their fortunes told, and although Clay and Sloane laughed at them, the two males were discovered a few minutes later gambling all their spare change on a balloon-busting dart-throwing contest. They drank fresh lemonade, cakewalked and applauded Amy, who was brave enough to have a glittering butterfly painted on her cheek. They watched little girls in lipstick and tutus perform a ballet to the music of *Swan Lake* and little boys in green derbies tap-dance to "The Sidewalks of New York." Afterward, they sat on the riverbank with a crowd of others and fished from numbered cane poles to try and land the largest catch of the day.

No fish, three volleyball games and four hot dogs later, they stood on the riverbank and watched the sun disappear behind the bald cypress, tupelo and water oak that lined the Wehachee. Frogs in the thick underbrush of cabbage palm and button bush began a symphony and a screech owl joined in with its mournful wail. The night was damp and velvet dark before they gathered their quilts and headed back to Sloane's car.

"Now to see the maiden," he said. "We have plenty of time. Would you like to go home first?"

"I'd like to change out of these shorts," Elise admitted. "It'll be chilly by midnight."

"Can you drop Amy and me at the springs?" Clay asked. "We told some people we'd meet them there."

"I guess that'd be all right."

Elise watched Clay slide out of the back seat and extend his hand to Amy. Amy took it as naturally as if she'd always held it. Clay and Amy were more than teenagers in love. They were kindred spirits. There was so little of the moody, exhilarating highs and debilitating lows of young love in their relationship. They were enchanted with each other, obviously emotional in their responses, but there was a steady quality, a certainty about their feelings that set them apart.

"Clay and Amy are going to feel like they've each been torn in half when Clay leaves," Elise observed, her head back against the seat of Sloane's car as he drove to her house.

"For once I'll understand exactly how Clay feels."

She smiled a little. "And I'll be able to sympathize with Amy. I'll remember just how it felt." She didn't add that she'd be feeling the same way again. It was part of the bargain she had made with herself and, unconsciously, with Sloane. She had no right to make him feel guilty about leaving. She would not tell him of the devastation she was going to feel when he walked away for the last time. It would serve no purpose; it would only spoil their last days together.

Minutes later Sloane and Elise were alone in her front hallway. "Do you mind if I help you change?" he asked, his hands already laying claim to her body in a way that announced that he expected no resistance.

Even as a lustful teenager, Sloane could not remember being this insatiable. It seemed to him that he always wanted Elise. He could make love to her, fill his body with the total peace that comes after good sex, and then an hour later—alone in his own bed—he would begin to crave the feel and smell and taste of her all over again. His fingers would tingle with the urge to stroke her smooth olive skin and feel it heat with her response. He wanted to smell her subtly exotic perfume of orange blossoms and jasmine, the fragrance of a hot Florida night that drifted around her when she moved. He wanted to taste the rich cream flavor of her skin, feel it linger on his tongue until she seemed a part of him.

He would lie in his bed and try to remember the little noises she made when he touched her, the sighs, the moans, the words of love she'd murmur. But it was never enough. Not nearly enough. His heart constricting, Sloane realized it never would be. When he left Miracle Springs, his longing was going to explode within him. She was staying behind; he was leaving. It was inevitable, as inevitable as the calm, sure flow of the Wehachee. If he asked Elise to come with him, history would repeat itself. In seventeen years, neither of them had changed enough to challenge fate.

Away from everything she knew, Elise would be like a bird raised in captivity who is set free to roam the skies. She would be stricken with fear, unable to fly in strange territory. Eventually her freedom would be her undoing. She would long for her cage, perishing without it, and she would never know the joys of the new gift she had been given.

But oh, how he wanted it to be different. How he wanted to challenge her to come, to defy the inevitable, to dare her to fly far and free.

"Sloane? You asked me a question, I answered it and you've been staring at me ever since." Elise frowned and stood on tiptoe to wipe parallel vertical lines from his forehead.

He pulled her close in a bone-crushing hug, and he knew that if his life depended on letting her go at that moment, that he could not. He held her and felt his eyes fill with tears. He never cried.

"Sloane?" Elise's arms crept hesitantly around his waist. She could feel him tremble with emotion. "What's wrong?"

He swallowed hard, banishing the moisture from his eyes. He wanted to tell her that he didn't want to leave Miracle Springs without her. He wanted to ask her to come. But he couldn't do that to either of them. He would not watch what they had together die in new surroundings. Instead he told her only a tiny part of the truth. "I was just thinking how lucky we've been. You've given me more happiness in these months together than most people get in a lifetime. I'll never forget them."

"Don't forget me," she whispered. "Don't ever forget me. Promise me that much."

"I won't forget you. I couldn't, not even if I wanted to."

He picked her up and carried her to the sofa. Their clothes were abandoned and their movements were, too. They made love, completely aware of each other as they searched for the response they needed to make the act of love perfect. It was a long time before they dressed again and walked in silence to the springs.

The springs was silent, too. The same boisterous crowd who had romped and laughed at the Inn's festivities had settled on every square foot of sand of the beach. There were only the hushed tones of an occasional voice to augment the sounds of a star-filled Florida night. Sloane and Elise found Amy and Clay near the water's edge, and they joined them on their quilt.

Now was the time of meditation, of crystallizing wishes until—if the maiden appeared—the wish would be so clear that it could be granted. Now was also the time of searching hearts for purity. No one on the tourist commission had ever defined exactly what a pure heart was, but each person on the beach had his or her own understanding of what that meant. Even those who had come to scoff fell into the mood of contemplation and wondered what their greatest heart's desire was and what they had done that year to prevent it from being realized.

There were already mists rising from the water. The temperature had turned cool enough to scare away mosquitoes and the air hummed only with expectations, crickets and frogs. Elise leaned against Sloane and closed her eyes. She had no idea if she qualified as having a pure heart. She knew she had tried to live up to her own beliefs. Finally, after much thought, it wasn't her own purity she questioned, but her wish. Like the cowardly lion in a different fable, she wished for the courage she knew she didn't have. She wished for the words to tell Sloane her feelings. She wished she could ask him if she could come with him. She wished for the fortitude to withstand his inevitable answer, his apologies, his sympathy. She wished that just this once—even knowing she was doomed to failure—she would reach out for what she wanted most in the world. And when that effort was unsuccessful—as she knew it would be—she wished she might have the courage to leave Miracle Springs anyway, to begin a life somewhere else, a life rich in possibility and growth.

Sloane felt Elise sigh, and he tightened his arm around her. He wondered what she wished for. Was it the impossible? Did she fantasize that life could go on always as it had in the last incredible months? If she did, it was close to his own deepest wish. But Sloane knew better than to put his faith in Indian maidens and tourist commissions. His wish tonight would be simpler and entirely plausible. He would wish that his parting with Elise would be quick and as painless for both of them as possible. He would take nothing of her back to New England, and his wish was that she would keep nothing of him here with her.

AMY STROKED CLAY'S HAIR. He had pillowed his head in her lap and the sensation was intimate and very special. Their parting lay before her, and it was all she could think of as she waited restlessly for the Indian maiden to appear. It wasn't fair. Clay had come unexpectedly into her life, and soon he would be gone. She would stay behind in a town that now seemed filled with restrictions and people who were nothing but strangers. Her wish was simple. She wished that the years would pass quickly and that someday she would find Clay again as an adult, free to live the life she chose.

Clay absorbed the pleasures of Amy's hand stroking his hair. When she touched him he could feel the effect all over his body, and he wondered what it would be like to feel all of her against him. The forbidden thought shot through him, translated into sensation. Someday he would be an adult. If he had any wish at all it was that when that day arrived, somehow Amy would be there to share his life with him.

Amy bent her head and put her mouth to his ear. "You'd better sit up or you won't see anything."

He did so reluctantly. They sat holding hands and watching the wisps of mist play over the water of the springs. The sliver of moon disappeared behind a cloud, and the frogs quieted until the sound that was dominant was the whisper of trees at the water's edge as a light wind blew in from the south. The mists danced, scampering over the water like small children. They formed and reformed, tantalizing the people on the beach with their antics. Near the island the mists gathered, covering and obscuring the palmetto and cypress knees until the island itself was wreathed in vapor and seemed a part of the river.

Midnight came and went. There were soft rustling sounds from the beach as some people left. Elise wondered if they were leaving because they had seen the maiden or because they had given up. She never wanted to leave. The sensuous beauty of the night, the comforting feel of Sloane's arms around her, the shared longing of humans—skeptical and not skeptical—who waited for a miracle, all blended together to fill her with a peace she had seldom known. She could sit there for hours, absorbing it into her soul to sustain her in the days ahead when she would need tranquillity most.

But as she watched, the mists on the island parted. The moon came from behind its cloud and grew in power until the island was brilliant with its beams. From the cypress knees and palmetto an iridescent wraith uncurled. It was vapor illuminated by moonlight, one delicate, human-shaped spiral of mist that looked strangely unlike mist at all. It moved to the edge of the island, a woman with her arms outstretched, and then as Elise watched, it floated above the island and was absorbed into the surrounding vapor. She felt the sting of tears in her eyes and then the wetness of her cheeks.

Sloane's arm tightened spasmodically around her. Suddenly he wished that he'd been less practical. Given the chance for a miracle, he'd chosen only to ask for a comfortable parting. He wanted to shout for the maiden to come back. He wanted to shout his sorrow to the heavens and ask for another chance.

"Did you see her?" Elise asked softly. "She's gone now. Tell me you saw her."

He took a deep breath and wondered at his own response. "I saw something."

"Amy, Clay?" Elise whispered. "Did you see her?"

She saw their heads nod in the darkness. Silently, with no need for more conversation, they all stood together. Sloane picked up the quilt and they found their way across the beach to the road.

No one else moved. Those still on the beach sat quietly, still waiting to see the maiden.

CHAPTER THIRTEEN

ELISE STARED at the telephone receiver until a loud buzzing informed her that the other party was no longer on the line and the phone had been off the hook long enough. She replaced the receiver gently and then stared at her hands, finally letting her eyes and her hands travel to her abdomen. The words she had just heard still rang in her head. *"The test was positive, Miss Ramsey."*

Positive? The doctor's words had been clear and precise, but how could she have heard him correctly? Still, he had warned her of this possibility at her annual checkup earlier that day. The telephone call had only been a confirmation of their earlier conversation. She'd thought of nothing but his warning since she'd left his office.

"I told you you'd have great difficulty getting pregnant. I didn't tell you it was impossible. These things can change as a woman grows older. It was years ago, but I'm sure I must have pointed out that if you wanted to be absolutely safe, you'd have to use birth control."

Elise shook her head as if to rid herself of the truth. Pregnant. Six weeks along, he had estimated. Hadn't she wondered when her period was late?

No, she hadn't. Sloane and Clay were leaving in a matter of days. Her periods had been late often enough, especially when she was under stress. She'd had no reason to worry about pregnancy and no symptoms that couldn't be explained by her unhappiness. She had not considered the fact that a child might be growing inside her. Sloane's child. Clay's brother or sister.

Why hadn't she postponed her appointment until Sloane was gone? Her decision now would be easier. She'd considered it. She hadn't wanted to make the drive into Ocala and miss an afternoon with him. But her doctor was popular and the appointment had been made months before. She had decided to go, using the traveling time to try and figure out how to say goodbye to Sloane when he left on Saturday.

The trip back home had been a nightmare. If what the doctor said was true, saying goodbye would be easy compared to telling Sloane he was to be a father again. She had refused to accept the doctor's diagnosis until the test was completed, but she had known at some deeper level that the phone call would confirm his prediction.

Sloane would not believe she hadn't done this on purpose. And perhaps he was correct. Wasn't it Freud who said there were no accidents? Had she hoped that Sloane's seed would find its way deep inside her and give her a part of him to keep forever? Against the odds, had she hoped for the miracle of life, for the miracle of joining herself with Sloane in the unmistakable commitment of a child?

She would never know. She had believed she would never conceive. But she had taken no additional precautions to insure it. She had left the final decision to fate.

A baby. Hers to love. She had loved and let go, loved and let go all her life. But this time she would not have to let go. The child would be hers forever. He or she would grow, move away and live its own life, but there would be a bond that would never be broken. Her child.

Sloane's child. The man who never wanted to be a father. The man who had admitted to relief when the wife he hadn't wanted to marry had miscarried. But also the man who yearned for the love of his teenage son, the man who felt cheated because he hadn't known Clay as a child. A man often at war with himself.

Elise stood and smoothed her skirt nervously. Sloane was coming for dinner. She was faced with two choices. She could tell him about the pregnancy—as his ex-wife had done—accept his obligatory offer of marriage and prepare herself for a life of one-sided love and resentment. Or she could refuse to tell him—as Willow had done—and deny him the chance to learn to love his own child.

Neither possibility was tenable. She could not bear trapping Sloane into marriage, nor could she bear cheating him out of knowing his son or daughter. And as she realized that both choices were impossible, her third choice became obvious to her.

She would tell Sloane, but not until the baby was born and she was established somewhere else. She could not live in Miracle Springs any longer. That was definite. Unmarried mothers did not make role models for the youth of the town. She would lose her job, her prestige, her place in the community. She had to leave town, and she had to do it before her pregnancy began to show.

She would move to another part of the country, find a job outside of teaching and set up a good situation for her child. Then, when her life was in order, she would tell Sloane. He would not be obligated to offer her marriage, and he would still have the option of getting to know his son or daughter. The choice would be his. She would not push or plead. If it was beyond him to love another child, she would understand. This child would have all her love; she could be father and mother to it.

There was a knock on the front door, and Elise realized just how long she had been standing in one place, contemplating her future. As she walked to the door she realized something else. She was no longer in shock. She was terrified at the coming changes, but more important, she was elated. Growing inside her was the child of the man standing on the other side of the door. Sloane would leave, but no matter where he went, no matter what happened in the future, she would always have a part of him in her life.

When she opened the door, her smile was genuine. She put her arms around Sloane's neck before he could say a word and kissed him. Then she drew away, and she knew that doing so was the more significant act.

"Let's pretend I just knocked," Sloane said, stepping forward to catch her by the waist before she retreated farther. "Instant replay." He bent and joined his mouth to hers. He encouraged her to part her lips and his tongue tasted them before it moved beyond to meet hers. Elise sighed and allowed him to pull her closer.

"Any man worthy of the name would kill for a greeting like that," Sloane said finally, after reluctantly pulling his mouth from hers.

"I'm afraid it was the highlight of the evening," Elise apologized. "I haven't gotten dinner started yet."

"Let me take you out."

"No." She stepped away and held out her hand. "I don't want to share you with crowds."

"We could go somewhere romantic and intimate."

"We'd have to drive miles to do that. Come help me." She led him into the kitchen.

"Hard day?" Sloane asked as they rummaged through the refrigerator.

She bit her lip to keep from blurting out an answer she would regret. "We only had a half day of school today, and I had an appointment in Ocala," she said finally. "I got home later than I'd intended."

Sloane took lettuce and cucumbers from her hands and set them on the counter.

"These tomatoes are fresh," she said, changing the subject. "The father of one of my students grew them in his garden. I've got peppers, too."

"What kind of an appointment?"

"Doctor's. Routine. How does steak sound? We can broil it."

"Are you all right?"

Elise felt her heart stop and start up again at double speed. She wet her lips and told him the truth. "I've never been better."

Sloane took the peppers and tomatoes out of her arms and lifted her to stand against the open door. "Dinner sounds great. Why don't you put some potatoes in the oven to go along with the steak?"

"That'll take a long time," she warned.

"My intentions exactly." He drew her toward him and shut the refrigerator.

And since she had never needed him more than she did at that moment, Elise went willingly into his arms.

"YOUR FATHER WON'T let you stay with your aunt and go to school here next year?"

Clay brushed Amy's curls with his fingertips. They were sitting in the front seat of his father's car. Clay had turned sixteen on the twenty-seventh of May, and Sloane had taken him for his driver's license the next day. The resulting sensation of power was overwhelming. "He wants me to come with him."

"I want you to stay."

"He's promised I can come here for Christmas."

"That's seven months away!"

"I can count, Amy."

Amy lay her head on Clay's shoulder and turned her face up to his. "I'm sorry."

Clay hugged her against him. "I'm not anxious to leave. You know that."

"My father says it's a good thing you're going."

"That doesn't surprise me. What else does he say?"

Amy hesitated and then giggled. "Something about a chastity belt."

Clay grinned. "Maybe he's not so out of it after all."

"He's going to be out here any minute to drag me inside."

Clay took the hint and turned her so that he could reach her lips. She ended up on his lap with the steering wheel pressed against her back.

"What a difference sixteen makes," Amy teased finally, pushing Clay away. She slid off his lap and straightened her clothes. "Maybe my father's right. Maybe it's a good thing you're going."

Clay fingered one bright-gold curl. "I'll miss you."

"We can write."

The front door of Amy's house slammed, and Amy swiveled to watch her father stalk down the sidewalk. She opened the door before he reached the car. "I was just coming in, Daddy."

Bob Cargil peered through the window. "You've been out here long enough!"

"Mr. Cargil?"

Bob frowned at Clay, his obvious dislike barely in check. "What?"

"We both care very much about her. We do have that much in common."

Clay could see the effect the simple statement had on the older man's face. Little by little Bob's frown disappeared until the resulting lack of expression was like a chalkboard wiped clean.

"You're a hard kid to figure out," Bob said finally.

Amy slid across the seat and stepped out onto the sidewalk. Bob slammed the door, and together he and Amy watched Clay drive away.

THERE WAS ONLY ONE PLACE to say goodbye. Only one way.

On Friday night Elise stood in her bedroom, adjusting the fit of the bathing suit she had bought for the occasion. Her old suit, a sleek black maillot, had emphasized the slight fullness of her stomach. The faint bulge was barely noticeable—she hadn't thought about it herself until the doctor's diagnosis. Still, someone who was familiar with every curve of her body might be able to tell the difference. Naked, she looked very much the same, but the clinging black fabric might point out the truth about her pregnancy to Sloane.

To compensate she had got a new suit, a dark blue and red Hawaiian print in a sarong style that softened the lines of her abdomen and the riper curves of her breasts. It set off her perpetual tan and the glossy length of her hair, and she covered it with a beach dress in the same pattern.

She was halfway downstairs when she heard Sloane's knock. He was early for once, and when she opened the door to greet him, Clay was standing by his side. She kissed them both, one more passionately than the other, and drew them inside. "Where's Amy?"

"We'll pick her up on the way."

"I've got everything packed to take."

"I picked up drinks."

"Champagne," Clay added.

Elise met Sloane's eyes without flinching or showing her distress. "Bon voyage."

"Something like that." He reached out and smoothed a lock of hair back from her face. The champagne had been an afterthought, and he wished he hadn't brought it. Tonight felt like anything but a celebration. And yet it would do nothing but harm to treat the occasion like the funeral it was.

"It's a good thing there's a graduation dance at the Inn tonight. The springs would be packed otherwise." Elise made her way into the kitchen and began to load Sloane and Clay with food to carry out to the car.

"Actually I thought we could go down the river to a spot I know," Sloane told her. "But I didn't realize you were packing all this food."

Elise knew just what spot he meant. "Well, you're going to be sitting in a car for days. You can use the exercise to get yourself in shape."

They managed to take all the food to the car in one trip. Amy was waiting for them in front of her house. Sloane had handed the car keys to his son at Elise's, and he and Elise had climbed into the back seat. Now they watched as Clay got out to open Amy's door.

"Polite boy, your son," Elise murmured. "Much politer than you ever were."

"Everything a father could want."

"He's the brightest student I ever had. If he decides to write, he's going to be well-known someday."

"I hope he's going to be happy someday," Sloane said cryptically.

"He's happy now."

"He tolerates his life. He wants to be free."

"Don't we all?" Elise laced her fingers through Sloane's and squeezed them tight. "Growing up is realizing you're never free and learning to live with your restrictions."

Sloane wondered if she was talking about herself or Clay or all of them. "Maybe growing up is learning to rise above restrictions," he parried.

"We've had this argument before."

"Continuously," Sloane said with a touch of bitterness.

"Don't." Elise withdrew her hand. "I thought we'd accepted our differences."

"I'm sorry. This is no time to fight."

No, this was the time to pretend that everything was fine. Elise accepted his apology with a nod.

Clay covered the miles to the springs with confidence. He was a good driver, careful, patient, thoughtful. Elise admired his skill and told him so. At the beach they unpacked, distributing the food into four loads. Then Sloane led them down the path to the riverbank.

"This is great," Amy said with enthusiasm. "How come you never showed us this before?"

"I thought every teenager in Miracle Springs already knew about this place," Elise told her. She spread the quilt she carried on the narrow strip of sand. There was just enough room.

"They've been keeping it private," Clay told Amy, dropping to the quilt to take off his shoes. "Race you to the water."

In a minute he and Amy were chasing each other into the river.

Sloane watched Clay play. He swam now as if he'd been born to the water. Best of all, he obviously enjoyed it. It was just one of many changes.

"Why didn't we show this place to them?" Sloane asked. He sat next to Elise and opened the small cooler, pulling out the bottle of champagne.

"Because we didn't want them doing what we did here. They're not old enough yet."

"How old do they have to be?"

"Old enough to realize how much they could hurt each other."

Sloane stopped work on freeing the plastic stopper from the bottle neck. "Did we hurt each other?"

Elise stretched out next to him and rolled to her side. "It's been worth any pain it caused. All of this has."

"Are you going to be all right, Lise?" Sloan set down the bottle. "Be honest."

"You don't have to worry about me." She wrapped her fingers around the open lapel of his shirt and pulled him down beside her. "I have no regrets."

"None?"

"None I want to talk about." She put one finger on his lips to silence his questions. "Do you remember Thanksgiving?" She went on without letting him answer. "I told you then that when it came time for you to go I'd let you. No tears, no recriminations. I've known this day was coming. I'm prepared."

Sloane kissed her finger then brushed it aside. "You have a standing invitation to visit me in Cambridge."

"Maybe I will." Neither of them believed her.

"Clay wants to come back for Christmas." Sloane couldn't stop himself from continuing the subject although Elise had obviously tried to bring it to a close.

"That would be nice."

Sloane frowned at her lack of enthusiasm. "I might come too."

What could she say? That next December she would be in her eighth month of pregnancy and settled somewhere far away? That if Sloane came, he would not find her here? "It's easier for me to believe this is over than to grasp at straws," she said at last.

"That's like you."

"And it's like you to criticize me for it." Elise sat up and grabbed her knees, staring at the river. "You're trying to start a fight. It'll be easier for you to leave if you're angry with me. I'd suggest you rise above the inclination."

Sloane sat up, too. He put his hand on her shoulder. "Is that what I'm doing? Maybe I'm genuinely upset to be saying goodbye."

"You don't have to say it, Sloane."

"What does that mean?"

Elise clamped her mouth shut and shook her head. What was she saying? With all the complications between them, why was she confronting him now?

Sloane's hand tightened on her shoulder. "What are you saying?"

She shook her head again and wished the conversation had never gone this far.

"I have to say goodbye. I can't stay here. My life is in Cambridge."

"Don't you think I know that?"

"Then what are you saying? That you'll come with me?" He cupped her chin and turned her face to his. "Do you honestly believe you'd be happy living away from everything you know and care about?"

Elise wondered how Sloane could have made love to her all these months and not realized that *he* was what she cared about. He clung to the belief that she was still the eighteen-year-old girl who had refused to leave her home for him. It was easier because then he could avoid thinking about making a commitment to her. He was a man who wanted no commitments. It was that part of him that made it impossible to take the final step with Clay—and that part of him that would hate knowing he was a father yet again.

She decided, having gone this far, that she owed him some of the truth. "I could be happy living anywhere with a man who loved and wanted me always. We both know that man isn't you."

In the twilight, Sloane's expression was difficult to read. Elise thought she saw anger, chased closely by regret. But she couldn't be sure.

"Maybe it's easier for you to believe that than to reach out for something you say you want." He removed his hand and turned back to the water. "I'm going for a swim."

"We can eat when you get back."

He stripped off his shirt and shorts and walked to the water's edge. Then he turned and held out his hand. "Come with me."

She wanted to refuse. She needed the time away from him to put everything back in perspective. But even as she was about to say no she stood and took his hand.

"I don't want this night to be spoiled," he said.

"Neither do I."

They walked into the water together, passing Amy and Clay who were on their way out. "Go ahead and start on the picnic," Elise encouraged them. "Just save us some."

Clay watched Elise and Sloane swimming toward the middle of the river. "They had a fight," he said.

"How can you tell?" Amy handed Clay a piece of fried chicken. "Do you want a Coke?"

He nodded. "Watch the way they swim. They're three feet apart, and they aren't talking."

"It's hard to talk and swim at the same time."

"Not when you're in love."

"Do people their age fall in love? I always thought they got together because they were lonely or something."

"I think they've always been in love. At least Elise loves Sloane. I'm not sure Sloane can love anybody." Clay punctuated his sentence by turning the Coke can bottom up and drinking most of it in one long swallow.

"He loves you."

Clay set down his can and began on the chicken. "Are you going to date other people while I'm away? I want you to."

Amy respected the abrupt change of subject. "Yeah. Did you think I was going to sit around and mope for two years?'' she teased. "And you. Are you going to find yourself another girlfriend at that fancy school you're going to?"

"Probably three or four, now that I know how."

"I like the three or four bit. Just don't get too serious about one."

"I'm already serious about one."

"Do you think? ..." Amy finished her chicken as she contemplated how to ask her question. "Do you think we'll still love each other when we're old enough to?"

"We're old enough now."

"That's not what I meant exactly. I don't feel old enough, not for... well, you know."

Clay smiled. "It's funny. The moment I turned sixteen I felt old enough for that."

"Well if that happens on *my* birthday, it could be a problem. I'll turn sixteen while you're away."

"There was a guy at Destiny who always used to lecture everybody about the beauties of self-denial. He was kind of a nut. Everybody listened to him and then went right on doing what they pleased. Maybe he had a point, though."

"Will you wait for me?" Amy wiped her hands on a napkin, taking great care with each finger, not looking at Clay. "I want to be your first. I want you to be my first."

Clay swallowed hard. "When?"

"When we're ready. We'll know, won't we?"

"I guess we'll know. I just hope we don't both get ready when we're living in different places." He reached out and covered Amy's hand.

She met his eyes. "Just make sure you get Sloane to let you come back to visit as often as you can."

"I will."

Amy giggled. ''That shouldn't be too hard. He and Elise are going to want to see each other.''

''I don't know. They went seventeen years without seeing each other. Who knows, maybe it'll be another seventeen.''

''What is it that keeps them from getting married?''

''They're both afraid.''

''That's dumb. They're so happy together.''

Clay and Amy turned to watch the two adults who were treading water in the middle of the river. ''I sure hope when we're that age we'll have more sense,'' Amy said, as Sloane kissed Elise and they disappeared under the water's surface for a moment. ''I don't ever want to be that messed up.''

ELISE CAME AROUND to the driver's seat of Sloane's car and leaned through the window to give Clay a goodbye kiss. ''I'll miss you,'' she said, her eyes bright with tears. ''Write me.''

''I will.'' Clay's voice was husky.

She stepped back and watched as he drove away. Sloane stood on the sidewalk. When Elise joined him he picked up the empty picnic basket and the quilt and started up the walkway to her house. He paused on the front porch. ''Do you want to say goodbye here?'' he asked without turning to look at her.

''We've been saying goodbye for weeks now. One more real goodbye won't hurt either of us.''

Sloane turned and held out his hand for her key. In a moment they were inside. He leaned against the door. ''I wanted to make love to you at the river tonight. I've never wanted anything that badly before.''

Elise tossed her hair over her shoulder. ''And how do you feel now?''

"The same."

The corners of her mouth curled up in a tiny smile. "Will my bed do?"

"The hard floor would do."

Elise started toward the stairs. "Let's be comfortable."

Upstairs they undressed each other slowly. Their agreement was unspoken. Both set out to make their lovemaking last as long as it possibly could. They traced each inch of skin and covered each other with kisses. They teased and played and brought each other to the brink of pleasure time and time again only to withdraw. Finally, even knowing that it was their last time, they could not hold off any longer.

"Now," Elise commanded, wrapping her legs around Sloane to take him inside her. "I need you now."

It was over too soon. With her release came tears. Elise pillowed her head on Sloane's shoulder and allowed them to fall.

"Don't cry, Lise." He held her tight.

"It's all right. It was just so beautiful." She almost choked on the words. "It's been so beautiful."

"It doesn't have to end. Come with me."

The room was silent.

He had said the words she most wanted to hear. She had taunted him at the river with his inability to ask her to come. And yet, he had no idea what her coming would entail. Even with the fierce flame of hope burning off her common sense, Elise knew that this was not the time to tell him about their child. Not when they were entwined, body and soul, and unable to think rationally. If she did and he still said he wanted her, she would never know if it was duty, passion or love that had made the decision for him.

"Not now." She turned on her side so that she could trace his jawline with her fingers. "I love you, Sloane. I've loved our time together. But we both need a chance to see this more clearly."

"You're afraid."

She was. "Yes."

"Again." His voice was bitter.

"Yes." She kissed his cheek.

"God, it's a repeat of last time."

"No, it's not. Please trust me. It's not the same, Sloane."

"Then what are you afraid of?"

"Of making a mistake."

Sloane sat up and swung his legs over the side of the bed. He rose and began to look for his clothes, slipping on his shorts, obviously angry. "Then it is the same. You won't take the risk. You're opting for the comfortable, the familiar."

"I'm just asking for some time."

"Funny, I've heard you ask for that before."

Elise could say no more without telling him the whole truth. She got out of bed and came around behind him, pressing her body against his. It flashed through her mind that their child was right between them. "This time you need the time. Think about us, Sloane. If you still want me, I'll be waiting."

"Don't hold your breath." He turned and placed his hands on her shoulders, shaking her. "Do you know how damned hard it was to ask you to come with me? I knew you'd say no again."

"I said not now."

"The first two letters of both words are N-O."

"Is this where you throw something at me and tell me it's all I'll ever have of you if I don't come?" Elise lifted her chin and stared unwaveringly into his eyes.

The tension left his body. He dropped his hands. "No, this is just where I tell you I'll miss you."

She relaxed too. "Then maybe we have grown up."

"I still feel the same inside."

"I'll miss you, too." She bent and picked up his shirt, fingering the soft cotton. She resisted the desire to smooth it against her face. She held it out, and he slipped it on. "Will you do me a favor?"

He shrugged.

"Will you kiss me once and then get out of here before I say something stupid?"

His arms locked around her and the kiss was fierce. When Elise finally opened her eyes, Sloane was gone.

CHAPTER FOURTEEN

DECEMBER 15TH: I miss Florida. I miss the storms that blew in suddenly, leaving just as suddenly with the air cleansed and fresh behind them. I miss the passion of those furious clouds, the golden split of lightning, the smell of the rain just before it drenches the earth. Most of all I miss the peace that comes afterward.

Here in Cambridge there are no thunderstorms—not this time of year anyway. There is snow and the cold snap of air as it bites at your skin. In the New England countryside there must be peace after the blizzards. Here there are only the sounds of the snow plows and salt trucks and then the rhythms of a city once again.

At home, with Sloane, there is no storm; there is no peace. There is only waiting. I think I lost my patience for waiting the day I turned sixteen.

Clay looked at the words he'd just written and shook his head. Keeping a journal was a habit he'd acquired in Elise's English class. Now, even though he was usually loaded with homework, he still found time each day to write a few paragraphs. It had become as necessary as breathing. It was the one chance he had to express his feelings now that he and Amy were so far apart.

Closing the journal he stood, in no hurry for what was ahead. He pulled on his jacket and gloves and slung his backpack over his shoulder. The walk to Sloane's condominium from the Harvard library wasn't a short one, but he preferred it to taking a bus. These days he preferred anything that got him home late.

Forty-five minutes later, he stripped off his gloves and blew on his fingers to restore circulation. No matter what he wore, no matter what precautions he took, he could not keep out the bone-chilling New England cold. He suspected it was going to get worse before it got better.

He reached in the pocket of his slacks for the key to the front door of the gray stone four-plex and pushed it in the keyhole. In a moment he was standing inside at the foot of the stairs that led up to Sloane's apartment. Someone had set up a Christmas tree at the side of the bottom steps. It was small, not up to the job of making the cold, empty hallway a festive sight, but Clay appreciated the gesture. It was a reminder that the holiday season was here and that soon he would be flying back to Miracle Springs.

Sloane would not be going with him. Clay trudged up the steps, his backpack less heavy than his spirits. He hoped that Sloane had worked late; he hoped that the apartment would be empty when he unlocked the door. He hoped he would not have to face his father at all that night.

He was not to have his wish. He was greeted by the sound of soft classical music and the sight of Sloane, a drink was in his hand, staring into sputtering flames in the fireplace. "You're late."

Clay closed the door behind him. "I stopped off at the library. I've got a research paper due, and I needed some more information."

Sloane nodded, still staring vacantly at the flames.

Clay went into his room and unpacked his book sack. He had his report to finish, and he was tempted to begin it immediately. But he was also growing, and his stomach was rumbling to confirm the fact. He changed out of his school uniform and into comfortable jeans. He liked his school. He was constantly challenged, and he had been accepted by the other kids immediately. But he also liked the end of the day when he could just be himself again. Of course he would like coming home even better if Sloane didn't make him feel so unwelcome.

Back in the living room he took stock of the situation. Sloane hadn't moved. The same drink was in his hand, his eyes were still trained on the flames. It was the portrait of an unhappy man. Clay wondered if Sloane was this way all day or only when he was forced to come home and face the son he didn't want. Something clenched convulsively inside him, but he ignored it and resolutely faced his father. "What are we doing about dinner?"

"I stopped and got Chinese. It's in the kitchen. You can heat it up in the microwave."

"Have you eaten?"

"No."

Clay went into the kitchen and took down plates for both of them, dishing up food from various cartons and shoving it into the microwave, one plate at a time. When it was ready, he took it to the dining-room table, pulling silverware out of a drawer in the buffet on the way. "It's ready."

Sloane looked up as if he were surprised he was not alone. "You go ahead."

Clay shrugged and began to eat. He would never think of this time in his life without tasting the exotic tang of soy sauce and M.S.G. He figured that in the last six months, he and Sloane had averaged four nights a week of shrimp-fried rice, moo shu pork and egg rolls.

"How is it?"

Clay was surprised by Sloane's question. Whenever Sloane spoke to him nowadays it was a surprise. "It's okay."

Sloane wandered over to the table, picking up his egg roll. He looked at it as if it were a radioactive isotope and dropped it back to the plate. "I was nineteen before I had my first Chinese food."

"You've made up for it."

Sloane's eyes narrowed, and he regarded his son. "Is that a complaint?"

"Would it do any good?"

Sloane was surprised at Clay's flippant answer. He sat down and leaned over the table. "I asked you a question."

"So you did." Clay leaned back, his eyes never flickering. "You'll have to excuse me, I'm out of practice at answering."

"What does that mean?"

Clay sighed. "It means whatever you want it to, Sloane. Look, I've got to get busy on my report. It's due before I leave for the holidays." He stood, then looked in surprise at his arm. Sloane's fingers were wrapped tightly around it

"Sit!"

Clay sat, and Sloane released him.

"What did you mean about being out of practice answering?"

Clay leaned back in his chair. "What did you think I meant?"

"Obviously there's some truth to what you say. I'll have to give you a refresher course on how to respond. You don't ask another question. You give an answer, a sentence with a period at the end. Now, what did you mean?"

Anger flickered across Clay's face. "I meant that you never ask me anything."

"I ask you how school is going."

"That's true. Sometimes you do ask me that. You did last month in fact."

Sloane had the grace to look sheepish. "Has it been that bad?"

Clay shrugged. "I'm used to it."

"I don't mean to be so distant."

"Don't you?" Clay picked up a fork and began to toss it from hand to hand.

"No, I don't. I've been . . . preoccupied. I haven't meant to ignore you."

"It seems to me that people always mean to act the way they do. I figured that out when I was about five and somebody apologized for spanking me. It could have been Willow, I don't even remember. It was a woman. She said she didn't mean it. She did. She enjoyed it. And you mean to be distant."

"What makes you think so?"

"I'm not stupid, Sloane. I'm not a little kid either. I know what's going on. I know you want me out of here."

Sloane exhaled with force. "No, Clay...I—"

For the first time in a long time, Clay told the adult in charge what he wanted to tell him, not what that adult wanted to hear. "Stop lying to me! You don't want me." The fork clattered to the floor. "You haven't wanted me from the first moment you found out you had a kid. You think you're supposed to want me so you try. Why don't you just stop trying, Sloane? I don't want you. I don't need you!"

Sloane felt a surge of fury at Clay's words. He didn't need this now. He wove his fingers together to keep from slapping Clay's face. "I think you'd better go to your room."

"If you recall, that was my idea in the first place." Clay pushed back his chair and slammed it against the wall behind him. He was gone in a second.

Sloane shut his eyes. The momentary rage that had crackled through his body was gone. He sagged against his chair and wondered if it was humanly possible to feel any lower.

He had always thought of himself as a winner. Through sheer determination he had won his heart's desire: freedom. Now freedom seemed a petty goal if it meant the absence of all the ties that made life worth living.

He stood and went back into the living room. He bent and stoked the fire, then he returned to the chair where he had spent so much of the evening. He wasn't a winner. He was a loser. He had lost Elise; now he knew he had never even had Clay. He was a man alone.

How do you set things right when you're incapable of communicating with the people you love most? He loved Clay, and yet somehow he had neglected to let Clay know. And Elise? Elise was gone, had been gone since September, and he had no idea where to find her. The past months had been like living in the middle of a nightmare.

In August, after a cocktail party where he had imbibed more than his usual limit, he had called Elise just to hear the sound of her voice. She had said nothing about leaving Miracle Springs, and of course, he hadn't asked. Their call had been friendly and impersonal. He had hung up feeling lonelier than he'd ever felt. He hadn't wanted to repeat the experience, but he hadn't wanted to lose touch with her either. In September he had tried to call again, only by that time her phone was disconnected.

He had assumed the recorded message telling him to check the number was just trouble with the phone lines. Elise would not leave the town of her birth. He was as sure of that as he was of anything in the universe. But the next day he had gotten a chatty letter from his Aunt Lillian containing all the news of Miracle Springs. The biggest story had been Elise's disappearance.

Evidently Lincoln Greeley, the high school principal, had known she was leaving because when the academic year started, there was a new teacher for tenth grade English. But no one knew where she had gone or why she had left. Lincoln, a master of small-town politics, had refused to discuss the matter. All Aunt Lillian knew was that Elise's house was up for sale and a nice young couple was probably going to buy it. Did Sloane know anything about it?

Sloane had gone through the month of September telling himself that when Elise wanted him to know where she was, she would tell him. At first he'd been pleased that she would spread her wings so mysteriously and fly away from everything that was familiar and dear. He half expected her to land on his door-step. The thought gave him pleasure. He was beginning to admit just how much he missed her, beginning to realize what she added to his life—beginning to believe that there was hope for them after all. But by the end of September, he was beginning to worry.

Where was she? By mid-October he was frantic. He was working harder than he'd ever worked, writing, teaching his classes, lecturing at nearby colleges and universities. All the work didn't even begin to make a dent in his fears. How could he ever have thought that he and Elise had no future together? Why hadn't he told her he loved her?

Why hadn't he realized he loved her?

He did. More than his freedom. More than his pride. More than his fears. He loved her. He wanted her. And for the first time he realized that it was his own fear that had stood between them this time. He had been afraid to ask her to come. He had been so afraid that when he finally asked, it was only at the very end of their time together, when she couldn't say yes without worrying about how genuine his request was.

He had been afraid to tell her he loved her. Love bound people together. He had been a man who wanted no ties, no boundaries. He was a man, but he had acted like the boy who could not wait to leave the town of his birth and its restrictions. He was a man, but he had acted like the boy who wanted to punish the girl who spoiled his grand escape. He had been reacting.

He had been a fool.

By November, Sloane had humbled himself to the point of calling Bob Cargil and begging him for information about Elise. Bob had refused to tell him anything. If it was possible to gloat over the telephone,

Bob had done it. Still Sloane sensed when he hung up
that Bob had known no more than he did.

Lincoln Greeley had known. Sloane called him, explained his desperation and pleaded for Lincoln's help.
With no explanation, Lincoln had refused. He could
not be swayed. Elise's realtor pleaded confidentiality
and hung up on him.

Now it was December. Once, at the beginning of the
month, a phone call had come late at night. Sloane had
picked up the receiver and when he held it to his ear he
could hear the peculiar crackle of a long-distance connection. There had been no voice, only a click and
then, later, the buzz of a dial tone. Every night now he
waited for the phone to ring again. This time he would
pick it up and call her name before she could hang up.
He would make her know he wanted her, needed her,
loved her. He would make her know that no matter
what problems stood between them, he would find a
way to make them all right.

If she didn't call before vacation started, he would
spend his holiday looking for her.

Now Sloane had a more immediate problem, but it
stemmed from the same source. He had never had the
courage to tell his son the one thing he needed to hear,
just as he had not had the courage to tell Elise the
same. It was time to make the final commitment to
Clay.

Sloane stood and walked down the hallway to Clay's
room. He listened, undecided about how to approach
the conversation that was long overdue. After a deep
breath, he knocked on the door. "Clay? Will you come
out here, please?"

There was a long interval. Sloane remembered well
what it was like to be a teenager. He remembered well

the heady feeling of power that comes from knowing an adult is waiting for you. He was surprised it had taken Clay this long to learn the same thing. Finally the door swung open.

Clay lounged in the doorway, his eyes carefully veiled. He wondered what fancy language Sloane would couch his rejection in. What words would he use to rid himself of the son he had never wanted, the son who had finally told him exactly what he thought? If Clay knew one thing about adults, it was that they didn't want to hear the truth. Sloane wouldn't want to chance having to hear it again. Clay only hoped that when his father found another place for him, that place would be in Miracle Springs.

"I want to talk to you." Sloane turned toward the living room, and Clay followed him. Sloane sat on the sofa and motioned for his son to join him. Clay sat on the far end.

"It's very easy to misconstrue..." Sloane stopped. He realized just how stilted he sounded. Clay was trying to look stoic, but even in his own agony Sloane could see the vulnerability in his son's eyes. He started again. "I've blown it."

Clay just looked at him.

"Look Clay, I've been acting like a jerk. It just never occurred to me that you'd think it had anything to do with you. I'm one hell of a lousy father."

Clay's eyes widened, and his expression encouraged Sloane.

"You see, I never had a father of my own. I never had anyone, really. My mother was always busy, distant. My aunts and uncles cared about me but they weren't usually there when I needed them. I... well, I made it on my own. But I never learned how to tell people what I was feeling. I never learned to be a father either, and I don't seem to have much talent.''

"What's this got to do with me?" Clay's voice was still tinged with anger, but Sloane could hear the hurt little boy under the insolence, and he slid a little closer and touched him on the shoulder.

"I've been wrong about one thing. Very, very wrong. Right from the beginning. I've never told you the most important thing you can tell someone. I've never told you I love you. I do. I loved you the minute I set eyes on you." He coughed to subdue the lump in his throat. "I've been torn up inside ever since thinking about all the time I've missed with you, thinking about how lonely you must have been, how lonely I was. I've tried to show you, but it hasn't been good enough. You may not need me, Clay, but I need you. I want you in my life forever."

Clay looked skeptical. Or was it that, having never been told he was loved, he didn't know how to answer? Sloane didn't know, but he did know that telling his son he loved him wasn't enough. He slid closer until he was next to him. Then he put his arms around Clay in a powerful bear hug. "I mean every word of it," he said, and he felt tears wet his cheeks. "And someday you'll know I mean it."

Clay sat in the circle of his father's arms and wondered why he felt he was going to cry too. He hadn't cried since he was a small child. He felt Sloane tentatively stroke his hair and he marveled at how good it felt. Before he knew what he was doing, he was patting Sloane's shoulder to comfort him.

"If you love me and you really want me here, then why have you been so awful to live with?" he asked after Sloane had drawn away a little

"I promise, it hasn't had anything to do with you."

"Do you need a refresher course on answering questions?" The insolence was gone. It was the voice of the Clay Sloane had known in Miracle Springs, humorous, ingenuous.

Sloane laughed a little, wiping away the tears that had felt so cleansing. "You want me to share my feelings with you?"

"Yeah. I could get to like it."

"I'll make a long story short. I'm upset about Elise."

"Why? She sounds fine. She likes Atlanta; she likes her job."

Sloane froze. "What?"

"It's hard to tell the truth from letters, but I think she's doing all right. She sounds a little lonely."

"What are you saying?"

Clay frowned. "I can't figure out why you're worried. Did she tell you something she didn't tell me?"

"She hasn't told me anything! I didn't know where she was! How do you know?"

"We've been writing ever since I left Miracle Springs. She sent me her new address when she moved. I just got a Christmas card from her yesterday."

"Damn!" Sloane stood and began pacing the living room, pounding his fist into his hand. "All this time."

"Too bad you didn't tell me before."

"Damn!"

Clay wondered just how far he could push Sloane. "See, if you'd told me, I could have saved you all this. I could have told you she's in Atlanta working for some publishing company. I could have given you her address. I haven't seen much of this love stuff but it does seem to me that if you love somebody you talk to them, tell them what's worrying you."

Sloane continued to pace. "Didn't I already tell you I'd blown it? Obviously it was worse than I thought."

"Well, why don't you make a short story long?" Clay lounged back in his seat. "Tell me the rest."

Sloane stopped pacing to shoot a grin at his son. He could almost see Clay relax under its power. "Do you really want to hear this?"

Clay nodded.

"All right, but it might take me awhile to get to the point. I'm still figuring it all out."

"Make it up as you go along. I've got the time."

Sloane began slowly. "Once upon a time there was a man, a hermit, who lived in a cave all by himself."

"A bedtime story?" Clay interrupted. "Aren't I a little old for that?"

"I missed all my other chances. I was cheated out of them. I'll never forgive Destiny Ranch for that!"

Clay was surprised by the strength of his father's words and the detour. "I was happy. . . ." He stopped.

"Were you?" Sloane faced him.

"No."

Sloane shut his eyes and nodded. "I know."

Clay tried to be honest. He realized that Sloane actually wanted the truth. It was a new experience, but one Clay thought he was going to enjoy thoroughly. "There were good things. I see the way kids are raised in other places, and what I had was better than a lot of that. Some of the people who came through the ranch were terrific. I learned so much from them. But I always missed," his voice caught and he swallowed, "I always missed having someone who thought I was special enough to keep with them"

"I think you're special enough." Sloane opened his eyes. "You can do what you want, be who you want to be, but no matter what you do or who you are, you're my son. That can't change."

Clay swallowed again. "Finish your story."

Sloane nodded, knowing that Clay already had enough to contemplate. He began to pace again. "This hermit I was telling you about liked his cave. It was huge and warm and it had a picture window where he could watch the world go by. At night sometimes he'd sit by the fire and write down what he'd seen. He'd send off his writing, and people would read it. They liked what he had to say."

"And then?"

"And then one day, the hermit was forced to go outside his cave. He didn't want to go. He was happy being alone, at least he thought he was. Outside he found out that the real world, the one he thought he'd been writing about was a difficult place to be. One minute he'd feel happier than he'd known he could be and the next minute he'd be in the depths of despair."

"Sounds like a place I've been myself," Clay murmured.

"Then you understand how this hermit felt."

"Anyone who's been there would."

Sloane nodded. "It took this hermit a long time to adjust. He was so used to being alone he didn't know what to say, what to do for other people. He didn't realize he lacked courage, that was something he always accused other people of lacking. But the truth was that he was afraid of all those highs and lows. He kept a big part of himself away from the people he grew to love, just to play it safe. Finally, he couldn't stand it any longer. He returned to his cave."

"But he wasn't happy?"

"No, he wasn't. Because you see, he'd changed. The picture window wasn't big enough anymore. He could see but he couldn't touch or smell or hear. In fact, he couldn't hear at all; his cave was silent. So he tried to go back to the real world again, find the people he loved, but one of them was gone, and he couldn't find the words to tell the other one what he was feeling."

"So he ignored him."

"Exactly."

"And the one that was gone. Why did she go without telling the hermit where he could find her?"

"Because the hermit seemed like a hopeless case, I guess."

"Was she right?"

"No."

Clay smiled. "Then one day, the hermit found a map. At the very center of the map in a kingdom called Georgia was a big X. The hermit journeyed night and day until he reached the spot. There he found the treasure he'd been seeking."

"Yes."

"When are you going to leave?"

"As soon as you take off for Florida. With any luck, Elise and I'll be joining you at Aunt Lillian's for Christmas."

"I don't know. Elise may have too much sense to get mixed up with a hermit again."

"You're a rotten kid!" Sloane tempered his words by ruffling Clay's hair. "*My* rotten kid, and don't you ever forget it."

Clay's smile got bigger. "People don't own people."

"Don't kid yourself. I've been owned body and soul for years, and I just figured it out. And you know what? It feels wonderful!"

CHAPTER FIFTEEN

ELISE LIFTED HER CUP of nonalcoholic punch along with everybody else in the room. She listened as her new boss made a toast to the Christmas season. Mechanically, she brought the cup to her lips and swallowed. It was red fruit punch, the kind the children had been served when she'd taught Sunday school in Miracle Springs. Someone had tried to make it Christmassy by floating lime sherbet in it. The result was a sickly brown scum where the sherbet and punch had blended together, and it took all Elise's fortitude to swallow it. She apologized silently to the baby inside her, who gave a mighty kick in response.

The party resumed. Elise found an unobtrusive spot to set her cup down. The buffet was classier than the punch and she was starving. Ignoring the warning voice that told her whatever she ate would show up when the nurse weighed her at the obstetrician's, she heaped a plate with cold boiled shrimp, salmon mousse and crackers, fruitcake and rum balls.

"Only a pregnant lady would eat that combination," her boss commented, coming to stand beside her.

"I believe I qualify," she said, patting the huge bulge that preceded her everywhere.

"You look like the Madonna." John Switt shook his head at his own words. "Just don't go having that baby in a stable somewhere."

"At this point, I'd be glad to have this baby anywhere, just to have it."

Mary Jo Switt came up behind her husband and laughed appreciatively at Elise's words. She took his arm. "I remember just how it feels to be that close. How much longer do you have?"

"Three weeks, two days. Give or take a month." Elise smiled at the Switts. They were a handsome couple in their fifties who resembled each other in the way that people long married often did. She envied them their togetherness.

Mary Jo was clucking like a mother hen. "Shouldn't you be on maternity leave? Has John been making your life difficult?"

"Never. I'm just happier working. I want as much time with the baby as I can have afterwards."

Mary Jo nodded. "I don't blame you."

"Southern Pines Press can do without you," John assured her, as he'd assured her every day for the last month. "You're the best copy editor we ever had, but we can make do with free-lancers till you get back. Don't hesitate to take off when you need to."

The baby kicked again, and for a minute, Elise couldn't speak. It was amazing how much a kick could hurt. "You're so kind," she said when she could talk again. "But don't worry, I promise I'm not going to deliver in the office."

"If you do," Mary Jo put in, "John'll know what to do. He almost delivered our last child himself. You'd think I'd have known better, but I kept telling myself the baby was just restless. By the time I realized what was going on, the poor little fellow was already on his way to meet us.''

''We got to the hospital just in time for Mary Jo to give one last push,'' John reminisced.

Elise wanted to hear more, but by the time she had weathered another kick, Mary Jo and John were gone, distracted by other employees. She finished the plate of food and helped herself to seconds on the fruitcake.

She was lucky to have landed this job. Because of her father's insurance money, she had decided to work more for her sanity than her financial stability. Still, even though she hadn't sought prestigious or high-paying positions, few employers had been willing to listen to the plight of a woman old-enough-to-know-better who was unmarried and expecting a child. They hadn't wanted the prospect of instant maternity leave, and Elise hadn't blamed them. But John had listened without making a moral judgment. He had hired her because he had believed she would do a good job, then he had made it clear that his door was always open to her. John and Mary Jo had helped make the adjustment to Atlanta easier.

Elise was pleased with her choice for a new location. Atlanta offered all the things that life in a small town never had. In addition, it offered the one thing she needed most of all: privacy. No one here cared that she was not married to the father of her baby, or if they did, they didn't make a point of it. After the child was born, she would explore all the sections of the city, check into school systems and buy a house where she could raise her son or daughter in peace. She would make friends. She would survive. If she sometimes missed the town of her birth, she still knew that this was better.

Miracle Springs was just a memory now. It was a cocoon where she had lived far too many years of her life. She had traded its comforts, its unchallenging sameness for the adventures of the unknown. Some days she awoke and wept for the ease of the life she had left behind. More often she sat up and stretched, eager for the joys of a new day.

She should have left years before. But as often as not, she put that thought behind her. She had finally made the break. She was free, independent and as happy as she would ever be without Sloane.

Elise realized she was tired. She traded repartee with her fellow employees, made plans to attend Christmas Eve Mass the following week with one of Southern Pine's editors, and then excused herself to head home. The drive through downtown Atlanta's traffic always tired her, but never more than it did this evening. The long day and the baby's activity had taken a toll on her limited energy. All she wanted was a chance to sit in a warm tub with her feet propped as high as she could prop them and a good night's sleep.

No, she wanted more than that. She wanted the impossible. She wanted to go home and find Sloane waiting for her. She wanted to melt into his arms and feel his hands soothe away the constant ache in her back and the pain in her heart. She wanted to hear him ask how she felt and how their child was doing. She wanted to know that in three weeks and two days he would be standing beside her, watching their baby come into the world.

She wanted the impossible. Clay had her address. Sloane would have no trouble finding her if he wanted to. Obviously he didn't. Elise edged her car into the right lane of the interstate and took the exit that would lead to the apartment complex where she was living. It was hard to get behind the wheel of a car now, hard to steer, hard to sit up straight. It would be hard to climb the stairs, hard to undress. Maybe she'd forgo the bath and go straight to bed.

She found a parking place immediately, which was unusual. Apparently some of the sprawling complex's tenants had already gone elsewhere for the holidays. For a moment, she envied them their freedom. She climbed the open stairway, which always made her think of a cheap motel that rented its rooms by the hour, and paused outside her door. She must be tired. The faint strains of Christmas carols had reached her ears, and for a moment, she had almost believed they were coming from inside her apartment. The sound was welcoming, pleasant. Maybe she would leave her radio on from now on so that when she came home, the apartment wouldn't be so silent, so foreboding.

She stuck the key in her lock and turned it. The sound of carols grew louder. She *had* left her radio on. That was funny, she didn't even remember having it on that morning. Inside she felt for the light switch. The resulting brightness made her close her eyes. She stayed that way as a sharp pain shot through her abdomen, and she felt her body bend in protest. She gasped as the pain continued for long seconds and then disappeared. *That was no kick.*

"Lord!" She straightened and opened her eyes to find her way to the sofa and the telephone. She forgot about both when she realized she was not alone. "Sloane!"

Sloane was standing next to the sofa, his face as white as Christmas snow. "What in the hell!"

"How did you get in here?"

"You're pregnant!"

"Did you pick my lock?"

"Why didn't you tell me?"

"That's why I heard carols. You turned on my radio."

"Who the hell cares how I got in and what I did while I waited? Why didn't you tell me?" Sloane's face was no longer completely white. There were two red spots of anger on his cheeks and the muscle in his jaw was jumping. "My God, you're as bad as Willow. You used me like a stud and then took my child!"

"No I didn't! I was going to tell you. I . . ." She stopped and her eyes widened. "My God!" She bent over again. "Sloane, I can't. Sloane . . ."

He was at her side in a split second. He put his arms around her waist. "Lean on me, Lise."

"I can't." Her knees began to tremble. Something inside her seemed to give way, and she felt a rush of fluid soak her undergarments. "It's not supposed to happen like this," she said on a moan. "It's supposed to happen slowly the first time. Especially when you're my age. I don't know what to do."

"Let's get you over to the sofa. Then tell me who to call."

She was no help at all. She couldn't move. Sloane finally picked her up, grunting at her new weight and carried her across the room. "Who do I call?" he asked after he had laid her down.

"It's by the phone. This is too soon. I'm not due for the better part of a month!"

"You knew, didn't you? You knew before I left town!" Sloane dialed as he spoke. "You knew, but you didn't tell me." He realized that he ought to stop himself, but he couldn't seem to halt the angry flood of words. "You kept this a secret . . . Hello? My name is Sloane Tyson, I'm calling for Elise Ramsey. I'd like to speak to," he covered the receiver with his hand. "Who the hell am I calling?"

"Dr. Pinchot." Elise closed her eyes.

"Dr. Pinchot," Sloane continued smoothly. "Miss Ramsey is about to become a mother," he hesitated, "and I'm about to become a father. Again," he said, looking straight at Elise.

The voice on the other end of the line asked him to wait.

"How long have you been in labor?" Sloane asked her.

"I don't know. I thought the baby was just kicking hard."

"How long?"

"Two hours or so."

"Where have you been?"

"At my office Christmas party."

"Did you eat anything?"

"Tons."

"Terrific. Hello, Dr. Pinchot? My name is Sloane Tyson. I'm the father of Elise Ramsey's baby." Sloane watched as Elsie turned her head to the back of the sofa. "She's in labor. Hard labor. Has been for a couple of hours but she didn't know it. She may already be in transition."

Elise's head spun around, and she stared at him.

Sloane covered the phone. "Did your water break?"

She nodded weakly, biting her lip as another pain ripped through her. Sloane looked at his watch and began to time the contraction. "I'd say her contractions are about three minutes apart and they're lasting around ninety seconds or so. But that's just a guess. I just started to time them.''

Sloane listened to the doctor as he watched the minute hand on his watch.

"Yeah, she ate. Tons, she says." He covered the receiver. "He wants to know if you've completed the Lamaze childbirth training."

The contraction ended and Elise nodded. "Last week."

"She says yes." He listened again. "We'll meet you there in—" he covered the receiver again. "How long will it take to get you to the hospital?"

"Twenty minutes."

"Twenty minutes," Sloane repeated into the receiver. "Pant and blow? I'll tell her. I've helped before." He hung up. "Come on, Lise. We're going bye-bye."

Elise couldn't sit up. Her whole body was trembling. "This is supposed to take hours."

"Or minutes. Depends." Sloane slid his arms under her back and helped her sit. She bent over as another contraction began. "Come on, love. Do as I say. Now, take a deep cleansing breath. That's right. Let it out slowly." Sloane began to massage her abdomen. "Now light pants, like an overheated Dalmatian. That's good." He could feel the contraction tearing at her until her belly was as hard as a rock. "Okay, three pants and a short blow. Come on, Lise." He demonstrated, and she followed his lead. They continued together until the contraction was finished. "Time to go."

Elise was too weak to stand. "I can't make it. You go ahead without me."

"I'll carry you if I have to."

"Sloane, I was going to tell you."

"When? When the kid needed tuition for college?"

Something purely imaginary burst inside her, and she began to cry.

"That's not going to help. Come on." Sloane helped her stand, and then he lifted her in his arms. "You realize I'm too old for this, don't you? I'll get a hernia."

She sniffed, trying hard to control her tears. "Why are you here?"

"I'm beginning to think I'm here to deliver this baby. Be quiet now. We'll talk later."

"How do you know so much?" They were at the doorway, and Sloane was fumbling for the knob with one hand.

"Destiny. I watched a baby being born once at a rock festival. I held the girl's hand and talked her through it. Later one of the Destiny midwives taught me the Lamaze techniques, but I never got to use them because I left right afterward."

"And you remembered it all those years?"

"You'd better hope I did." He felt her stiffen. "Okay, take a deep breath." They began to pant together.

The trip to the hospital was the most difficult twenty minutes either of them had ever spent. Sloane alternately cursed traffic and panted. Elise felt every bump, every twist of the road. Finally Sloane roared into the parking lot with the speed of an ambulance and ran around the side of the car to scoop Elise out. They were in the emergency room in less than a minute.

"Dr. Pinchot's patient is here, her contractions are two minutes apart and lasting ninety seconds or more," he yelled to the admitting nurse.

"They don't start and they don't stop," Elise corrected him on an indrawn breath.

The nurse, gray-haired and somber, took one look at the man holding the woman in his arms and called for a gurney. "Take her right to delivery," she instructed the orderly who arrived a moment later. "Pronto."

Sloane laid Elise carefully on the hard, sheeted surface, and touched her hair. "Only a little longer."

"We've got to take her up now," the orderly told him.

"I'm coming too."

"Just a minute," the nurse began. "Did Dr. Pinchot give his permission?"

"Of course," Sloane said smoothly. "I'm the baby's father."

"Then you can go to admitting first."

"I already did all the paperwork," Elise said between gasps. "Elise Ramsey."

"We'll have to check. Mr. Ramsey, if you would wait."

"Sloane!" Elise grabbed his hand. "Come with me."

"Of course." He bent and kissed her forehead. "We have to talk, don't we? I'm not going to let you out of my sight until you answer a few questions." He straightened. "I'll be down as soon as the baby's born," he told the nurse. Without waiting for the orderly, he began to push the gurney himself.

"This is irregular...!" the nurse shouted.

"Highly!" Sloane agreed. The orderly took his place and Sloane grabbed Elise's hand. "Okay, Lise. This time, start the pant-blow sequence as soon as it gets rough."

She was beyond response. She could only feel the intense pain in her abdomen and the warmth of Sloane's hand around hers. She did as she was told.

The delivery room was icy cold. Dr. Pinchot was already in hospital blues, and he chased Sloane out immediately, insisting that he cover his clothes, hair and shoes before he was allowed to come back in. With a nurse's help, Sloane was back in a minute. Elise had been stripped, garbed in a hospital gown and covered with a sheet. She was gasping for breath.

"No anesthesia," Dr. Pinchot said when Sloane returned. "Too far along and too stuffed with dinner."

The doctor turned back to Elise. "Okay sweetheart. When I tell you, I want you to push. You," he pointed at Sloane, "get behind her and lift her up. Elise, grab your knees."

"I don't know how to push," she wailed.

"Your body's going to teach you how. Just follow its lead," Dr. Pinchot said calmly.

"Sloane, I'm sorry I asked you to come. You don't have to stay. Oh!"

"Try and toss me out! Take a deep breath and hold it." Sloane looked to the doctor for confirmation. "Okay, Lise. Bear down hard!"

The first pushing session went well. Elise welcomed working with the contractions. "How much longer?" she gasped when the doctor told her to stop.

"Depends on how well you do," he said nonchalantly.

"Is the baby okay?"

"No reason to worry."

"Sloane, I'm sorry."

She felt his hands massaging her shoulders. "We'll talk later. Just worry about the baby now. This is Clay's brother or sister you're having."

Elise closed her eyes and waited for the next contraction. When it began, her body took over and pushed for her. All she could do was help it a little. She felt Sloane lift her, and she heard his voice soothing her although she couldn't understand any of the words.

"Good job, Elise. You're that much closer. One more push should do it," Dr. Pinchot told her.

She drew in her breath on a sob. "Sloane. I'm scared."

"So am I." He came around to her side. "I love you, Lise. It's going to be all right."

She didn't have time to absorb his words.

"Okay, Elise. Give it one more good, hard push and then I'll let you hold your kid." Dr. Pinchot stationed himself between her legs. "Looking good. Don't shut your eyes. Look above you in the mirror and watch this baby come into the world."

Sloane wiped her forehead. "Push, Lise. Harder. Harder!"

"Open your eyes!"

Elise did as she was told and watched the biggest miracle of all. She heard a cry: the baby's. She heard a sob: her own. She heard a laugh: Sloane's.

She heard a calm professional voice. "It's a girl. Looks full term. With a mop of black hair and a powerful set of lungs."

Elise felt something warm and wonderful on her stomach. Sloane held her up a little and she saw their daughter, eyes open and staring in her direction. Her skin was mottled and covered with a pasty white film, but she was without doubt the most beautiful baby in the world.

"Oh, Sloane, look at her!"

"Just lie back, Elise. You can hold her as soon as I cut the cord," Dr. Pinchot said cheerfully.

Sloane eased Elise back to the table. "She looks like her mother."

"You can't tell that already."

"She does."

"I wanted a boy who looked like you." Her voice trembled.

Sloane was filled with emotion at her words. He hadn't known he could feel so intensely. His knees felt weak from it. "Don't tell me you're disappointed," he said at last. "I won't have you be disappointed she's a girl. She's perfect."

"What's Clay going to say?"

"He'll be as surprised as I was," he said with irony.

"Okay, you two. Here she is. Not a thing wrong with her either except that she's pretty cold and more than a little mad."

The delivery room nurse who had efficiently hovered in the background cranked up the table so that Elise could recline. Elise opened her arms and held her daughter for the first time. "She does look like me." She touched the wailing little bundle on the forehead with her index finger. "Please don't cry, honey," she soothed. The baby continued wailing as if she were insulted by the request.

"Go ahead and nurse her," Dr. Pinchot prodded Elise. "She can't cry if her mouth's full."

Sloane untied Elise's gown and watched as tentatively she put the baby to her breast. Elise gasped as her daughter grabbed hold and began to suckle like an expert.

"It's good for both of you," Dr. Pinchot explained. "Makes your uterus contract, quiets her, and hopefully it will keep your mind off the stitches I'm about to put in."

"Stitches?"

Sloane bent closer to watch his daughter eat her dinner and distract Elise. "She has my personality. Look at her. She knows exactly what she wants."

"Sloane, help me hold her. My arms are trembling," Elise pleaded.

Sloane reached down and steadied the infant who was ignoring everything except her new connection to her mother.

"When I got off the plane and rented a car, I had no idea what I was getting myself into," Sloane told her. "This is incredible. What a way to spend an evening!"

"You hate me."

"I don't understand why you did it. I expect a complete explanation in about three hours. But no, I don't hate you. I love you."

Elise shut her eyes. "You don't have to say that. This doesn't change anything."

"It doesn't change the fact I love you. It changes just how fast we're going to get married, though." He straightened. "When does she get out of here?" he asked the doctor who was just finishing up.

"Three or four days. The pediatrician will have a look at the baby. If all goes well, it should only be three."

"How long before Elise is on her feet again?"

"She'll be tired for awhile. But she's done real well for an old gal."

Elise opened her eyes and narrowed them. Dr. Pinchot laughed. "Thought that might pep you up." He came around and plucked the baby from Elise's breast. "We've got to weigh and measure her." The baby was quiet as if she felt sleepy already. "I'll have her back in a jiffy, and then you two can go into recovery with her."

"Have you got a name picked out for her?" Sloane asked Elise.

She pulled the gaping neckline of her gown closed, aware that Sloane's eyes were lingering there. "I'm not going to marry you."

"No?" He smoothed her forehead in a gesture that was distinctly humoring. "Why not?"

"The whole reason I did this was to keep you from marrying me out of duty. I'm set up here. I have a job, a decent income. I have my own apartment, my own friends. I even have a woman who'll baby-sit for me when I'm working. I'm free, independent and quite capable of taking care of myself and my daughter. You don't have to worry. I'm not the scared, fragile little girl I used to be."

"And you didn't think I had the right to know anything about my child?"

"I was going to tell you." She grabbed his hand. "I wasn't going to do what Willow did. I just wanted to be sure you believed me when I told you that you didn't have to marry me."

"How long would you have waited?"

"As soon as I'd recovered from the birth."

Sloane picked up a lock of her hair and held it to his lips. "Why did you have to recover first?"

"I didn't want to be weak. Don't, Sloane."

"Are you weak now?"

"Extremely."

He bent a little closer. "Good. Marry me."

She tried to shake her head, but the movement pulled the hair held tightly in his hand. "Sloane, you told me yourself you married once to give a baby a name. You didn't want that baby or that wife. How do I know you want me and our daughter?"

"Because I love you."

"Even if that's true . . . what about her?" She nodded to the other side of the room.

"I already love her." Sloane saw the disbelief on Elise's face and he smoothed it away. "Look, Lise. When my ex-wife miscarried, I felt relieved. I knew our marriage wasn't going to be a good one. I didn't want to bring a child into it. But I know now there was a part of me that mourned that baby. I tried to ignore it, to tell myself it was for the best, but I was depressed for a long time. In my own blind way, I covered over those feelings. I told myself I wasn't father material. But now I have another chance, another child. And you're the two ladies I want to spend my life with. Don't shut me out of your lives."

"Sloane . . ."

"Marry me. Be my love, my wife, my adored companion, the mother of my children, my heart, my own private miracle."

It was the last word that convinced her. She was too tired to prevent tears. "When did you decide you wanted me?"

"Months ago. Only I couldn't find you."

"Clay knew."

"Clay and I were hardly speaking."

"Sloane . . ."

"We're speaking now. He told me where you were. I told him I'd bring you to Miracle Springs for Christmas. We'll get married there—unless the thought embarrasses you."

"Do you really love me?"

He nodded.

"And the baby? You want the baby?"

"Try and keep me away."

"I could have made it on my own."

"I couldn't have." He brushed her lips with his, then did it again. "I never want to make it on my own again. Only with you, with Clay and with that screaming little bundle over there." They both listened to their daughter begin a new set of rebellious roars.

"She does have your personality."

"You're going to have your hands full with both of us."

Elise felt a peace she hadn't known was possible wash over her. She shut her eyes and grasped Sloane's hand. "This isn't a dream, is it?"

"Ask me that after three months of wet diapers and midnight feedings."

"It isn't a dream. It's a miracle," she said, bringing his hand to her lips. "The maiden couldn't have done any better."

"We made this one happen ourselves."

Elise smiled. "'Tis the season."

"It's always the season."

Elise heard a rustle, a roar and then a quiet cooing. She opened her eyes and looked up to see Sloane proudly holding their daughter, who had nestled against him as if she knew just exactly who he was. "You're going to make a good father," she said sleepily.

"I am a good father," he corrected her with a grin. "I'm going to make a good husband."

"I believe you will." Elise yawned and closed her eyes again.

"I take it that means you'll marry me."

"That's right."

"I love you."

"I love you."

Sloane watched Elise drift off to sleep. He swayed back and forth with their baby and planned their wedding. It couldn't be soon enough to suit him.

EPILOGUE

CLAY'S JOURNAL: It's Christmas. The second one I've spent with my father. For a present this year he gave me a mother and a sister. After a lifetime alone I'm suddenly overwhelmed with family. It's a funny thing about having all these people who matter to you. At first I wasn't sure there was room inside me for them. I thought that part of me was just inoperative—like a short circuit on a robot. Now I know that's not true.

I called Sloane "Dad" yesterday, and his face lit up like the brightest of Christmas trees. The smallest things seem to give him pleasure now. When I see him holding Rhea and smiling at her, I get the strangest feeling. I wonder what it would have been like to have him hold me that way. He seems to be trying to make up for it though. I haven't had so many hugs in my entire life.

And now Elise is my mother. She says stepmother is an honorable title, that it's the best step she ever took. We're staying at the Miracle Springs Inn, and she and I walked down to the river together this morning before Sloane and Rhea woke up. Elise wanted me to know that as much as she loves Rhea, she loved me first. I told her she could quit worrying about sibling rivalry, and she laughed and kissed my cheek.

Rhea is beautiful. I named her. It's Latin for "that which flows from the earth: the river." Rhea Elise Tyson. Elise says her name is perfect; Sloane says it sounds like something straight out of Destiny Ranch. But he says it with a smile.

Today at two Elise and Sloane are going to say their vows down at the riverbank. They already got married by a justice of the peace in Atlanta so that people here wouldn't talk, but their real wedding is going to be today. Just Amy and me and Sloane and Elise. And, of course, Aunt Lillian and Rhea.

Amy hasn't changed at all. She's still the most beautiful girl I've ever seen. We've both been going out with other people since I moved away, but it doesn't seem to matter at all. When we're together it's like we've never been apart. When I kissed her for the first time in months, it felt like I'd never stopped.

She has more freedom than she used to. Mr. Cargil asked Carol to marry him to keep her away from the man with the male Pekingese. They were married December first. Amy says Carol was smart. Making her father jealous was the only way to get him to pop the question. Now Carol keeps him busy and well fed, and Amy can live her own life. Mr. Cargil has even given Amy permission to spend Easter vacation in Cambridge with us. Amy giggled and said she thinks Carol's going to make him use that time to work on his textbook.

I'm glad to be back here. Late last night when everyone was sleeping I walked down to the springs. Christmas Eve is like holding your breath, waiting for something to happen. The night was very black and very still. There was part of a moon hanging in the sky and the water was a black satin ribbon. I know the date's not right, but as I looked at the island, the mists surrounding it parted. I thought I saw the maiden.

Just in case, I thanked her.

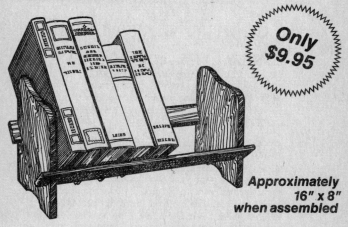

Harlequin
Superromance

COMING NEXT MONTH

#242 LOVE CHILD • Janice Kaiser
Jessica Brandon desperately needs money to care for her crippled son. Chase Hamilton desperately wants a child of his own. Surrogate motherhood seems the perfect solution for them both—until love creates a whole new set of problems.

#243 WEAVER OF DREAMS • Sally Garrett
Growing up dirt-poor on a Kentucky farm has instilled in professional weaver Abbie Hardesty the need for financial independence. She dreams of overseeing every aspect of her own crafts business, but she needs to learn about wool production first. So she becomes Montana sheep rancher Dane Grasten's intern student, and they both end up learning more than they'd bargained for...in each other's arms!

#244 TIME WILL TELL • Karen Field
Attorney Corinne Daye no longer knows whom to trust: Derek Moar, the devastatingly attractive stranger who bears an amazing resemblance to her dead husband, or Margaret Krens, her loyal assistant, who insists that Derek is on the wrong side of the law. She only hopes that when the dust finally settles, Derek will be there to fill the emptiness that stretches endlessly before her....

#245 THE FOREVER BOND • Eleni Carr
With her daughter grown up and her career finally established, Eve Raptis is ripe for a change. Carefree Carl Masters supplies it, but the responsibilities of Eve's past unexpectedly reappear to dim her precious freedom....

AUTHOR'S CHRISTMAS MESSAGE

Softly falling snow and carolers bundled against winter temperatures. Fires in the fireplace and fir trees cut from neighboring farms. That's one kind of Christmas, and I've spent many of mine just that wonderful way. But then there were the Christmases when the Florida sun shone brightly, and my brother and I played outside with our new toys, wearing nothing more than shorts and T-shirts. Brilliant red poinsettias bloomed around our house instead of in pots on coffee tables, and Christmas Day often ended with a walk along the beach to watch the surf and the sea gulls.

I live in New Orleans now, a city that celebrates everything. Christmas traditions here include Christmas Eve bonfires along the Mississippi River levees and fanciful depictions of a Cajun Santa whose sleigh is pulled by alligators instead of reindeer. No matter where I am, Christmas never fails to touch me, to make me believe in the miracles of birth and beginnings, to give me faith that someday the world will celebrate peace on Earth 365 days a year. This year my family and I will be celebrating Christmas in Australia. It will be the same wonderful holiday. May yours be likewise.

Love,

Emilie

Take 4 books & a surprise gift FREE

SPECIAL LIMITED-TIME OFFER

Mail to   **Harlequin Reader Service**®

In the U.S.	In Canada
901 Fuhrmann Blvd.	P.O. Box 609
P.O. Box 1394	Fort Erie, Ontario
Buffalo, N.Y. 14240-1394	L2A 9Z9

YES! Please send me 4 free Harlequin American Romance® novels and my free surprise gift. Then send me 4 brand-new novels as they come off the presses. Bill me at the low price of $2.25 each —a 11% saving off the retail price. There are no shipping, handling or other hidden costs. There is no minimum number of books I must purchase. I can always return a shipment and cancel at any time. Even if I never buy another book from Harlequin, the 4 free novels and the surprise gift are mine to keep forever

---

Name   (PLEASE PRINT)

Address   Apt. No.

City   State/Prov.   Zip/Postal Code